D.C. STONE

EVERNIGHT PUBLISHING ®

www.evernightpublishing.com

INTIMATE ESCAPE

D.C. STONE

DEDICATION

This book is dedicated to coffee, rice crispy treats … and "Joe" who introduced me to La Llorona—thanks for the nightmares, dude.
And my husband—I love you.

D.C. STONE

INTIMATE ESCAPE

Empire Blue, 4

D.C. Stone

Copyright © 2022

❯❮·•◆•·❯❮

Chapter One

Healing is learning to trust life.
—Jeanne Achterberg

Nestled outside Queens, New York, sat the bane of Drug Enforcement Agency Agent Matthew Gonzalez's existence—JFK Airport. Not that he had anything against the airport itself or the city it serviced, but managing the proper timing of getting in and out of the epicenter for world travel was a tedious task. A task that sometimes could take up to two hours once he was over the GW Bridge. Though there was one time it took *five*.

The traffic wasn't his only reason for hating the six-billion-dollar nightmare. No, that other right was given to the constant barrage of people who commuted through the terminals, half as many somehow managing to either not see him, which resulted in constant bumping to his body—shoulders, back, hips, and *hello there*, one time with his groin. Or they saw him and felt like somehow challenging his presence by delivering those well-timed impacts with not-too-subtle checks of their corresponding body parts.

He didn't hate people. Let's get that clear. He hated *rude* people. Ones who had no common sense, manners, or consideration for others.

Okay, maybe he needed to be a bit more honest. He hated New Yorkers. And since he was a New Yorker himself, he could give the blanket statement for what it was: the truth.

So, despite the fact he had to make a trip to JFK during the busiest time of day, on a Friday before a three-day holiday weekend leading up to the Fourth of July, all for a case that may or may not pan out, really set his nerves on edge. That he had to leave his brother's barbeque an hour earlier didn't help matters.

So help him, if Lawless Lou—his confidential informant—sent him on a goose-chase with this latest piece of intel, he would throw every available resource at his disposal at the no-good-piece-of-shit.

Then again, if this panned out, the good ole bank of Uncle Sam would make Lou one happy pig in shit.

Well, technically, Matt was the pig here.

He smirked. Cop humor.

Unfortunately, CIs—otherwise known as confidential informants—were what made his world, or in this case, his job, go round. Feeding agents information was one way they were able to get a leg up on this war on drugs. There'd been references of these CIs being the foot soldiers in this war, but he saw them for what they were. Low-lying, garbage-feeding scums just trying to make it in this big, imperfect world.

Lou had been informing Matt going on four years now. Outside of Lou constantly looking over his shoulder, seeing as snitching was pretty dangerous work, he averaged about fifty thousand dollars a year for his efforts. With his CI, they'd managed to put away quite a few dealers, some of which were preying on local schools around the area, as well as a few wanted for murder, and one for rape. Great accolades all around, yes, yes—insert sarcasm here—but anytime Matt had to deal with Lou, better referred to as Lawless, he felt as if he needed a head-to-toe stainless-steel scrub like the ones his ma used on her scorched pans.

Even outside all the icky-yucky sensations, their partnership—if one wanted to call it such—had been pretty successful. So, when Lawless wanted to talk, Matt listened. And seeing as he'd received a 2:00 AM call telling him a description of the subject he needed to be looking for and the amount of product coming in from the good neighbor of the United States, Mexico, then a call only two hours prior telling him the flight number, Matt hadn't had much time to prepare.

It was now five o'clock in the afternoon and he was slowly making his way through terminal four toward his POC—point of contact—who would get him through security and to the jet bridge of their soon-to-arrive suspect.

He checked his watch. "Fuck, let's hope this plane isn't early," he told his partner, Don Watson. Watson's scowl matched his as he shoved and pushed his way through the ever-thickening crowd.

Watson thinned his already thin lips until they practically disappeared. Despite his annoyance levels being near maximum, Matt fought the chuckle bubbling its way from his gut. His colleague may be one bad-ass DEA agent, but with the asymmetry of his face, all hard angles, high-brow, and permanent scowl, whoever had a hand in making him had missed out on the finishing touches to his face. Namely, his mouth. It was distracting as hell, and the boys back at the office let him know all the damn time. Then again, when one worked a high-intensity job such as drug enforcement, there had to be some ways to let off steam. Cracking on your brothers-in-arms was just one in many of those ways.

"I'll peel off and check the arrivals listing. You head back in case they get in early," Watson said, nodding in the direction of the security checkpoint.

Matt nodded and renewed his approach to get through, dodging luggage, side-stepping strollers, and trying to plan out his route. A few minutes later, he stepped up to Agent Sanchez, the DEA contact assigned to JFK, who had those pretty little escort privileges to get him through security. A badge meant nothing at an airport. Access authority said it all.

Agent Sanchez leaned against the wall outside the executive entrances, his low-lidded gaze saying he'd much rather be taking a nap in one of the back offices. Then again, with the constant activity coming in and out of JFK, especially with drugs, Matt could only imagine some things Daniel Sanchez had seen, done, or heard—fuck, any of it. Yet another lovely thing about living near such a big city was the big-named criminal lords pushing their product into the neighborhoods. The whole buy-sell-demand thing was a living, breathing demon in New York.

"Plane is about fifteen minutes out," Sanchez said as a greeting. "You ready?"

Matt nodded and looked over his shoulder for his partner. Truth was, he was always ready. At a young age, he'd developed this drive deep inside of him to stay a step ahead of others. Not in the sense of *I always have to be better than you*, but from a perspective of wanting to know what drove some to make the decisions they did. Later, in college, that drive narrowed in on criminal behavior and trying to understand criminals' motivations.

If one understood someone's motivation, they could most likely anticipate their actions. In the world of Criminal Justice, this was imperative to prevent crimes and deaths. Sometimes, even prevent activities worse than death, because yes, that kind of shit existed. Rapes, mutilation, and torture were just a few of the things he saw on a daily basis. Especially in his line of work with drug enforcement. And more than ever with those he investigated, which focused on none other than the Mexican cartel.

Watson rounded the corner and practically bulldozed his way to Sanchez and Matt. Color rose high on his cheeks, and his breath puffed from his mouth in heavy pants. Matt fought the chuckle, or at least he tried, but somehow failed seeing as Watson tossed him a glare.

"Do people have no sense of personal space in this godforsaken airport?"

Matt lost his fight with the chuckle and let out a sharp bark of laughter. Sanchez shook his head and turned, holding that pretty little access badge. Watson and Matt sobered. *Game on.*

****

Juliette Scaglione bit her lip and stared at the conveyor belt, waiting for her nondescript black luggage to come out from the back. Not that she was looking forward to hauling it off the belt after the exhausting eight-hour flight from Cancun, but it wasn't like she had anyone else to help her.

Damn you, Jorge.
And damn you, Jimmy. Good riddance.
She'd gone to Cancun in a party-plus-two but

ended up coming back by herself. Three Dog Night's "One" played on repeat in her head the entire flight and cued up again.

When Jimmy, her now *ex*-boyfriend, approached her and Jorge about taking a vacation in Cancun, she'd been ecstatic. Between working non-stop, pulling twelve-hour shifts at the office, and trying to get everything prepared for their upcoming regulatory review, she'd been ready for some time away. Not that being a bank auditor was difficult. One simply had to make sure policies were followed, but when the auditor became the auditee, perspectives changed. Especially with the heightened increase in regulatory compliance over the past few years.

With the review over—and her unit passing with flying colors, thank you very much—she'd jumped at the opportunity to get away with her boyfriend and brother. The two were inseparable, and even though three was a crowd, she figured her brother would find things to do, or rather, someone to do, to allow her and Jimmy the chance to reconnect.

Of course, seeing as Jimmy didn't have a job, she ended up fronting the bill for him as well, but why have money when you didn't spend it, right?

She hadn't wanted to make a big deal out of paying for him, either. Since he'd lost his job at the manufacturing plant two years ago, whenever finances were brought up, his anger took over. Between the hours she'd been pulling, the stress they were both under, and feeling as if their relationship was slipping away, she didn't utter a peep. Instead, she produced her AMEX card for the travel agent.

She should have paid closer attention to it all.

The late-night phone calls.

The constant way Jimmy was always on his

phone.

The beer on his breath and coming in late.

She'd been so blind by their five-year relationship, so deaf to the warnings that she hadn't thought her boyfriend would break up with her on day two of their vacation when all she'd done was stand by his side and support him for the past few years.

Ugh!

Not only did he break up with her, though. Oh, no. He managed to take the cash she had kept specifically for this trip, broke up with her over a text, of all things, and she didn't see him again after that.

And Jorge being Jorge, in his laid-back, carefree way, didn't seem concerned. Instead, her brother had pulled her out of her room, took her sightseeing, got her out to a few clubs, and helped her push the too-recent memory of Jimmy away.

Back at the airport, someone stepped up a little too close to her back. *Yikes!* Sure, the city wasn't known for allowing personal space, but when she moved away, the other body followed. Ugh. She tried to take him in but couldn't make out the guy's face because he wore a black sweatshirt with the hood pulled up and over his head until the shadows danced in eerie phantoms across his face. She squinted, thinking her mind must be playing tricks on her because the guy's face looked covered in tattoos.

Yikes again.

She edged away, moving to the other side of the belt, and turned her focus to searching for her bag and on her recent drama.

Now, back in the "real world" of New York City, everything Jimmy had done burned a path up her throat. She wanted to punch something or maybe cry-cry-cry just so she could have her pity party and call it a day.

Instead of being able to lie back and do nothing, she was forced to grab her bag that somehow, despite her not shopping too much, seemed heavier than she remembered. Then again, Jorge had asked her to bring some of his stuff back with her.

Don't even get her started on that whole mess. Jorge had decided to stay in Cancun for another week to enjoy the life. How he managed to take three weeks off from work was beyond her, but being the good little sister she was, she agreed to do as he asked.

Stupid, stupid her.

She spied her bag and stepped forward to grab it, heaving it off the belt with a grunt. It came down hard, landing on top of her right toe. Her Keds did nothing to protect the digit from the heavy weight. "Shit!" she yelped and tilted the bag away to pull her foot back.

She dropped to her haunches and rubbed at the offended toe. Her purse slid down her shoulder, pulling down her black sweater to bare her arm, and hit the floor next to her. The weight of her backpack threatened to topple her over. Tears smarted her eyes.

Instead of crying, she breathed through the pain, both in her foot and her chest, then took a deep breath. She focused on moving, staring at her favorite red leggings, then stood.

A tall shadow caught in her peripheral before a form moved to her side. She did a double-take, looking for the same guy from earlier. It wasn't unheard of for other New Yorkers to get too close to each other. It was a small city, after all. But that guy had made her uneasy.

She froze, and the second look confirmed it wasn't the creep-tastic dude, but someone else. A third look due to the fact that this guy was H-O-T hot. *Well, hold on.*

Hello there.

This guy had to be about six-foot-four, six-foot-five. He had a wide jaw with the most luscious lips she'd ever seen. Seriously, if they had to make a song about lips, it'd be Sir-Mix A Lot singing about Baby Got Lips, because *daymn*. From there, the view only got better. Eyes the color of a maple tree's late fall leaves set in perfect symmetry over a nose with a slight bump. The bump, she thought with a tilt of her head, looked more like he'd had his nose broken before and hadn't bothered to get it set properly. Lashes—that just had to be curled with a curler, because come on, life couldn't be that unfair—framed those gorgeous whiskey-colored eyes.

And with no small jolt, she realized his hair wasn't the typical short style most men wore nowadays but was held back in a ponytail at his nape, and dark, so dark she couldn't quite make out if it was deep brown or black. She'd kill for hair like that—silky and almost as if it were soft to the touch. How would her fingers feel pushing through it?

All along his arms were tons of colorful imprints, two full sleeves' worth she guessed, and as many ran under his short sleeve tan t-shirt. That shirt strained to contain his biceps that flexed under her perusal.

He cleared his throat. "Miss Scaglione?"

Oh, his voice. It was like *butt-ah*, baby. The sensual tone slid along her arms like phantom fingers, finding all the right spots to make her purr. She'd always been sensitive to the tone and timber of voices. Some people used music to soothe their souls. For her, it was the cadence, tone, and inflections of voices, and the reason why she was such a big fan of audiobooks.

She never understood this but chalked it up to how her mother used to sing her to sleep each night. And her mother had such a beautiful voice.

This guy's voice, though, she wanted more. She

stared at his mouth, hoping he'd say something else. She wanted to feel those fingers slide over her skin again.

He cocked his head, and the side of his beautiful mouth quirked. "Juliette? Juliette Scaglione?"

"Oh, dear God. Yes, that's me." She shuddered.

A startled laugh escaped him, the sound deep and moving through the air with enough electrical currents to power the entire airport. He shook his head and hooked a thumb over his shoulder. "Do you mind coming with us so we can ask you a few questions?"

Juliette blinked at *that* request and focused. Flanking her stood another fairly good-looking man, this one the light to the other's dark, though his lips were thinner. Mr. Light seemed to block the exit to the side, whereas Mr. Dark, she noticed, had blocked the other exit. If she refused to follow them, the only way she'd be able to go was toward the back of the baggage claim, which was administrative offices and lost luggage.

She furrowed her brow. "Um, who exactly are you and why do you want to ask me questions?"

Mr. Dark nodded and pulled out a black wallet as if he expected her question. He flipped it open, and about a million flashbacks of *Law and Order* reruns popped into her mind, along with the song. *Du, du, duuuuh. Du, Du, duh, duh, duh.* "Special Agent Matt Gonzalez with the Drug Enforcement Agency. My partner over there"—he nodded toward Mr. Light—"is Agent Watson. We just need to speak with you for a few minutes."

She spied both of them, the entire request a little surreal. And seriously, Agent Watson? "You're kidding me, right? Am I being punked?"

Agent Gonzalez's brows went up, and he shook his head. "Afraid not, ma'am."

She winced and held up a hand, which caused her damn purse to slide again. The strap caught at her elbow and she struggled to pull it back up. Dang thing weighed close to twenty pounds. "Okay, one, please don't call me ma'am. Everyone calls me Juliette. You call me ma'am, and I'm going to start feeling old. Two"—she pointed at Agent Watson—"are you for real with his name? Does no one else feel the absurdity of it with his so-called profession?"

He eyed her as if she'd lost her mind. Okay, she probably had. After everything she'd been through in the past two weeks and that hellish flight, now this? Someone should really put her out of her misery and check her into a psychiatric ward somewhere.

As if he could read her thoughts, Agent Gonzalez looked like he was seriously considering her silent plea when his face lit up. Just like that, everything and everyone around her ceased to exist. They weren't in one of the busiest airports in the world, there weren't people walking and bumping into them from all directions, and Sherlock Holmes's famous friend/DEA Agent wasn't watching them from a few feet away. Instead, Matt Gonzalez's face transformed into something so beautiful, a smile so blinding, surely nature had forgotten to add it to one of the Wonders of the World.

"Watson. I get it. Like Doctor Watson with Sherlock Holmes. That's a good one. I'm going to have to remember it for later." Then the guy did something she didn't anticipate. Something that caused her stomach to go on a tilt-a-whirl ride. Something she'd never expect from a big, bad DEA Agent.

He winked at her. Actually winked.

Her breath caught in her throat.

Agent Gonzalez stepped forward and reached for her luggage. She watched from a distance, his proximity making everything seem as if it was running in slow motion. The subtle scent of his cologne floated over and she took a deep breath in, finding his smell delicious. "Don't let him hear you make that reference, though. He's *kinda* sensitive already."

That damnable smile was still on his face, and it grew as he looked over her shoulder at what she had to suspect was Agent Watson. He chuckled, the sound sliding over her skin like a caress.

Matt straightened, her luggage firmly in his hand, and held out a hand for her to fall into place beside him. "This way, Ms. Scaglione."

Oh, what the hell. She decided to just go with it. How much trouble could she possibly get into with two Special Agents in the middle of the airport? "Please call me Juliette."

Agent Gonzalez nodded. "Juliette." The sound of her name on his lips sent a shiver along her spine.

A few minutes, more than half a dozen doors, and what had to be a super security clearance later, Juliette followed Agent Gonzalez into a small room with four plain white walls, a moderate-sized wood table, and three chairs. She took five steps inside and stopped as everything caught up. This was an interrogation room, right on down to the lone lightbulb hanging from the ceiling.

"Wait, what's going on?" she asked, eyeing the handsome Agent Gonzalez as he placed her bag on the table.

"Well, Juliette," he responded, "as I told you earlier, I'm with the DEA. We have received some credible intel that has led us to wanting to speak with you. Before we begin, and for the safety of all in this room, do we have permission to search your bags and yourself?"

Surreal. It appeared her brain moved about three steps behind normal functionality because another piece of the puzzle clicked into place. Agent Gonzalez and Watson worked for the DEA. She knew little about the agency other than they dealt with some scary stuff, including hardcore drugs. She'd never even smoked weed, so why would he want to talk to her?

"What do you expect to find in my bags?" she asked.

Agent Gonzalez stared at her, and rather than answer what she thought was a pretty logical question, he threw another softball. "I'll ask you one more time. Do you give your consent to allow us to search your bags? I'm warning you now that I have a federal judge on standby in the event you say no, so one way or another, I will search these bags today. It's just a matter of whether this will go quickly or take a few hours. Up to you."

Her heart pounded against the inside of her chest, wanting to run away. She felt much the same way. Not that she thought he'd find anything. It was the absolute certainty she saw on his face that said he *knew* he'd find *something*.

"What's going on?" she asked, hating the meek sound in her voice.

"Juliette—"

"Yes! Yes, you can search my bags, my—my body, but you won't find anything in, or rather, on them."

Agent Gonzalez unzipped her suitcase.

"After you find nothing, I expect an explanation for what's going on." There, that sounded firm. Not shaky, like what her insides were doing.

Agent Watson relieved her of her backpack and purse but placed them on the table and didn't go through them. Instead, he kept his attention on what Agent Gonzalez was doing, though she knew without a doubt she had his full attention too.

Gonzalez removed her clothing in a systematic fashion, placing items one at a time on the table next to the suitcase. Out came her dirty clothes, which lay on top, jeans, dresses, and her underwear. Her cheeks heated as he continued, his movements slow and thorough.

He got to the bottom, having removed everything from within. Her things were scattered across the table like some bizarre game of Clue.

"See?" she said. "Nothing."

Agent Watson didn't move, but Gonzalez sure did. He reached inside her suitcase and felt around the corners, then yanked. The sound of fabric tore.

"Hey! What are you doing?"

He tossed the fabric aside, and black plastic square packages were stacked inside in a neat and orderly fashion. Had to be about a dozen of them, at least five to six inches in width.

Shock rooted her to the spot for a few moments. "Wait. What is that?" she asked and took a step forward.

Watson held up a hand in front of her. "Ma'am, please stay back."

"What is that?" she asked him again, hearing the rising hysteria in her voice.

Gonzalez pulled out one package and produced a pocketknife from somewhere, then cut into the wrapping. Everything around her moved in slow motion until she swore the world had ceased to spin. Her attention stayed riveted to the white powder that came out on the shiny blade.

"Gonna need a test kit," he said to Watson. The other agent immediately set the bags beside the table, at the farthest reach from her, and left the room.

"Agent Gonzalez," she said, sounding like she pleaded, because she did. She'd never seen that stuff before in her life. "That's not mine. What's going on?"

He pulled out twelve packages, and yes, she counted every single one, before grabbing another black trash bag that someone had taped to the inside of her luggage frame. Once he opened that, several brown baggies came tumbling out. She gasped.

No wonder her bag had been so heavy.

Only then, after the whole horrid nightmare was laid out on the table, all the ugliness next to her things, her clothes, and her bag of toiletries, did he look up at her. "Ms. Scaglione," he said, reverting to formalities, "the intel we received was there would be someone on your plane, matching your description and carrying a suitcase with over ten kilos of cocaine and about a hundred baggies of heroin. Although I haven't tested it yet, I can tell you I'd bet my next paycheck that's what is right here."

"But it's not mine." Dryness coated the inside of her mouth, as if cotton balls had been shoved inside and sucked up all the moisture.

"Are those your clothes?" he asked.

She nodded.

"This your bag?"

She nodded, getting where he headed. "Yes, but those drugs are not mine!"

"Of course, they aren't." But he said the words as if he didn't believe her.

"They aren't!" she yelled.

He slammed his hands on the table and leaned toward her. The sound made her jump, and she cowered back. Everything before this moment had shown Agent Matt Gonzalez to be a man who lived carefree and full of humor. His whiskey eyes had even danced with laughter a short fifteen minutes earlier. Don't ask her how she knew deep down this man was happy, despite having a dark aurora, she just did. She could read people sometimes. Well, except if that person were taking her to Cancun to break up.

She smacked her forehead as the light dawned. "I don't know about those drugs, but I think you may want to talk to my boyfriend."

Gonzalez arched a brow. "Your boyfriend. Was he on the plane with you?"

She winced. "Well, he's not my boyfriend anymore, and no, he wasn't on the plane. He stayed in Cancun. We actually broke up on day two after arriving. I came back early. My brother and Jimmy stayed down there."

"Your brother is in Cancun with your ex-boyfriend?" If anyone could perfect the expression of disbelieving a story, Agent Gonzalez was their role model. His face, despite remaining hard, showed expressions of doubt. She got it. She really did. If she were in his shoes, she might not believe her either. The story seemed ridiculous.

She held up her hands, giving in and going with the pleading route. "Look, I know how it sounds. But if we can just get ahold of my brother, he'll confirm it all. I've never touched drugs or even been in the same room as the stuff. This isn't mine. I don't know where it came from."

He lifted to his full height again and tilted his head, studying her. "Tell me, Ms. Scaglione, why would someone set you up to mule drugs from Cancun? How would they go about getting those drugs from you after you get here if you were unaware of them? What purpose would it serve?"

"I ... I don't know," she finished lamely.

"Right," he said and nodded. "You have the right to remain silent."

"No," she whispered, horrified at this turn of

events.

He reached into his back pocket, pulled out a shiny pair of handcuffs. "Anything you say can and will—"

The room plunged into darkness. She let out a startled scream. An odd popping noise followed, and an alertness pulsed from the man standing across from her.

"Ms. Scaglione, please come stand behind me. Quickly now."

The popping grew louder until the noises changed into what sounded like gunfire. Alarm skittered through her, seizing her muscles with fear. She lurched forward and slammed into the edge of the table, then let out a cry of pain. The edge dug its way into the side of her pelvis. Despite the room going dark, shadows formed as her vision adjusted.

Agent Gonzalez's hand wrapped around her bicep, and he roughly yanked her behind him as the doors to the room slammed open. She screamed again. His body went solid. Gunfire erupted. Then pain slammed into her head, and all went dark.

Chapter Two

What was it, a week later, maybe ten days after that fateful attack in JFK? Matt opened his gritty eyes and took in the same wooden door he'd seen over and over again each time he'd woken over the past however many days. He'd hoped it'd all been one big ole nightmare, but no such luck. His mind, hazy with dehydration, sleep deprivation, and minimal food, scrambled to take stock of his surroundings. But the damn organ operated as if he'd been drugged. Maybe he had been. Did they move him again? He'd lost count of the days after the third sunrise and sixth beating.

He'd been bounced from one identical room to another, or so it seemed. The last thing he remembered before coming to this hellhole was a dark truck where they spent hours and hours driving. Non-stop. God, it seemed as if they'd keep going forever.

Where was Watson?

He tried to lift his head to see if he could find the man but dropped it after he determined the movement required too much energy.

The last time he felt anything remotely similar to how much his body ached, pain seeming to come from every muscle and joint and his head, was after the academy, when he'd been jumped from behind by three beefy DEA trainers. They'd tied his hands behind his back. He'd left that room with a black eye, a broken nose, a bunch of bruises, and a bit of pride. Where he thought he'd been on top of his game, that room and what had happened knocked him down a peg or two.

Prior to that day, he'd been so confident in his abilities to defend himself and others, no matter what. Thought that growing up in a family with a handful of brothers taught him enough. Thought that all those schoolyard fights had given him enough know-it-all to make his way through the academy without drawing too much attention to himself.

He'd been horribly wrong.

That lesson taught him he wasn't invisible. He would not be handed anything, and he had to work to achieve what he wanted. That for every one of him, there'd be three times as many trying to take him down. All things he already knew, but that day in that room, the reinstated message was clear.

In his current place, only God knew where, he eyed the battered wooden door. If he had any motivation, he'd get up and bust down what looked to be a door toddlers built with two-by-fours. But as it stood, he had no energy, barely enough to take in the ragged, dusty air into his lungs. None to fight back anymore, not even enough to put an end to this horrid existence he'd found himself in. He closed his eyes, and his body sagged against the warm, hard brick again. Even in the darkness, his vision swam. His body pitched and rolled in time with his stomach as if he were on a cruise ship at sea during a storm. The meager excuse of food he'd been given earlier threatened to make its appearance.

Food.

God, how long since he'd had something of nutrition? Not simply bread and broth. He'd kill for a steak, French fries, corn on the cob…

His stomach growled, the sound like a lion's roar in the silence. It bounced off the walls and pushed through his head, causing the dizziness to get worse.

Warm butter dripped off the corn, running in rivulets between kernels as if seeking its way through trenches of the streams he and his brothers used to play in back home. Steamed fries kissed with spices. The scent embedded its way into his nostrils. A perfect cut of steak, a porterhouse. The outside seared long enough to keep things red on the inside. His mouth watered. Matt lifted the blade of his steak knife and cut into the meat. Juices leaked out, the pink stain thickening before his eyes. Blood seeped its way across the plate, invading the fries, the corn...

Blood.

Open your eyes, you spineless coward.

Matt snapped his teeth together, the sound banging through his head and causing the dull ache to pulse in response. He winced and opened his eyes, testing the waters, waiting, and praying this was all a dream.

No fucking luck.

Damn it.

The lone light bulb, that insulting glass piece, still hung in the center of his cell, bringing him back to a painful reality. It taunted him, always on, keeping his surroundings illuminated. He could do without seeing the scorpions crawl across the floor, the dark iron stains standing out in stark contrast to the terracotta-colored cement.

Those stains. They spoke volumes of what had occurred in this room before him.

Don't get him started on the rats hanging around. Those fuckers would make a New York City rat run for cover.

"Matt?" a weak, questioning sound came through the wall.

He groaned and closed his eyes again, wishing himself anywhere but here. *She* did this. This all had to be connected to her. Logically, there was more to consider. Of course, there was. She was locked up too, or appeared to be.

He frowned.

Couldn't focus. Couldn't think straight.

They'd hardly let him sleep, playing the music so damn loud. He'd been trained in the art of interrogation and knew everything being done was a part of breaking him down to his most vulnerable. Making him weak. And even then, there was more that could be done. To him. Her.

If she really was a victim in all of this…

He tried to get his brain together but struggled to form coherent thoughts.

All her fault.

Right? Right?

She had to be tricking him. Wanted to get something out of him.

What was it again?

"Agent… Matt, please. Answer me." Her gentle sob almost broke his heart. She sounded so genuine, so frightened, and so real.

It was all a game, though. Had to be. She'd set him up on purpose.

She carried those drugs in, distracted him with her words, her looks. Her body.

He groaned and turned his face away from the sound of her heart-wrenching sobs. The room spun again despite him already being horizontal. He fought against some invisible force as the movement threatened to topple him over to his back again.

He shifted. On his front. He couldn't decide.

So damn hungry, thirsty. Heat sweltered in the air, wrapping around him in a thick blanket he didn't need. His face slammed into the dirt floor, and white spots danced behind his closed lids. Pain burst from his nose. Matt coughed and choked as the inhale brought sand into his mouth with a straight path to his lungs.

Fucking great.

He dug his toes in the ground and attempted to push himself toward the silver bowl sitting to the side of the door. It was a gift after day three, when he'd attacked the third guard to come into his room. He'd fought so damn hard, understanding if he hadn't given his all, he'd never leave this godforsaken hellhole. He'd gripped the guard's arm, heard a snap, and felt something break beneath his hands before it was lights out again.

The guards had learned when to come into the room. Not that he did much nowadays, in his current condition.

He tried to focus again.

Flies hovered above the bowl and the word *Fido* blurred.

Sadistic assholes.

A sweet, panicked voice pitched through the wall, her screams calling to some protective instinct deep inside him. He lifted his hand, the movement feeling as if he were bogged down with cement blocks. The door snapped open and sent the bowl scattering across the floor, precious drops of water sinking into the sand and concrete as if it never existed.

"No!"

Matt rolled to his back as the shout took the last of his energy and found himself staring into a pair of soulless night eyes before darkness claimed him again.

****

Shards of what felt like cold glass slammed across his face, spilling down his chest. He came awake with a gasp. Matt lifted his head, and the room spun—*not this shit again*—as he tried like hell to focus.

A dark-haired man tossed the bucket against another brick wall, then leaned down, his smile holding an ugly twist as if he expected something.

"You think to get away so easy, *puto*?"

The only response Matt could give was a pathetic groan.

Nice, dude. Want to hand over your man-card now?

A blow landed across his cheek, and his head slammed to the side. His ears rang as if he was attending his baby brother's trumpet lesson. Baby brother? Luke wouldn't find that reference amusing at all, seeing as those lessons had been ten years ago, and the man was now in his late twenties. But at least it distracted Matt for a few precious moments.

Liquid dripped on his upper lip, and as his head rolled, the bright spatter of crimson splayed across his chest. If he had any energy, he would have shown surprise he had any liquid inside him at all. As it was, his lips were cracked, his mouth dry as cotton, and his skin looked as if he'd aged twenty years overnight.

Fingers wrapped in his hair and yanked his head back to meet the same pair of soulless eyes from earlier, except now, they held a harsh squint and begged for trouble.

"*Suficiente*, Jose. Enough."

Jose looked over his shoulder. Rapid Spanish, too quick for Matt to understand, bounced between the two. As the conversation went on, all he could understand was the anger rising, the tension spreading through the air. Voices rose in crescendo. The fingers tightening in his hair didn't fail his notice, either.

As abrupt as his wake-up call had been, the conversation ceased, and Jose stepped away with a scowl. Matt's head bobbed like a buoy in the ocean before it came to rest on his shoulder. An older gentleman pulled up a chair and sat in front of him. The man's dark hair carried sprinkles of gray above his ears, eyes so blue Matt swore he could see the ocean's floor. Impeccably dressed, the three-piece charcoal suit stood out worse than a Dallas Cowboy cheerleader at a funeral.

"Agent Gonzalez," the man began.

Ah hell, they know my name.

"It seems you and I have some business to discuss."

"Who—" Matt choked on the dryness in his mouth. The cough spread through his chest with a dry, hacking sound. To his ears, it was thunderous, horrible, and disgustingly wrong. For what seemed like hours, he coughed until his chest ached, feeling as if his lungs would be the next to come up.

"Excuse my rudeness, Agent. I seem to have forgotten my manners." The man lifted a hand and snapped fingers over his head. Shuffling ensued in the background. "Let me introduce myself. My name is Antonio Ruben Cardalas Gonzalez, the third."

A plate slid on a table in front of him, and a glass of water came within inches of his face. Condensation dripped along the side of the cup, and his eyes practically bulged out of his head. Matt tried to lift his hand but failed, wanting to curse his weakness. It was as if cocaine had been placed in front of a recovering drug addict who'd been tied down. He smacked his lips and grunted.

Antonio reached for the glass and leaned forward to set the cup to Matt's lips. Water rushed into his mouth, cool like a spring day in New York. He took greedy gulps and followed forward as the glass was removed.

"No."

"You must slow down, my friend. We wouldn't want you to be sick."

Matt lifted his hands and rested them on the table. Even that infinitesimal movement left him in a state of exhaustion. Someone settled the glass between his hands, and he fumbled for it before they plopped a straw inside. He lifted his questioning gaze up to Antonio, who smiled in response and gestured to the table.

"Please, eat and drink your fill. Then we'll discuss business."

Matt's head lolled, and he took in the plate. Atop the plastic material sat a steak brimming with juices, red oozing out from the sides—just how he liked it. There was also mashed potatoes, beans, rice.

Carb heaven.

And like the dog they made him to be, he dug in using his hands. Picking up the steak, he gnawed at it, biting out big chunks of meat, barely chewing it, and hardly tasting before swallowing the pieces whole. Never had food tasted so good. Stronger, by the hair of a Barbie at least, he reached over and gulped the water like the lake that had dried up in California, if it still existed. Folsom Lake or something like that. He remembered watching a newscast on it as they'd found a missing plane from years before.

His mind struggled to keep up with his thoughts, to put them in order.

All the while, Antonio watched him with a slight smirk. He sat in a chair, one leg crossed over the other, as if he had all the time and patience in the world.

When the food was gone, Matt lifted the plate and licked it.

Hell, I'll give them Fido. Perhaps I'll even lift my leg and piss on something.

The thought brought a smile to his lips, and he sat back to wait, wondering what kind of business this man would want to discuss in this god-awful place.

Antonio lifted a brow. "All done?"

Matt nodded.

"Would you like some more?"

This perked him up. Was the guy serious? "Uh, sure."

Antonio nodded and turned to the side. "In a few moments. There is something I'd like to discuss first. Jose, bring him in."

A door opened. Jose reached out to the darkened space and gave a tug on something. Metal clanged against itself, and they led a man into the room with his hands tied off by steel rings in front of him. On his feet were much of the same restraints, and across his face was a black sash. Matt frowned as some sound reached him. A low, thumping beat, lyrics of a singer better known as Prince filling the air. He realized with sudden clarity the sound was coming from headphones sitting on the man's head.

Jose yanked the blindfold from the man's eyes, and Matt cursed. Those eyes looked familiar. The hair. The features.

The guy's eyes widened as he stared back at Matt and screamed, "Help me! Please!"

Matt tensed but stilled as the telling feel of steel tapped his temple. Beside him, a low laugh, then a familiar voice.

"I don't think you'll be helping him. You recognize him, no?"

Matt clenched his teeth, then ground out, "Yes."

"Such a mess, is it not?"

A trick question. He didn't answer.

"You see," Antonio said and sat beside him. "I asked Jorge here to do a small task. One he assured me would get done. Did it, Agent Gonzalez? Do you think the task got done?"

Matt ground his teeth together until pain lanced through his jaw. If he got out of here alive, he was going to need a superb dentist.

"No," Antonio answered, "it didn't. You see, Jorge has a thing for always getting himself into binds. He swore this time things would go off without a hitch. But my package never got to its destination. Because you, Agent Gonzalez, interceded. I don't like it when my plans don't work out. It makes me very, very angry."

Antonio gave a brief nod, and the room filled with Jorge's begging pleas again. Someone stuffed a red rag into the man's wide mouth, and his legs gave way as they pulled him away. The sickening sound of bone meeting concrete filled the air before another door, this one on the opposite wall, opened, and they dragged Jorge through. Matt watched it all unfold, feeling helpless to stop any of it. He knew all too well the situation he was in now, and there wasn't a single fucking thing he could do about it.

A large barrel sat in the middle of the room, one like he had seen a long time ago in a picture from when his brother, Chris, had served a special tour in Iraq. The kind filled with black oil. A shudder worked its way along his spine as two men lifted the lid.

Oh, sweet Jesus.

Matt slammed his eyes shut, knowing what was to come. He had read numerous reports, watched things unfold along the border, and understood he was powerless to stop any of this from happening.

Jorge's muffled screams grew frantic, and the cool steel barrel pressed harder against his temple.

"Open your eyes, Agent. This, this you will watch. This is what you caused."

The telltale sound of a cocking gun had Matt watching in horror as they lifted Jorge and set him inside the barrel. Oil splashed out, overfilling as the weight distribution settled. The cover went back over the top and for a moment, Matt breathed a sigh of relief, happy he wouldn't have to watch the terror unfold.

Jorge's head popped through the center and his earlier hope died.

Our father, who art in Heaven, hallowed be thy name…

A match struck against the barrel, the orange flame licking the air, searching.

Thy kingdom come…

Jose flicked the lit match through the air, his maniacal laughter following behind. Matt rushed on through the prayer as time suspended.

The flame disappeared as it hit the rim of the barrel and Matt clamped his jaw shut as Jorge's muffled, terror-filled scream charged through the air.

Chapter Three

Juliette stared at the wooden door, her lower lip and chin trembling as the last of the screams died down. Fear trickled up her spine, causing her entire body to freeze. She could not move, could barely breathe.

Holy crap. The horror that had saturated the air, the absolute pain engulfing the sound, had her pressing back to the cool brick wall and cowering like a frightened animal. Hell, it scared her shitless. After hearing that, after waking in this god-awful place far from home, locked away in some underground cell deep in the recesses of Mexico, for only God knew what reason, she doubted anyone would blame her.

Surely she wasn't in Kansas anymore. She did an internal eye roll. She obviously wasn't in the United States of America. Only reason she grasped that was because she'd heard the guards talking when they didn't think she was awake. The drive to their destination had been long and included hitting every pothole known to man until she felt the vibrations still in her sleep. No doubt about it, she was going to need a good adjustment for her spine after getting out of this place. The first few nights, she'd been unable to fall into a deep slumber, waking up as her body jerked and rolled with the phantom, lingering feeling.

Voices sounded from outside the room, jarring her back to the present.

She had to get out of here. The other option wasn't something she wanted to accept.

Jorge, what have you gotten me into now?

Her brother had a knack for getting into trouble, which seemed to orbit around him. As if he were a magnetic force to draw in problems. It didn't matter that he didn't look for it. Trouble always found him. And always had.

As a kid, he'd drawn the school bullies his way with a perpetual look of disgust on his face. It wasn't intentional. She'd talked to him over and over about trying to school his features, but it was almost like he couldn't control it.

As an adult, that same look and ego of his drew the roughest criminals in the neighborhood. The two of them were so different, him the night to her bright and sunshiny day. Amazing they held the same DNA labeling him as her twin.

After what those agents had found in her bag and what followed, she knew, just knew he was connected to this.

She pulled on her wrists and winced as pain spread, scoring up the length of her arms like glass pulsing through her veins. Juliette studied the rusted shackles. Where they scraped against her skin were bright red lacerations. That couldn't be good. The way the veins beneath her skin inflamed, drawing a red line up her forearm, didn't look too promising either.

Oh, joy. What was a blood infection on top of a kidnapping?

Maybe she'd try her luck in the lottery next.

She winced and followed the chain attached to those shackles. The length gave her about three feet of movement around the confined space until tethering off to the wall. The hook that held the chain in place didn't look to be in much better shape than the shackles, but in the week or so since they'd been here, with her movements and tugging on it, the hook began to loosen. Hope sparked in her chest like a lone light in the middle of a dark forest.

She shifted closer to the wall again and peeked

through to the next room. There were a couple of missing bricks here and there, almost like someone had taken the time to remove them. For what reason, she didn't know, but she was grateful to see into the room where they kept Matt.

His room was different from hers. She had bars lining the length of what she now referred to as her cage. His was only lined with bricks, mud, and concrete.

Pushing her face to the opening lower near the ground, she ignored the scraping against her skin. She didn't see anything, but that didn't mean he wasn't there.

"Matt?"

Something scurried past her head, and a scream bubbled in her throat.

"Matt!"

Her voice choked off as a metallic clank rumbled in the lock to her cage. Juliette scrambled back again, hovering in a dark corner as the door opened to reveal a man. She tried not to cower, fought to hold her fear at bay, but this was the same man who brought her in here when they first arrived. The same one who grabbed her and Agent Gonzalez from that room in JFK airport and smuggled them into Mexico. He was the same man who visited her cell every night and listed off all his promises.

She shuddered as some imaginary clock ticked down what remained until he actually followed through with those vile threats.

"*Mi mujer*, come with me."

Juliette swallowed the thick revulsion in her throat. "I'm not your woman, Jose."

His eyes flashed, and something malevolent slid across his black gaze before he grinned. The smile did nothing to reassure her. Instead, it held secrets, as if the joke was on her. He crossed the room, and she pulled the chains taut to get as far away as possible before being forced to stand still. She was trapped between the bricks at her back and the man approaching. Her gaze darted around the room, looking for anything, something to use so she could fight back. She wouldn't go down like a victim.

The room was bare, save for a bucket she used as a toilet and a small red blanket. She hadn't used that blanket for anything other than wrapping around her waist, as she needed to relieve herself. The guards stationed outside her cell door often liked to watch through the windows in the wall and whispered crude things through the small bars.

Jose stepped up, and despite having a good six inches of height on him, she felt vulnerable, weak. She hunched her shoulders inward to get farther from him. He oozed power, his strength pulsing in waves. Jose stood at about five-foot-four, but he was bulky, his black t-shirt screaming at the seams of the arms and the threads stretching across a muscle-honed chest.

He grinned as if he saw the fear she desperately tried to hide. Like a snake, he reached out quickly and caught the chain between her shackles, then gave a hard yank until she stumbled forward. Her body came into contact with his, and a hiss escaped as lightning pain originated from her wrists. They throbbed, her pulse screaming, the rust feeling as if a thousand needles punctured her at once.

Jose dropped his face into her neck, and she fought a wave of nausea as he grazed his lips against her ear. Hot breath puffed against her skin and the stale scent of sweat filled her nostrils.

"*Nuestro tiempo esta llegando, hermosa.*"

Her stomach lurched, and she forced down the rising bile. "Never. Our time will never come."

He chuckled, and she silently cursed the tremor in

her voice. A click of another lock, and Jose stepped behind her, then pushed forward, his hand catching a feel of her butt in the process.

She tripped over the heavy chain lying on the floor but caught herself as she walked out of her cage. A quick glance down both sides of the hallway revealed nothing but brown-bricked tunnels. Haloed lights hung every fifty feet or so, and dirt lined the floor. Her heart sank like an anchor as hope for escape dwindled. There were no signs telling her which way was the exit. She'd more than likely piss someone off by getting loose in what looked like a maze of tunnels before she'd break free.

Another taller guard stood off to the side with a rifle in his arms, waiting opposite the wall from where they came out. This one looked so young, like he couldn't be any older than seventeen, maybe eighteen years old.

Jose stopped next to her and gestured to the right. "This way."

She stepped forward, taking in anything she could identify as a weakness. They moved past Matt's cell. The door was ajar, the room empty. Her heartbeat thundered in her ears. Where had they taken him? Was he still alive? Could her time be next?

Some two hundred feet down the hall, Jose stepped ahead and opened a door. Sunlight caused her to squint as the natural light seemed overwhelming. She stepped into the room after Mr. Rifle Guy shoved the offending weapon into her back. She glared at him over her shoulder, then turned to survey her surroundings. Her breath caught in her chest.

She noticed Agent Gonzalez first. He sat in a wooden chair along the wall from where she had walked in. His hands were clenched into tight fists and lying on a metal table in front of him. Between his large frame and the small furniture, it would be a laughable situation had they been anywhere else. The chair and table looked as if they had been made for an elementary school child.

His whiskey eyes hardened, and he stared back at her. She tossed him a silent question, and he shook his head ever so slightly, so small of a movement that if she blinked, she would have missed it.

She hated to admit it, even here in an unknowing place with these foul men around her, but Matt had this rugged look going on about him. Dark hair came in along his cheeks and jaw. Shadows pushed on his cheeks as if he'd lost some weight in the short time they'd been here. He looked leaner, stronger, meaner.

It all worked really well for him, and she honestly needed her head examined. To be thinking that now was not the time. Not the place. She did not need to be checking out the hot agent who'd been kidnapped with her while there were men with wicked-looking guns watching them.

"Ms. Scaglione, I presume?"

Juliette reluctantly tore her gaze from Matt.

A man, one who threw off sparks of power, way more than Jose, leaned against the brick as if his three-piece suit didn't stand out in this dirty room. He had sprinkles of gray at his temples, and his blue eyes were so cold she shivered. Her gaze bounced between Jose and this newcomer as if questioning the lesser of two evils. "Yes, that's me."

Mr. Suit grinned. "I've heard so much about you."

She frowned.

"It's a pleasure to finally make your acquaintance."

A dark cloud crept over her at the unknown.

What was going on? Her gaze darted to Matt, but he wasn't watching her. No, his eyes were on Mr. Suit, and the storm brewing there reminded her of a hurricane's anger. It shook her, that wrath she saw there. She'd never been on the receiving end of something like it, and she decided right then she'd do everything in her power to never be so.

She straightened, drawn back to Mr. Suit when he called her name.

"How do you know me? What do you want? Where am I?"

Mr. Suit inched his way around the room, as if he were taking a stroll in the park and not some hellhole in the middle of nowhere.

"I was a business associate of your brother's."

She knew it! Her spine stiffened. "You know Jorge? Is he here?"

Mr. Suit gave a low, throaty chuckle, his head shaking as if he were amused by her questions. "I did know Jorge. And yes, actually he is. Would you like to see him?"

"Juliette, no!" A grunt whipped her head around. Jose pulled his hand away from Matt's face and shook it. Matt's head lolled on his shoulders before he glared up at the shorter man. Her heart slammed against her chest.

What's going on here?
What does Matt mean, no?
Where's Jorge?

Mr. Suit motioned, a grin curving his lips up at the corners. "Come, Juliette."

Her skin crawled with unease.

"I'll let you see your brother, and after that's settled, we'll discuss business."

She shuffled forward slowly and looked over at Matt again, but this time his eyes were closed, and a look of pain crossed his scrunched-up features. Jose wasn't touching him, though. Instead, Jose eyed a door next to Mr. Suit as if it hid treasures. Was Jorge in there? Was he hurt?

Mr. Suit looked at her, his eyes dancing. "Let this be a lesson. A reminder, Ms. Scaglione. I'm not one to be crossed. You'd do well to remember that."

Her heart caught in her throat, and the door opened. She turned with wide eyes into the room. Breath punched out from her lungs in a rush, the meager rice from hours before rising like a geyser in her throat. She fell to her knees and retched. Jose chuckled behind her. Matt cursed, but Mr. Suit said nothing. He just stood next to her like a demon shadow.

The scream billowed up from her chest and exploded out as her vision grew hazy. Tears filled her vision, and she was thankful. She didn't want to see any more. She had seen enough, and the sight of her brother's charred remains, the Saint Christopher she'd given him ten years ago still wrapped around his neck, was one she knew would forever be etched into her brain.

Her brother. Dear God, what had he done to deserve such a horrifying death? She gulped in a heavy breath of air, trying to ease the pressure in her chest. Dust came in swiftly, causing her lungs to seize and her throat to coat with grime. She coughed violently, caught between the ache of the loss of her brother and the physical pain in her body. All of this was too much. The trip gone wrong to Cancun, the questions in JFK, the attack, kidnapping, guards watching while she tried to handle her basic needs, the vile promises from Jose, the silence from Agent Gonzalez. Now this…

"I have no one," she said under her breath.

"What's that, dear?" Suit asked next to her, but she could barely hear him through the whooshing in her ears. What was that? Her heart beating? Couldn't be. Her heart felt as if it had broken instead.

She had no one to rely on anymore. Her parents were long gone from this world. Her asshole of a boyfriend had abandoned her, and now her twin—the walls around her closed in until the despair of her situation ripped through her chest. The pain. It felt as if someone had dragged a serrated blade through her chest.

"Wha—what did he do?" she cried, unable to see through the tears. Mr. Suit's watery image stepped closer.

"Don't play coy, Ms. Scaglione."

"What do you mean?" She tried to stand on shaky legs, grateful when someone assisted and continued to support her weight. She'd probably go down hard if let go.

"Jose," he said instead of answering. "Take Ms. Scaglione back to her cell and teach her all about lessons."

Like hell. She went solid just as the grip on her waist tightened. Mr. Suit's order left nothing to the imagination. The last thing she wanted was to go anywhere alone with Jose.

"No," she whispered, horrified. To be taken against one's will was the very nightmare every woman prayed they'd never experience. She'd always been careful, locking her doors, carrying mace, and parking in well-lit lots. Now this, after coming home early from an awful vacation. Every safe act she'd taken before meant nothing.

"Don't you fucking touch her!"

She turned in time to see the butt of a rifle slam into Matt's temple. He fell to the floor as if a boulder had plowed into him, then didn't get back up. She started struggling in earnest, hitting anything in her path, kicking out. Someone else grabbed her legs, but she fought for all she was worth, then realized nobody was coming to save her. No one would help.

So, she screamed.

The sound was raw and full of anguish.

The lights above her head came in pulsing waves as they moved her toward her cell again. She could barely move her limbs, and panic caused a nauseating swirl of bile to turn in her stomach. She couldn't think, could barely concentrate on fighting, breathing.

Moments later, she was slammed atop the thin cot mattress. Pain shot through her hip and tailbone, but she immediately recovered, rolling over and scooting backward until her spine met the brick wall. Her hair caught against the abrasive stone and pulled against her scalp.

Jose said something to the other guy, and she didn't quite catch the words before the second one left them alone, walking out with a lascivious grin in her direction.

She shuddered.

Jose took a step toward her.

"Stay away from me!"

He lifted his hands in front of him but glanced over his shoulder. "Listen to me, very carefully. I'm not going to take you now, but this situation you're in can either get better or much, much worse. It all depends on how much better you want it to be. And that depends on just what you're willing to do. Hear me now, I can make it better. Or you can make it worse. The choice is yours."

Chapter Four

A pulse throbbed in Matt's temple as a soft sob broke through the silence, drawing his attention back to the woman who seemed to be linked to everything.

Shit.

He leaned over and peeked through the brick-sized hole in the wall.

She pressed a slender, pale hand to her stomach and sat on the small cot. Her movements were that of someone in either a world of pain or emotionally broken beyond belief.

"Juliette," he called.

She stared straight ahead, lips quivering, tears tracking down her face.

She looked like she'd completely given up.

Not good.

Shit. Shit!

He shifted on the bed and stared through the hole, trying to get a wider view of her room. It looked different from his. Wide gray bricks instead of the small orange ones. He suspected, from the heavy clicking metal sound he heard earlier, that her cell was lined with metal bars rather than a heavy wooden door and bricks like his. The differences told him everything he needed to know. These cells were additions to what was most likely a building built for some other reason, maybe a dwelling for a family. Lucky for them, depending on the age of the materials used and the craftsmanship of the individuals who built it.

He'd take some time to look around, try to find some weaknesses in the room, ways for them to escape. But first, he felt compelled to help Juliette Scaglione.

"Juliette," he called again.

She didn't answer, didn't look his way. He couldn't blame her, not after how long he'd ignored her. Looking back on the days that had bled together, he couldn't drum up a run-of-the-mill excuse that even made sense for why he'd acted that way. Shock, maybe?

He shook his head and scooted closer to the hole, trying to "throw" his voice to her while still speaking softly. He didn't want to draw the guards back. "Come on, Scaggs, please talk to me."

She sniffed and looked over at him with narrowed eyes. He felt mediocre satisfaction at her attention. Pissed off was better than defeated.

The heavy burden of her hair, riots of curls that looked as soft as the wild rabbits that scurried through his ma's garden, had begun to escape the haphazard twisty thing she'd pulled it into. He wouldn't have been able to say when she did that, as he hadn't been paying attention and had been acting like the selfish asshole he was. Noticing it now, the style drew his gaze to the slender line of her neck, the arch of her cheekbones, the lushness of her lips, and the cat tilt of her eyes. She really was a beautiful woman, but sitting there looking both pissed and lost, he couldn't ignore the draw he felt toward her.

Not something he needed as a distraction. He refocused his thoughts and tried again.

"Do you know if anyone can hear you if you talk?" he asked.

She threw a quick glance in what he assumed was the direction of the bars of her cell. Before she responded, though, she shocked him by standing atop her cot and looking out of the window lined with bars above. Smart girl. She sat back down, this time closer to the wall where he and the hole were. "No," she said, her voice pitched low. "What about you?"

"No, unless someone is standing outside the door here, but the wood is thick enough I don't believe anyone could make out what I'm saying." He paused. "Do you know where we are?"

She shook her head, and a lone tendril of hair dropped off her shoulder to fall along her back, landing beneath where the strap of her bra would be. He gritted his teeth and pulled his focus back to her as she spoke.

"Mexico somewhere. I'm uncertain where. Whatever they gave me really made me drowsy, so I can't be sure of how long we were driving."

He remembered much of the same. Not good news, but not horrible either. "Same here. Have you been out at all? Outside?"

She shifted closer still, dropped to an elbow, and all he could see was the side of her face, the slope of her shoulder. Her white t-shirt looked closer to beige at this point and had dark marks of dirt or something staining it. "Today was the first time they've taken me anywhere." She drew in an audibly shaky breath.

"Hold it together, Juliette," he warned and wondered briefly how he would have reacted if he'd seen what she had with one of his brothers. Probably similar. Maybe worse. Especially if it was Luke, his non-blooded twin. They were so close in age and mannerisms that many had called them twins as they'd grown up.

And then he remembered. That *had* been her twin, information having come down from the analyst assigned to his team moments before the attack.

With that in mind, he tried to show he wasn't a heartless bastard while keeping them on the right path. "I know it's hard. I can't imagine the pain you're going through. But we need to hold it together and think straight so we can find a way out of here. Because we will get out of here. There is no doubt in my mind."

That was when her head snapped over to the entrance of her cell. She froze, and he strained to listen. Whistling broke through the thunder of breath in his ears. A familiar tune he had to strain to take in. He knew that melody from somewhere but couldn't—

"What is that song?" he asked.

"I know it from somewhere but can't place it. Jose whistles it every time he comes to visit." She shuddered and crept back toward the corner of her bed. Matt took a deep breath, trying to work on calming down so he could think.

The whistling grew louder just as the song clicked. As if these guards could get any more sadistic.

Clang. Clang. Clang.

Sounded like a baton or something hitting each of the bars of her cell. But the sound moved on, as did the whistling, until he couldn't hear Jose anymore.

They both spoke at the same time.

"'Twisted Nerve.'"

"From *Kill Bill*."

He chuckled, heard her do the same, and was glad they had a little humor to toss into their personal hell.

Their snickers died off and silence reigned. He'd never heard such quiet where he grew up, just north of New York City, a place called Nyack. It was as suburban, small-town living as one could imagine in the northeast. He'd been to a few different places around the good ole U.S. of A, but he'd never come across towns like they had in the northeast.

Even so, the "town" wasn't so small anymore and turned into a lively hotspot at night, drawing the crowds of local colleges to the Main Street-lined pubs and restaurants. The street his parents lived off wasn't too far from the center of town, and as a result, you could always hear cars passing, the occasional large groups chattering, or even the waves rocking upon the shore from the Hudson River. Never this kind of quiet, the lack of sound one that would make a man insane.

But the silence told him as much as it didn't. They were obviously somewhere far from civilization. Though there were areas in Mexico where people would just turn an eye, anyway. But humanity living and breathing had a certain sound that could not be silenced.

Here, all that existed were the ones in this building. That meant he and Juliette were on their own unless Watson was around somewhere. God, he hoped not. He hadn't recalled seeing the big guy at all.

"Are you still there?" she asked. Her voice sounded as if rocks were caught in her throat, reminiscent of an old jazz singer his ma used to listen to.

"Yeah," he responded, leaning down more and attempting to get a better sight into her cell. He'd already scooped his out, and there was no way he could get out unless someone opened the heavy door. A long, thin arm sat on the other side of the hole, along with two legs clad in red leggings crossed at the ankles. "We need to find a way out of here. Any ideas?"

She dropped further, and the fall of loose curls tumbled to block his vision. She must have pulled it down. Call him demented, but he had a powerful urge to see her hair all loose and wild. Put his hands in it. He forced the wants aside and refocused.

His only *want* needed to remain the *need* to get out of this place.

"Maybe I can distract Jose or something?" she said, the words coming out as if torn from her.

He narrowed his eyes, trying to hear what she wasn't saying. "Exactly how are you going to distract him?"

She sighed and dropped again until her head

rested on the bed, her hair so close all he had to do was reach out and he'd be able to see if the curls were as soft as they looked.

"Well, you know. You heard him."

His pulse thundered in his ears, and he had to force his voice to stay low, not bellow like he wanted. "Absolutely not."

"It's our only—"

The whistling came back around, the same song, the same demented thoughts that came along with it. He couldn't help but picture the very scene in *Kill Bill* while Jose strolled by their cells. Each *clink, clink, clink* of the baton against the bars had Juliette flinching further away. No way could he allow her to offer herself as the sacrificial lamb. But damn it, if not that, then what?

He waited until the whistling had faded again before speaking. "What if you did try to go through with it? What's the plan then? Take his keys?"

She tilted her head. A small pert nose came into view. Nothing too big but the right size with a sweet slope. "Maybe I can find something to tie him up with. Or switch the chains to him."

He cringed and wanted to laugh. "Really?" he asked, voice full of disbelief. "He may be on the shorter side, but the guy is clearly clever and strong. He'd overtake you in seconds, and then where would you be in the face of a pissed-off, sexually aroused asshole who gets off on the pain of others?"

She blew out a breath. "Wow. I mean, you have a point and you're right, but just, wow."

He felt like the same kind of asshole he'd just accused Jose of being.

"I'm sorry. I just, I don't want you to have to go through that. The thought of having to sit here while he violated you is enough to drive me crazy just thinking about it. I just—" He pulled in a deep breath to force his mind to settle, to get the right words out. Hearing her get raped would toss him back in the past, into a nightmare so ugly he wouldn't wish it on his worst enemy. "I don't think I'm strong enough to handle that." A soft admission, but from her lack of movement—it didn't even look like she breathed—he knew she heard him. "Choose something else," he said.

She tilted more toward him, and this close, the ring around her irises looked a pretty dark brown. Some might even call her eye color light brown, but he could definitely say it was closer to hazel. And entirely captivating.

"There's nothing else," she said in an apology.

He ignored the apology. It wasn't needed. But he couldn't disregard what she told him. Her seducing Jose was literally the only way outside of him attempting brute force on the guards when they came for him again. That hadn't worked out so well the first few times he tried it, and now that they were on to him, he doubted any overpowering would work at all. He was weak, restless, and with little sleep, deprived of proper meals and sunlight, and dehydrated despite slurping up those two glasses of water earlier. No way would he be able to use his strength to get them out of here, with the element of surprise or not.

Resigned to the fact he was going to help her put herself in danger, in this despicable position, he dropped his head against the wall and closed his eyes. "Okay, walk me through your plan. Let's talk details."

"Well, I notice he pays attention to what I say and do. His eyes are always on me, except when he and I are alone. Then his eyes are on my..." She cleared her throat. "Breasts."

The last word came out so strangled and quiet he

wanted to laugh. He held it back. "He's got the hots for you. I get it. Go on."

"I can start talking to him, maybe catch him as he walks by. Get him interested in spending some time with me. Maybe it'll relax him some."

He mentally shrugged. Anything was possible at this point. Didn't mean he liked this plan, though.

"Maybe he'll come in and relax, and anything can happen then. Maybe I can get ahold of the keys and get us both out of here, or hit him over the head with something." She let out a heavy breath. "I don't know. Something."

He rolled onto his back and ran a hand down his face. The plan was shit. "It's all a risk." He shook his head. One hell of a risk. Who knew how many times they'd done exactly this? Kidnapped men and women and used their fear and pain to get information. "Shit," he said under his breath.

The heavy lock to his door slammed free with a loud bang, and he was up and out of his bed before the sound stopped echoing in his room. The walls around him spun as he stood, men coming straight at him looking as if they were wormy humans swimming through the air.

"What the—" he asked just as one grabbed his arm and yanked him forward.

Jose stood at the door with a smirk. Matt shook his head, trying to clear it. The whole world spun. Either he was more dehydrated than he thought or they had put something in his food.

All too late, he realized he'd been played. The scene earlier had served a purpose that would play out later, probably something that satisfied the anger in Antonio first. But bringing him food, giving him something to drink. That had been meant for this right here. The exact spectacle of them taking him out of his cell groggy with God only knew what in his system. A truth serum, maybe? Or just something to make it easier to cut up into tiny pieces?

Fuck, now his mind was catching up for the ride and wanted to play a game too. Every awful scenario started rolling through his head as they dragged him down the hall. His feet gave out. Whether it was from the fear of what was to come or the drugs, he didn't know.

Nothing worked right anymore. Not his vision, not his head, not even his body.

Fuck.

Chapter Five

The screams started several hours after they'd taken him.

Juliette had never heard such pain come through in a sound. The soul-shredding violence made her want to cover her ears to shut it out. But she forced herself to listen, to hear. Matt was going through whatever torture had been dreamt up. Matt, who'd been trying to comfort her earlier. Who was now doing his best to shield her from his pain. That'd been made clear as she'd heard voices yelling at him to scream, the taunts and encouragements once he did.

Another pain-filled shriek rent through the air, this one causing her spine to stiffen and her mouth to dry in horror. If they caused that kind of sound from him, what must they be doing?

What would they do to her?

Logic told her they were looking for something or someone. What or who, she didn't know. That her brother was, or rather, *had* been involved, made everything that much more confusing. She'd never guessed he'd know men like this, be involved in an operation like this. Her sweet brother may ask for trouble, but she didn't think he'd cross this kind of ethical line.

And it made her wonder … where was Jimmy?

She tried like hell to make sense of it all. The drugs found in her bag. She'd never seen drugs in person before. Well, that was a lie. She'd seen marijuana, but that'd been at a party or two and she didn't touch it. Not that she had a problem with it or anyone who wanted to smoke the stuff. It was just something she'd never felt the need or want to do.

No doubt the luggage was hers as she'd recognized her panties and shirts. A bit embarrassing, but what had caused her cheeks to heat before was now only a minor inconvenience.

What would have happened had Matt and his partner not pulled her inside that room? Would someone else have made contact? Was she the mule in this situation? Unknowingly?

That was the only logical conclusion she could come up with. Someone had placed those drugs in her bag, then somehow or another, tipped Matt off about it.

The questions were who did it and why?

She didn't want to think it was her brother or ex. She'd never seen them with drugs, but why would her brother be here? Why would they have killed him if he wasn't involved?

Another scream filled the air, but raucous laughter followed this one.

And suddenly, the earlier despair about Matt being tortured switched to anger and disgust. Yeah, it would suck to see what they had planned for her, but she couldn't consider that. She'd never get her mind straight if she kept that line of thinking. Instead, she needed to find a way out of here.

Minutes later, while she tried to work through the logistics of her earlier plan to grab the keys from Jose, voices sounded from down the hall, then grew closer.

A strange, out-of-place dragging noise filled the quick pauses of what was obviously a conversation going back and forth. She couldn't tell what they said, but it was obvious they were trying to keep their voices low.

She made her way to the cell bars, wanting to see who was coming and if they had Matt. Thinking they may put him back in his cell, she let out a startled gasp as Jose came into view along with two other burly guards.

Between them was an unconscious Matt, his head lolling against his chest and his legs dragging behind.

The guards held him by his arms and were careless in their handling. Blood soaked his head and body, running in rivulets down his bare chest and legs. The only piece of clothing he wore was a pair of black basketball shorts. He hadn't been wearing those before, and she had a moment of insanity in wondering who they belonged to.

Instead of taking Matt to his own cell, Jose motioned for her to move back, then unlocked her door. She stood aside as the other two dragged Matt into her prison, then dropped him like a sack of potatoes in the middle of the floor. The two left without another word.

Juliette wanted to go to him and check to see if he still held a pulse. Surely someone couldn't bleed so much and survive. But how was she to know? She wasn't a doctor. Head wounds bled a lot, that much she knew. She held firm and stared at Jose, who stood watchful next to the entrance to her cell.

His gaze switched between her and Matt, as if deciding something.

Finally, after she thought she'd scream under the intense scrutiny and pressure, he spoke. "Like I said." He shrugged. "You can make things easier or harder. Up to you. And," he said with a tilt of his head toward Matt, "it's also up to you on whether you want to help this *puto*."

Jose locked the cell and strolled down the hall, whistling that eerie tune from earlier. As soon as the sound faded, she rushed to Matt's side and fell to her knees. Blood covered his skin. Most had to be from the long-serrated gash in his scalp. It didn't look too deep, but it had made a mess. Combined with his split ear, which looked like it had a pair of rusty scissors taken to it, his head wounds caused quite the scene. Someone somewhere had once told her head wounds caused a lot of bleeding when, outside of concussions, they were relatively not as bad as they seemed.

She took comfort in that, though it was a small amount since Matt still looked really bad.

He lay on his stomach, one arm stuck beneath his heavy body, the other out to the side. His face was also turned toward her, and breath puffed in ragged motions, drawing dust and dirt up before his face. His mouth was slack in sleep, and had he not been covered in blood and they not stuck in this godforsaken prison, she would have considered his features and position almost—*dare I say it?*—cute.

As it was, she was still concerned about the state of him and what they had done. She tried to push him over, but either he was heavier than he looked or she weaker than she realized because she couldn't budge him at all. She strained and grunted, screamed out in frustration trying to turn him to his back, but nothing worked. Sweat dotted her brow and rolled along her back. The air in her little prison grew heavy with humidity and darker as the sun set.

This was the worst time in this hell—a time when she couldn't see in front of her face. It made her claustrophobic and played tricks on her mind. Combined with the heat and dampness in the air, she almost felt like she was being suffocated inside a box.

Matt here didn't help matters because now she worried what critters would come for him on the floor. She usually stayed on the bed and listened to them rustling around. And when the sound grew close, she made enough noise to wake the dead and have the night guard yelling for her to be quiet.

"Matt," she said again and shook him just enough

to wake him. "Please."

He didn't move, didn't respond.

The meager light coming through her barred window quivered with its last few moments, cutting a small path in a sharp line across his back. It bathed his skin with a torturing kind of freedom, one she wanted to feel on her face, out in the fresh air.

The light turned a vivid shade of red, almost a burning reminder of the sun's spectacular beauty. If she looked out the window, there was no doubt the sunset would be as beautiful as the ones she'd seen as a kid in the high valley deserts of Arizona.

"Whiskey," she whimpered, wanting to see his beautiful eyes open and acknowledge her. Where that nickname had come from, she didn't know. But it felt right. She shook him again, watching as the red faded away. Deep blue and charcoal black worked their way across the exposed flesh of his back, night coming in to take over, the sun fleeing from the day's false promise. Of freedom. Of hope.

The air hung in suspense with the tiniest of slivers.

"Agent Gonzalez," she begged, panic a very real serpent slithering up her spine.

Nothing.

The shimmering light fell dark with the sun falling asleep, then all went black.

The first few hours passed in a blur of listening. She tried to hear the critters coming out, but everything was drowned out by a storm outside. The walls were illuminated in jagged spurts of light, then shook with deafening thunder that went on and on. On one hand, she was happy with the brief seconds of light, but on the other, she couldn't hear any of the hissing or chattering of the rodents that came out.

Something brushed by her foot and had her yelping and screaming, the sound hidden by the storm, but that had been hours ago.

She continued to check on Matt's breathing by leaning in close to where she knew his face lay, then felt along his forearm and down to his wrist for a pulse. The steady pumping of his heart gave her measured relief each time. She was almost sure she'd find nothing.

Exhaustion pushed at her after the storm passed, perhaps from being weak with a lack of food or from the adrenaline rush of the day and evening, but she had to fight to keep her eyes open in the pitch black. Her mind and body wanted to shut down, begging her for a few minutes of sleep, but she didn't know what would happen if she allowed herself to catch some Zs. Would the creature or creatures hiding in her cell come out to bite Matt? Were they riddled with disease?

She had to keep watch and make sure he made it through the night, then tomorrow, she'd come up with another plan. Or better yet, maybe he'd wake by then.

What time was it, anyway? It had to be the very early morning, or maybe that was her wishful thinking, especially with how fuzzy her mind had gone. Something chattered to her right, down by Matt's legs. She moved quickly and felt the brush of fur beneath her palm.

"Get away!" she screamed. Whatever scampered off with an indignant sound. She passed her hands over Matt's frame, making sure nothing else was on top of him. Only when she found him clear did she return to her previous position.

God, she just wanted out of this place. She wanted to go home. Wanted to sleep in her own bed. Eat a proper meal. Watch mindless television. Anything but stay here and wonder about the worst possible outcomes.

A shuffling sounded to her left, above Matt's

head. She dove forward and wrapped her arms around him, holding her own body as a shelter. "Leave us alone!"

Matt shifted beneath her and groaned. She startled and jumped back. "Whiskey," she called, leaning toward his face. The room had grown lighter, still held a weighted darkness, but gray had begun to seep in, meaning the sun would soon rise.

Relief rushed through her at the promise of daylight and the hope Matt would wake soon.

She lay next to him, stretched out her legs with a groan, her muscles twinging and protesting at being curled beneath her all night. A golden light gradually replaced the gray, filling the room with yet another promise, as it did yesterday and the day before.

She took the edge of the blanket she'd yet to use to keep warm and dipped it in a water bowl. Trying not to think of how dirty the water was or if she would make matters worse rather than help, she cleaned away dried blood on his cheeks and nose. She stayed away from the gash, afraid she may introduce something into the open sore. They would need to clean it sooner rather than later, but that would be a problem they'd solve later.

Matt groaned again as the golden light grew. This morning, he seemed better than he had yesterday. Or maybe that was her imagination and quick clean-up job on his face.

"Matt," she called again.

His eyelids fluttered.

Something with a minor heaviness scampered up her leg then. She kicked out, but not fast enough to knock whatever off. Scrambling to her feet, the weight fell from her hip. She spun around and screamed as several enormous rats stared back at her.

Chapter Six

Juliette's soft sobs chipped through the hazy veil of sleep. Matt let the heartbreaking sound pull him from his deep sleep. He realized briefly his rest had been so he hadn't dreamed. Or if he did, he didn't remember any of it. Not unusual, seeing as half the time, he fell into bed exhausted. Sometimes to the point where he blinked, then his alarm was blaring in his ear for him to get up and start all over again.

He didn't mind it. The staying busy, keeping active, exhausting himself half the time. He liked his work, liked to push his body, and both worked to his advantage.

However, this sleep was deep only because they had pushed him during that torture session. So much he had feared they'd go too far and he'd die in the forsaken hellhole.

He shifted, testing his body's response, and felt the hard ground beneath him. At least it wasn't the torture chair they'd had him in.

Another soft sob. Juliette sounded close.

So, he wasn't in that room from before. Where they questioned him. Did things to his body he never wanted to think of again.

How had he known who was carrying the drugs? Who was his source? How many agents worked in the New York field office? On and on, none of which he could answer. Well, not that he couldn't, but wouldn't. Shouldn't. No matter what. It wasn't only his life on the line with the information he had. And that was something he had to keep reminding himself.

Families were at stake. Children. Other unsuspecting agents. Well, none of them were unsuspecting. They all knew what kind of job they signed up for, the war they were in against drugs. A brutal one. One they had a very tiny chance of winning. Despite that, they all believed in the cause.

Another sob, almost as if the sound were being choked down. He really didn't need to be worrying about Juliette right now. These guys meant business, and they were hell-bent on getting anything out of him. He should harden his resolve against the draw he felt toward her, in making sure she was protected and safe. No way could he do either at the moment. He was having a hard time keeping his own head off the chopping block.

But those damn sounds she kept making—they chipped away his hardened resolve. After the bastards had revealed her brother, her screams had filled the air with such an agonizing pain it had taken every bit of his control to stay in his chair.

But the heartbreaking sobs, so low and soft, they forced him to focus on opening his eyes. Slowly, oh so slowly, he lifted his eyelids. Even that fucking hurt. They felt heavy as fuck, too. Like there were negligible weights attached to his lashes, pulling them back down.

Juliette kneeled beside him, head bowed, body leaning toward him. An arm jutted out on the other side of his hip. They were in her cell, not his.

Rapid-fire Spanish sounded close, and Matt turned his head, bracing against the excruciating pain that shot down his spine. Christ, he was a mess. No way would he be of any use to anyone in his present state.

Jose stood at the entrance to the room, speaking rapid Spanish to someone down the hall, and Matt let the momentary lapse in attention feed to his favor. His gaze drifted around the room at a speed that felt like molasses, searching for a weapon, anything they could use to get out of here.

How much of a laughable attempt would this be? He couldn't even be certain his limbs would answer the call.

Once again, he moved his attention back to her like a magnetic force he couldn't turn from. But something caught his attention.

Sitting under the bed right next to her was a plate and a fork. He braced for pain and tried to tune everything out but getting to his goal.

Shifting, he pressed his hands to the floor just as Juliette jumped back, effectively letting him sit up under a wave of almost blackout pain. He grabbed the forgotten fork—hey, you couldn't get too picky when you had no options—and without warning her, rolled to her side and wrapped an arm around her shoulders, feigning as if he were giving comfort.

Hell, he did feel bad for her, but the contact and comfort weren't the reason he needed to be so close.

Her body shook with a ragged inhale, and she cast tear-filled eyes up in his direction. The sun spread in a halo behind her dark head. Beautiful hazel eyes, rimmed with tears, stared at him in question and shock. She looked like a ravaged angel sent to read him his last rites.

"You're awake," she choked out in what he thought was a bizarre statement. She lifted her hands as if she wanted to touch him, but hovered above his face, hers awash in worry with a crumbled brow and a pouty frown that looked entirely too kissable.

His icy resolve melted a bit more, but before he could completely get caught up in the moment, he dropped his left hand to her waist. She stiffened. He slid the metal utensil into her waistband and spoke low in her ear as he watched the doorway to the cell.

"Say nothing." Damn, his voice sounded worse

than his throat felt. He must have slept longer than he thought, or they damaged his voice box from all the screaming yesterday. He leaned more toward the latter. "This is our only chance to grab a weapon. It may not be much, but it's all I need."

She turned her head toward his and whispered urgently, "What are you doing? They'll kill you. You're in no state—"

His arms tightened around her in warning. "Trust me. We're as good as dead if we don't get out of here." She stiffened, and he winced at the reminder of what happened to her brother. "I'm sorry about Jorge, but right now, we need to focus." He lifted a hand and idly ran his fingers through her hair, hoping like hell it would pass for an attempt at comfort. The calluses on his palm snagged against the soft curls, softer than he would have thought. He felt like a barbarian next to her. "I've seen the way Jose has been watching you. He's getting sloppy, letting his guard down. Even now, his back is to the door, and he isn't paying us any attention. I want you to feed into that. Distract him more." He hated, absolutely hated asking her to do anything that may put her safety in jeopardy, but he needed her help. There was absolutely no way he'd get the both of them out alive by himself.

"What!" she hissed and drew back. He caught her and tugged her back to his chest. She smelled of fresh spring and gardenias. Vaguely, he wondered how she did it in a world where there was nothing but dirt.

"Quiet." Matt held her still as he watched the door. He paused as an abrupt round of laughter rang out. "This is the cartel and when they are done with me and whatever they have planned, you're going to wish for death. You should know this. Being involved and all."

"Now you listen here," she said and drew back again. Matt arched a brow at the slash of angry lines marring her forehead. She opened her mouth, but Jose cut her off.

"Hey, *puto*. Get the fuck away from her, yes?"

Blinding pain seared the right side of his face as a sickening crunch filled the room. Matt slammed back to the dirt floor with a thud and blinked against the white stars dancing in his vision. Or maybe it was birds. He couldn't tell because the entire room swayed side-to-side. The lights dimmed. Juliette crouched in front of him and held up a hand.

"Stop. He wasn't doing anything. He was only trying to comfort me because my brother is dead and I spent the entire night fighting off *rats*"—she spat the word—"from eating him alive. I'm exhausted, hungry, and I really just want to go home." Her last word broke as if she was losing her battle with her emotions.

Matt blinked and rolled to a sitting position. *Wait, what?* She stayed up all night to protect him? From rats? He looked around but didn't see any of the furry creatures running around. Not that he would now, he thought, with the sun up. But he still shuddered, picturing the rats in New York City's subway system. Those things were the size of small dogs.

Incredulous, he stared at the back of her head and laid gentle fingers on his throbbing cheek.

"Get up," Jose said.

Juliette stood, and Matt shook the remaining dizziness away. Something was happening, and there were entirely too many guards in the room for a simple good morning. If any time was good to get a plan in motion in an attempt to escape, that time was now. And with the dark hungry look in Jose's eyes as he gazed upon the only female here, Matt had a sudden surge of adrenaline. He would enjoy taking that man down.

"Now you."

Matt met Jose's eyes and stood, lifting his hands as a young guard raised an AK-47 in his direction. The guard looked barely old enough to drive, and his hands shook worse than a virgin trying to put a condom on for the first time.

"Watch it with the twitchy hands. You want to point that thing another way? It's not like I've got anything to go against you with."

The kid's eyes narrowed, but his hands stayed put. Matt turned as Jose led Juliette toward the door of the cell.

There was absolutely no way he could allow Jose to take her somewhere. An ugly feeling settled in his gut. If she left now with Jose, she'd come back a different woman, possibly broken beyond repair. And having that light, the innocence that shone from her, taken away would be a damn tragedy.

"Go," the kid with the AK barked at him, motioning for him to follow Jose and Juliette. He shuffled behind, taking stock of his body, making sure all the right parts worked for what he'd need to do. His arms seemed to function okay, and he was steady on his legs. He felt weaker than he'd ever been before, and his peripheral vision wasn't quite clear. A dull ache had established itself at the base of his neck, and he knew without sleep or Advil that baby would turn into a full-blown migraine within the hour.

Whelp, nothing to do about it now. All his aches and pains were going to have to take a backseat. He needed to draw on every ounce of energy to get them out of this.

She looked back at him as she exited the cell and Jose drew her to the left. The kid behind redirected him from following them, then motioned to the right, back toward where his cell was. He stopped in the middle of the hall, facing the opposite wall, but his head turned toward Juliette's progress. Jose had his arm around her waist.

He was pulling her down the darkening corridor.

No…

The kid jammed the AK into his back again, and a sharp pain radiated from the area. *Shit, I hope that wasn't my kidney.* "Go to your cell. Now!"

Matt closed his eyes, took a deep breath, then he moved.

Chapter Seven

Juliette loved to watch thrillers whenever she got the chance. Occasionally, she threw in a cop show or two. Her favorite go-to was *Chicago PD* and *Chicago Fire*. There was something about Taylor Kinney in the role of Kelly Severide with the occasional tortured-soul-slash-I-really-want-to-be-at-peace-with-myself-but-am-having-a-hard-time-loving-myself-how-can-I-love-you type of deal going on. With his dark, clean-cut good looks, Taylor was her secret celebrity crush. Things got a little weird for a bit with him posing nude on the cover of a magazine with his then-fiancée, but she supposed everyone went through that phase in their life. The outward, I-don't-give-a-damn-what-you-think phase. Not necessarily something awful, but the confidence he exuded, the openness of sex and—she did a mental cough—orgasms with Lady Gaga had caused her to blush even as she poured over every detail of that article.

She wasn't a prude. Far from it. But raised in her strict Catholic household, the weekly mass attendings, and her religious schooling background, she'd never been so open and free with it. Bedroom activities were something left to the bedroom. Not to be openly talked about with millions of people.

Back to the topic at hand. She'd also never been exposed to violence. Living so close to New York City, news stories regarding horrific accounts of attacks were common, even expected. But she'd lived in her own little world, her head up in the clouds as her dad used to say. Protected by her brother.

Her breath stole away at that last thought, pain ricocheting through her system with a fresh wave of grief. Her brother who was no more. Gone from this world, no matter how beautiful or ugly it could be.

Now she only had herself to depend on. Something she was quickly losing faith in, especially as Jose started to lead her down the dark, dank hallway. Her time of putting off the inevitable promise in Jose's eyes had just come to a halt. He was going to take his pound of flesh from her—literally—and no amount of prior sheltering and protecting would prepare her for what she knew and expected would come next. The ultimate horrifying experience every woman feared.

She couldn't even think the word, much less the actions.

Panic quickly rose in her throat, choking the air from her lungs. Her body trembled, and her feet shuffled, tripping over imaginary obstacles before her. Dirt from the floor caught on her Keds, and she distantly focused on that minor detail. How something so normal occurred in a place she hadn't known existed until then. But Jose pulled her along, urging her forward and speaking in low tones, telling her the vile and disgusting things he would do to her, everything he looked forward to, things she'd never be able to repeat without throwing up.

Which was exactly what she wanted to do. Nausea swirled in her stomach and acid ate its way up her throat. She looked around for a weapon, anything to get her out of what was sure to be misery. The meager fork in her waistband burned a hole against her skin, unused and pathetic.

As she turned her head, time seemed to slow as she met Matt's whiskey-colored gaze. His tortured expression seemed to communicate something, but seeing as she couldn't read minds, she was lost.

One second, two. Then…

Awe-inspiring. Revolting. Violent to the ninth degree. There was no other way to describe the way he moved. Matt had barely reacted to the boy behind him, slamming the gun into his back before he raced up to her and Jose with a wild look in his eye. She blinked, finding the kid knocked out on the ground, the gun in Matt's hands, and him attacking Jose between one space and the next.

How did he move so fast?

Jose wretched her away from him, meeting the force that was Matt. She crashed against the dirt wall, her head slamming against the side with a jolting ring. Her vision spun and her ears rang as if she were at the horse races back home.

Matt and Jose tore into each other with a brutal efficiency that, had she been anyone else, would have left her amazed. Instead, she was stunned at the violent brutality.

She staggered out of the way as Jose thumped against the wall next to her with a force that caused the ground to shake and a gust of wind blow her hair past her face. A grunt sounded. She turned, finding Jose on the ground and red seeping out from under his head. Her mind didn't want to accept any of this. The kidnapping, the horror of the past however many days, and now, the thick blood blooming in a scarlet scar from Jose's skull, seeping as if the sand-covered walkway called for its moisture. Was he dead?

Did she care?

Stunned, she turned to ask Matt how he still stood. He took the fork she held and tossed it aside. She didn't know when she'd grabbed it from her waistband. Her mind refused to compute her actions from the past few minutes.

Matt grabbed her arm and started dragging her down the hallway.

As if in a daze, her world narrowed to the sole

focus of walking, following—actually, being pulled, almost dragged. How did he know where to go? They'd blindfolded her when she'd been led in. And now, with minimal sleep, very little food, and hardly any water in the past however many days or weeks, she was out of it. Her brain seemed to process things slower than what was normal. Instead, she felt as if she moved through molasses with her thoughts, and her body wasn't doing much better. She stumbled, muttering an apology when Matt barely paused, but pushed on relentlessly. She should be grateful. But she couldn't seem to get herself together. Couldn't get thoughts in order. Couldn't get her body to work quite right.

"Shit," he said ahead of her and pulled her inside a room off the hall. Inside sat crate upon crate. Warm, roughened hands cupped the sides of her cheeks and forced her gaze up to his.

"I need you to focus, Juliette."

She blinked. Focus? She was focused on him. "Um…"

He sighed and glanced out the doorway. "I need you to concentrate on me, Scaggs." He felt her forehead, then frowned and leaned in closer and narrowed his gaze, as if he could see inside her mind.

He sure had some pretty eyes. Gold broke out from around the brown in jagged spikes as if bursting with the life of a firework. Lashes curled up with enough talent to make any woman envious.

An uncomfortable feeling tightened her chest, and she tried to blow air out to ease the pressure. Unfortunately, blowing the air out made it feel as if she couldn't pull enough back in. She tried to take shorter breaths quicker, wanting oxygen like nobody's business, but the air just wouldn't come.

"Matt," she gasped, her eyes widening. It felt like

she was about to drown standing with air surrounding her but unable to take any in.

"You're in shock," he said, the lines around his mouth tight. Odd that she picked up on that. Details about him were all she could focus on, as if time moved exceedingly slow. Was this what it felt like to die? Was that what was happening to her? Was her body shutting down now that it had been through so much abuse in the past few days?

"Oh, oh, God," she cried.

His gaze snapped over her shoulder before cutting back to hers. He looked grim, as if he didn't want to deal with any of what occurred.

Welcome to the club, buddy, she wanted to say, but more, she just wanted oxygen.

One of his hands shifted and slid back to her nape, then he pushed until she bent in half. "Keep your head down. Try to take deep breaths," he instructed. The upside-down world spun around her, but the pressure in her chest eased and slowly, she could pull in deeper and deeper breaths. He finally released her, and she rose to a standing position. Everything seemed somehow clearer, which was weird, seeing as nothing had changed.

He rooted around in the crates and pulled out a rifle, what looked to be a backpack, and a few more things. She concentrated on taking air deep into her lungs. "What now?" she asked once she had herself under control.

He looked over and took her in, making some silent assessment of her mental abilities, most likely. She didn't blame him. Obviously, she was off-her-knockers kind of crazy. Her body still shook with what had to be a rush of adrenaline.

Whatever he saw must have convinced him she was better. "Now, we escape. Glad to see you could get yourself under control. The body does crazy things when it's in the flight-or-fight response."

The deep timber of his voice washed over her senses and settled something deep inside.

"You'll be sore," he said. "Outside of everything else we've been through, you're going to feel as if you've been hit with a boulder in a few hours. We'll try to get somewhere so you can rest and hydrate. I just need you to hang with me for a bit longer. Think you're up for it?"

She made a show of looking around like she was seriously considering, what, staying? Then she looked back at him and gave him a face to convey what she thought about his question. He chuckled—the guy actually chuckled. Pushing aside how nice *that* sound was, she asked, "Seriously?"

The side of his mouth kicked up, and she purposely ignored that, too. He was entirely too good-looking. This was all stuff she couldn't—and shouldn't—be thinking about while trying to escape from this hellhole of a place.

"Can I get one of those?" she asked, nodding at the gun.

He shook his head. "I think I'll take my chances with only one of us being trained on how to use these and not in shock. But here." He handed her a wicked-looking blade, about five inches in length. She took a deep breath as if to reassure her body she could still take in air.

"I really am glad you were able to break out of it, Juliette."

She looked up from her perusal of the sharp blade and met his stunning gaze. "What would you have done if I hadn't? Leave me?" The last came out oddly vulnerable. She hardly knew this guy, but surely, he was a good one, right?

He cut her a perplexed look, then reached down to do something that caused all kinds of hard knocking sounds to come from the gun. Perhaps it was better he hadn't given her one. She probably would have ended up shooting the wrong person. "Nah," he said. Then he had the audacity, in this place after all they'd been through and still faced, to wink at her.

He actually winked.

At her.

Then nodded toward the door and moved in the same direction.

"I would have just kissed you to break you out of it."

She tripped over her feet trying to follow him.

Chapter Eight

All jokes aside, Matt knew he was operating on minimal time. The stress of the past week or so, combined with lack of food and water, had drained his energy until it took every bit of his concentration to stay on his feet. With the beating—strike that, the torture—he'd been put through, he found the whole scene with him taking Jose down as lucky. Nothing but a blind miracle with success. Adding everything up, the only reason he could think as clearly as he was, the only reason he still moved with a make-believe confidence in planning their escape, was due to nothing but adrenaline.

He would collapse soon. And once he did, he would crash hard. He took stock of his injuries: cuts and bruises over nearly every inch of his skin, maybe a broken rib, definitely a few missing fingernails, and then he thought through their choices. Staying here any longer wasn't an option. They'd both be dead within days. There was no reason to keep them alive. How they'd stayed breathing until now was only because these guys were curious about how much the US Government knew about the operation here, and because Jose had plans with Juliette's body.

He bit back his anger at the thought of Jose. Thank goodness Matt had an opportunity to stop it. Getting her into this situation by failing her back in the airport and then again with her brother. He would have felt completely worthless had he let Jose do what he intended.

Matt shook his head, focusing on making sure the AR-15 was fully loaded and the extra magazines full of ammo were stuffed within the pockets of his shorts. There was no time to search for additional food outside the packages of granola bars he'd found. Instead, he shoved an empty canteen her way, along with a backpack and a rudimentary first-aid kit. "Keep hold of that and stay close. If I tell you to do something, I need you to do it right away. Understand?"

She blinked her big doe eyes and nodded. He sure hoped they made it out of here. He'd come to rely on his partner—he couldn't stop to think about Watson right now—working as a team to get out of hairy situations, and this situation definitely classified as hairy. Without his partner, he prayed he could fulfill the hope in Juliette's eyes.

He pulled on a discarded blue shirt that hung entirely too big on his frame and grabbed a pair of discarded sneakers that surprisingly fit. He'd thank his luck later, when he had a chance to look back on this entire event with fond memories—not. Ducking his head out into the hall, he took a quick glance up and down the length of it before pulling back again.

Clear.

With a deep breath, he moved out into the hall and continued the way they'd originally been going. Hopefully, this was the way to get out. He was only guessing at this point.

It had to be really early, or the compound wasn't as manned as he'd thought before because they didn't run into another person for several minutes. The hall slanted upward until they came around another corner to a large steel door. *Thank Christ!* Every minute they spent in that hall was like a bullseye into the tunnel of death.

He pushed the door open and slid outside. The sun, bright and high in the sky, shone against his face, its warmth landing against his body as if a lover long denied a kiss. He wanted to lie back and let the heat sink into him with an abandoned sense of calm. He had a feeling they'd gotten lucky, and he didn't want that luck to run out.

Car doors sounded from around the corner of the brick and clay building. He and Juliette faced an abandoned field, tall wisps of grass and leaves—not nearly enough for cover should they need it—between them and a thick forest with tall trees, trunks as round as large pressure pipes used underground back in New York City.

Humidity in the air promised water was close, but the dry cracks breaking the Earth's floor told him the desert would also bring some high temps to their location. Where the hell were they?

Voices from the direction of the slamming car doors sounded as if they came closer. He had seconds to decide.

Go back inside.

Try to make a run for it in the forest.

Or dart around the side of the building opposite from the voices and take his chance—hopefully his luck would still stand—to hide around the corner.

He deliberated for what felt like too long. Yet not enough time. He didn't know where they were. Hadn't had an opportunity to study satellite images of the area, so there was no knowing what they'd run into with the forest.

Needing just a bit more time, he grabbed Juliette's hand and shuffled quickly to the corner, then took a quick glance around before moving them to the other side.

They'd gotten around just in time. Voices sounded as if they were right on top of them. Then the creak of the steel door opened.

Matt glanced at the forest again. With them inside now, he didn't know how long they'd have before they found the kid and Jose on the floor outside the cells.

This side of the building was nothing but roads and fencing. The forest was their best chance. Scratch that. If they wanted any chance to survive any of this, that forest was their *only* chance.

He waited thirty seconds, no more, after the voices died away before he took a chance to peek back around the corner. Clear.

He turned to Juliette and absently pushed her hair back behind her ear before he leaned in close. "See that tree line?"

She nodded.

"We're going to make a run for it. Right now. Go."

Her eyes widened, but bless her, she didn't hesitate to take off. He followed behind, keeping his attention split between not tripping and to the side of the building he hadn't been able to see earlier. Cars started coming into view the farther they moved from the wall.

A man shuffled slowly around in a tight circle, smoking a cigarette. Matt glanced toward the tree line and Juliette. The tree line seemed so far. Maybe another 800 meters ahead of them, not as close as it'd seemed earlier.

A shout rang out behind them.

"Shit. Run faster, Jules."

And like a good horror film actress, her feet chose that moment to get tangled beneath her as she tripped and went down hard. He stopped and spun around, lifting the AR at the same time. Sure enough, the man who'd been smoking now ran their way with a walkie-talkie in front of his face. He fired off rapid Spanish, the words too fast and he too far for Matt to understand. But none of it boded well. He fired off a suppression of shots in a line, causing the guy to dive for the ground. The walkie-talkie went flying, but Matt didn't stop to see where it landed. He spun around again, glad to see her up and running toward the forest. She didn't look to be injured, which was a good thing. Their luck was holding out a little longer.

About a hundred meters from the tree line, a loud slam sounded behind them—most likely the door opening. He chanced a quick glance, which confirmed a half-dozen people pouring out of the building and all their gazes on him.

"Keep going!" he shouted as the trees swallowed both of them. "We have to find somewhere to hide, but they will know these woods better than you or me, so we have to push forward faster."

Obviously, someone from above looked down on them with a smile because she pushed forward without complaint, her long legs eating up the ground like a damn gazelle. She seemed to be in her moment, and he made a mental note to ask her later if she did cross-country because she sure moved like she'd been made for the sport.

He ran every morning, five days a week, not because he enjoyed it but because it was a necessity, as it proved to be now. They hurdled over fallen logs, darted around large trees, and avoided thick bushes. Long, thorny vines ripped across his exposed skin. The sweltering heat blanketed the air around his face, filling his lungs with a heavy woodsy smell. They ran until his thighs burned with fatigue. The up and down of the hills leading into the mountains caused his quads to shake with exertion. His legs felt like jelly, but Juliette still moved ahead as if she could keep going.

He wouldn't last much longer. How long had they been running? Five miles? Six? Which direction had they been heading? Surely, they had lost their pursuers by now. No way those guys had followed them this deep into the forest.

Right?

The ground rose in a steady hill before them, and he stumbled as his legs started to give dire warnings. His body wouldn't keep going. Couldn't. They had to find a place to hide. But where?

"Hold up," he said, breathing heavily. His chest felt tight, and his heart pounded. They both slowed, then stopped. Around them, silence reigned but for the brush of leaves against the wind, and farther, the sound of water. Maybe a river. Yeah, the forest was never this quiet. He'd spent a lot of time camping with his brothers in upstate New York. The only time this kind of hush pursued was when man was present. He looked up the mountain they'd have to climb, searching for a place for them to hunker down. Meanwhile, he strained to hear if they were still being followed.

A bird cawed overhead, the sound like bones rattling. Far off in the distance, a loud growl. He turned to face downhill and waited. They had to have outrun them. He couldn't go on. His body had reached its limit.

Seconds ticked by in stillness.

He met her worried gaze.

Then, sounds of yelling came from lower down the mountain.

He closed his eyes. They hadn't outrun them after all.

Shit.

Chapter Nine

Juliette wanted to cry out in anguished exhaustion. She was so certain they had escaped. How long had they been running? Her legs felt like those rubber noodles her mama used to put in the pool back home. Her lungs ached to find a rhythm of their own, and her heart sped as if a horse galloped through her chest on its own cross-country sprint.

Her head pounded out a beat that relayed she was more than dehydrated, despite the feel of heavy humidity causing sweat to run in rivulets down her spine. The air pressed in on her chest and face with a shockingly brutal intensity, as if there were a curtain of water in the air. She struggled to draw in steady breaths and fought back the black dots dancing in her peripheral vision.

"We need to find someplace to hide," Matt said, urgency in his voice.

Well, *yeah*, if the sound of the yelling coming up the mountain behind them was any sign, they needed to be gone or hidden, and they needed to do it fast.

Dark clouds rumbled in the distance, and the dense air filled with the scents of moss and fresh spring charged with an electricity that promised a storm was well on its way. She pushed farther up the mountain, following behind Matt, her quads and calves screaming with each additional step. The backpack seemed to weigh fifty pounds.

Matt didn't look to be doing much better. Growing dark spots on his midnight-blue shirt drew her gaze again and again.

Was it just sweat? Until they settled down and she got an opportunity to take a look, there was no way to know. Unfortunately, their time for rest didn't seem to be coming soon. All around were tall, thick trees, full bushes, or vast open areas. No caves, which could be both a blessing and a curse, seeing as there was no clue what might be inside.

Another step, and her leg went out from under her, but she caught herself, felt the scrap of rock against her sensitive palms, and winced at the sharp sting of pain. Knowing there could be no downtime, she pushed up and waved off Matt, who'd turned. His lips thinned with a grim understanding. The same understanding she had: their time in freedom was limited unless they did something soon.

He sighed and tugged her out from the original path they'd been on, which was nothing but a natural curve through shrubs and trees. They stopped at the base of a large fallen tree, one of the biggest she'd ever seen, and probably as wide as her mini coupe back home. That width was only at the base. The tree drastically slimmed down about halfway up.

She met Matt's somber gaze, already knowing what he was going to say before he spoke.

"This is our only chance. It's not ideal," he said.

She groaned low. "Oh, man." Those black dots she'd managed to beat back suddenly came back with a vengeance. She gulped. "Did I happen to mention just how claustrophobic I am?" She looked at the tree.

"If we had another choice, I'd offer it. I'm not too keen on getting in there either."

Her breathing picked up, coming out choppy and too fast.

"I'm sorry, Juliette. This is our only chance. We need to rest and hide."

He took the bag from her shoulders, leaned down, and peered inside. She took a quick look, then silently cursed herself. He was right. They needed to do this. But the thought of going inside that tree, even looking at it from the outside and seeing just how small it got, gave her a rising panic. Not that she didn't like the inside of the tree. She was sure it would be okay, maybe even comfortable. Oh, no, it was that despite knowing better, her mind thought she wouldn't be able to get enough fresh air. That she'd suffocate if she went in there. That she'd get stuck and *die*.

"Oh, God," she said with a whimper, then looked around for some other place to hide. Maybe behind a bush. Maybe they could actually make a run for it.

But even as she thought it, even as Matt rose with a grim look on his handsome face, she knew—*she knew*—there was no other option but this tree.

She blew out a breath and stared at the trunk, trying to talk herself into getting inside it. Only for a little while. "You can do this, Juliette Leon Scaglione. Clearly, there's an opening down here. Air will come in. You will be able to breathe."

She took several deep breaths, then Matt pushed on her head and directed her to move inside.

Time was up.

She whimpered under her breath and climbed on her hands and knees for what seemed like forever, but surely was only a few feet before she was forced to move forward on her stomach.

"Keep going," Matt called from behind her. He held a flashlight and illuminated the space in front of her, which helped. But for how much longer? It was surprisingly dark inside this hollowed-out tree, and from what she could glimpse, there didn't seem to be any rodents or insects crawling around, but who knew how long that would last.

She scooted forward on her stomach, feeling the rough bark bite into her shredded hands.

"More, Juliette."

"More?" she asked somewhat hysterically. Already, the tree felt as if it were closing around her head, stealing all of her air. She couldn't do this. They had to find another way. Her head spun, and her skin tingled as if a thousand ants stung her at once. "Oh, God."

"Shit," Matt said behind her, then she felt his hand on her ankle, her calf, her hip. Him coming up next to her didn't help matters because he was stealing all of her oxygen. She gulped in breath after breath, but it didn't help. The air was too thick and hot, disappearing faster than she could take it in.

"I can't do this," she said, her voice rising with hysteria. His face was a silhouette against the darkness. The flashlight had disappeared. He shoved the backpack between their bodies and laid it above their heads, then grabbed her face and brought her close to him until their foreheads touched.

The scent of male sweat, iron, and soap filled her nostrils, momentarily muting her rising panic.

"Juliette, please," he said in an urgent, hushed voice. "I'm not going to let them take us again, but we need a chance to rest and recoup, and this is the only place we can do it. Just for a few hours."

Her mouth moved as if to take in air or respond. She didn't know. But tears filled her eyes and spilled over at her helplessness. How had she gotten into this position? She'd only wanted to go home, bury herself in a pint of Ben and Jerry's Tonight Dough, and lose herself in a Netflix marathon of *Vampire Diaries*. She didn't ask to be involved in whatever her brother had mixed them up in. Or to have gotten twisted into some sort of interaction with a Special Agent, and now trying to escape with her life in this godforsaken jungle.

A sob forced its way out from her raw throat, and she found her face shoved into Matt's sweaty neck. Her hair stuck to her damp cheeks and forehead, her shirt soggy with sweat. The charge in the air grew heavier with humidity until it felt as if she could cut through it with a knife. Matt's arm went tight around her at mid-back. The other held her face to his neck, scrunching a fist against her curls.

"I'm sorry," she said, hiccupping through another harsh sob.

He groaned, then let out a soft curse that sounded surprisingly odd coming from his mouth when he'd been nothing but professional so far.

Well, as professional as one could be when kidnapped, taken to some secret prison in another country, and tortured, then escaping with barely a shirt on his back—literally. Then yeah, he'd been pretty professional.

"You have nothing to apologize for. This entire situation is fucked up." His voice dropped. "I hear them coming. Please try to calm yourself. Just for a little while."

Now that he mentioned it, voices grew closer and shuffling feet sounded somewhat loud against the silent forest. It was as if the animals held themselves on a precipice, waiting to see whether or not they'd get caught.

She scooted closer to Matt until her body pressed against the length of his. Sure, the situation was unlike any other and all social rules went right out the window, but being closer to him made her feel better. Odd, but it was what it was. She wouldn't question it because her body needed to feel that peace, that sense of calm.

He turned his head toward her and spoke lowly as his lips brushed against the apple of her cheek. "Don't move." In a moment of pure insanity, she wondered what he'd do if she tilted her head just a fraction of an inch so their mouths could touch. An exhilarating thought. A naughty and inappropriate one, too.

Now was not the time to be thinking about kissing a hot guy. It was probably the definition of when *not* to think of that kind of stuff. But she couldn't help it. Maybe her mind did it as a coping mechanism, trying its best to keep her alive and from freaking out, giving up their hidey-hole. And once the thought was in her head, it was all she could imagine.

The hand she'd curled against his solid chest rose of its own volition in the direction of his mouth.

How insane was she?

Properly and thoroughly, most likely, but this need to touch his lips was a compulsion she couldn't resist.

Her fingers brushed over the abrasive definition of his powerful jaw. His grip in her hair tightened a fraction, as did the arm around her back. As it was, her breasts pressed against a chest that felt as if it were made of brick. Her rounded hips were cradled to his harder ones, their bodies aligned as if they'd been made to do exactly this.

What *this* was … was pure craziness. Did people actually know they were losing it when it happened? Because that was what she felt. Like she was losing her will to care about anything going on around them when the urge to stay alive should have been at the forefront of her mind.

Instead, her fingers drifted over his mouth, which parted with what felt like a shocked breath. Air stuttered over her fingers, which traced the top upper lip, then the bottom pouty one. His mouth was well defined, the top and bottom lips made with a perfection she hadn't seen on any other man. As if he could kiss a woman silly with those lips or drive her to levels of insanity.

A bubble of laughter worked its way into her chest following that thought, but she forced it down and smothered the sound with her curiosity to learn Matt's mouth.

Her fingernail caught on his bottom lip, drawing it down. His grip tightened even further in her hair, and she shifted closer, adjusting her mouth until she could take his. Because she wanted to. Wanted to live wild and fearlessly in this moment. If they were caught, then this was it. She'd most likely be raped and killed. Wouldn't get to experience the promise that was a kiss from a man as handsome and brave as Matt, a man she'd never thought to end up in the arms of. She'd settled with her ex-boyfriend, thinking she'd never get the opportunity to obtain better.

But now, she had this chance. And from the feel of Matt, from how he adjusted his head toward her, and from how his breathing had changed, she knew he was thinking of the opportunity, too.

She shifted her head and felt him right there. His breath fanned over her lower face. All he had to do was lower his head an inch and they'd touch.

Her hand moved from the side of his mouth and wrapped around his nape, sweat-drenched strands wet against her palm. She put pressure there. He didn't resist, not even for a moment. And the lack of hesitation moved something within her. His mouth pressed against hers.

Her toes curled.

****

I'll take things I'd never thought I'd be doing in the middle of a Mexico forest after being kidnapped by a violent cartel for $500, Alex.

Pretty sure kissing a gorgeous woman, who was

also a suspect in a drug trafficking investigation, within a hollowed-out fallen tree trunk while surrounded by violent cartel members would be the answer to that question on the next episode of Jeopardy, may Mr. Trebek rest in peace, Matt thought somberly.

He used to sit and watch the episodes with his pops every time a new show was on air. Didn't matter whatever else was occurring. That time was reserved for him and Papa Gonzalez, as the family all jokingly referred to him. They'd curl up in front of the TV with some soda and popcorn, then tried to one-up each other with each question asked.

He had maybe answered one question, perhaps two—per episode. His pops, though, that man had an amazing amount of data in his head. He'd spurt random information off, no matter the subject, as if the material was just waiting to escape his lips.

Speaking of lips, the ones attached to the curvy woman beside him cushioned his mouth with a pillowy softness. He'd been shocked at the first touch of her fingers against him, then figured with as much as she'd been scared to get in the log that the kiss was a way to distract herself from her fears. He got that. There were a lot of nightmares in his head, too, and he wasn't very keen on the situation they'd ended in or where they had to end up hiding.

Outside their wood habitat, thunder rumbled, and murmuring from their trackers filled the silent forest.

Matt cupped the side of Juliette's cheek and shifted his head from one side to the other, then back again, keeping his attention half on the closed-mouth kisses and half on any movement or sound coming from the end of their shelter.

The sounds of their chasers grew close, so close it felt as if they were standing right on top of them. He froze, his mouth pressed to hers, breathing heavily through his nose and trying like hell to urge Juliette to not make a sound. Adrenaline pumped through his injured body, but the pain was minimal at present, manageable only because he was trying to survive, trying to escape their clutches. Later, he'd pay severely for what they'd put him through, both physically and mentally. But that wasn't something he could think about now.

The sounds of the men moved away. From what he'd been able to piece together with the different voices, there were about three of them in pursuit. There was no knowing how far they were going to move away or if they'd backtrack or seek shelter themselves from the storm brewing above them all.

Electricity charged the air with the promise of a good show, causing the hairs on the back of his neck to shake with anticipation.

He lifted his head and could just make out the outline of Juliette's face. He kept his voice pitched low enough only for her ears. "I think they may have moved off, but we should probably stay put until the storm passes."

She gripped his wrist. "In here?" she asked, and the sound of her trembling voice caused his gut to tumble. She had to be having a rough time in here with what he guessed was a claustrophobic attack.

He swept his thumb along the curve of her cheek, amazed at the softness. "It's probably best. We can catch some sleep for a few hours, and hopefully by then, the storm will have passed and our pursuers will be long gone. We'll get our bearings and try to find a way home."

Her grip on his wrist tightened, and she slid closer along his body. "A few hours?" she squeaked. "I don't know if I can stay in here for a few more minutes, much less a few hours."

Despite the situation, he couldn't help it and smiled. "I think you're stronger than you think. You've survived this far. You can spend a few more hours in here. Just try to close your eyes and get some sleep. It'll go by faster than you think."

"Matt…"

"I could give you a distraction again, if you like."

"A what?"

"I could kiss you. You kissed me earlier as a distraction." Then he teased, "I could totally sacrifice myself for the greater good and kiss you again."

Silence. She was so still if he hadn't been touching her face, he would've thought she wasn't there. "Juliette."

"I'll be okay," she said, her words pitched lower than before. There was a thread of something he couldn't quite place in her tone. Something that had him pulling her closer until the lengths of their bodies pressed tight against one another. There wasn't a whole lot of room to begin with, but now they were cozy and in somewhat of an intimate position. He opened his mouth to ask her what was wrong when she spoke again.

"Can you just tell me a story, something to take my mind off…" She took in a shaky breath, then let it out. Air skittered over his jaw. "To take my mind off where we are."

He let his hand slide back until his fingers threaded through her hair. A hint of coconuts and cream wafted toward him. Most likely her shampoo. He decided he liked it, then lay on his side and pushed his other arm beneath her head until she curled up against him and under his chin. Definitely her shampoo. "What kind of story would you like to hear?" he asked.

She shook her head against his chest, taking in

and letting out deep, controlled breaths. It was obvious she still struggled being in their hiding place, so he searched quickly for a story to try to help.

"I'm one of six siblings."

She let out a surprised laugh, the air puffing against his neck. He smiled.

"Six? Wow. It was just me and…" Her words trailed off, and he gave her a gentle squeeze.

"Yeah." He took a deep breath, letting the sad moment flow through them both. "All boys in that group." He paused, letting that sink in. "My parents are saints."

"They sound like it," she responded. "Where do you fall in that group? The youngest?"

"Ha. That's surprising you'd think that. I'm actually right in the middle. Third from the youngest or fourth oldest, depending on what kind of day I'm having."

"Are you all close?"

An entirely different warmth went through his chest at her question, one that held nothing against the hot humidity outside. "Yeah, we're pretty close. Especially since every single one of us was adopted."

Her hand convulsed on his t-shirt. "Seriously?"

"Yes."

"Wow, you're right. They are saints."

His parents. "Right." He smiled again. "Anyhow, my oldest brother, Chris, served in the military."

"Served?" she asked, and he heard the alarm in her voice.

"Served, yes. He's alive, but no longer in. Another story for another time. I need to save these up in case you don't fall asleep after this one," he teased.

She chuckled. "Okay."

That was it. Just *okay*. Like she expected to hear

that story later. The thought moved him more than he expected it would. He shook out of it and continued. "When Chris first came back from basic training and his schooling to be a military police officer, he'd learned all these cool new moves. Of course, being the oldest and the first to leave home and come back, albeit for a short time before he left for his first duty station, we were all in awe of not only who he'd become but of what he'd learned.

"I remember looking up at him and seeing my brother stand before me, but he was also different, someone I hadn't seen before. Like the military had stripped him completely down to the core and rebuilt him to be this stronger man, both physically and mentally." He shook his head, trying to describe what he'd seen, what he'd felt. "It's hard to explain, but I was in awe of this power that surrounded Chris. Of course, he *is* quite older than I am, so that may have something to do with it."

She chuckled as he intended, and he joined in.

"How much older is he?"

He grinned. "About five or six years."

She guffawed. "*So* much older."

He chuckled again. "Yeah. Anyway, he taught us these moves, pressure points that would cause someone to immediately comply, grips on parts of the body that would force someone to stop doing whatever they were doing, usually causing a physical problem, and holds guaranteed to put someone on the ground. We all ate it up. Everything he taught us, we practiced on each other for hours. Spent so much time just hanging with one another after being apart for almost a year. It was like being whole again. I didn't realize how much we'd missed Chris in our own way until he'd come home that day."

"Sounds like you all are extremely close."

"We are," he confirmed. "But of course, after learning this stuff, I just had to go show my friends, right?"

"Oh, no," she said through laughter.

He echoed her. "Oh, yes. We went up to this old, abandoned cabin just outside our village, and I took turns on both Evan and Alec, showing them everything Chris had taught me. We weren't paying attention to anything going on around us and ended up stirring up a hornet's nest nearby."

She gasped.

"Yeah, no matter how badass I felt after spending all that time beating the crap out of my friends with new moves my powerful older brother, who was now a hero, had taught me, the first zing and sting of one of those hornets had the three of us scrambling down the hill faster than I'd ever seen any of us run. By the time we got to the bottom and were on the verge of jumping into the Hudson—which, darling, is something no one ever wants to do—we'd lost the hornets. And a bit of our pride. The three of us had snot and tears running down our swelling faces. My parents took one look at us, and everything came tumbling out, about the secret cabin, the fight moves Chris taught us, the hornets."

"Oh, no." She laughed. "What happened?"

"Whelp, turns out even heroes can get grounded."

She laughed, the sound muffled in his chest. He smiled and soaked it up like he would sunshine. Anything sounded better than her screams and tears. "You ready to sleep yet?"

She went taut against him. "Not yet," she said. "Can you tell me another story?"

He curled his body around hers. "Of course." And he did. He told her of his brothers and stories of happy laughter rippling through the house from years long ago. He spoke on and on until he felt her breathing even out and went lax wrapped up in his arms.

Chapter Ten

Sometime later, Matt woke from a light sleep to a sharp and shocked feminine curse.

"Shit, what was that? Ow, that hurt."

He let out a low groan and tried to stretch as much as he could in their cramped quarters. As it was, his back burned as if on fire with what he was sure had turned into an infection. The knives they'd used on him hadn't looked clean at all.

His legs and shoulders screamed with exhaustion—an exertion that felt ten times worse than any hardcore gym workout he'd been through.

They had to get moving. Staying in one place would up their chances of getting caught. Surely their kidnappers had given up on them, especially after the storm let loose a few hours ago.

More cursing sounded next to him.

"What hurts?" he asked.

"Jesus, I think something bit me, or stung me. I've never felt anything like it. I hope my stinkin' ear doesn't fall off."

"Your ear?"

"Thing must have stung—or bit—me right inside. The *whooshing* sound is going to get annoying real fast. Ugh, just what we need, right? Me getting some random venom in me from some deep-forest bug no one has ever heard of, and there is no anti-venom, so of course, I'll probably end up growing weird hair in some questionable spots where weird hair should not grow— you know, because it's weird … hair. Ouch. Gosh, that hurt."

What the hell was she rambling about?

"And then I'll start losing my nails or something,

maybe grow some wings. God, we should look for the thing, whatever it is, to see what I may or may not turn into, of course."

"What?" he asked, trying hard not to laugh. As it was, his chest shook with it.

"Though, I really want to see if we can follow it to its lair, you know? Just to see what I may end up craving to eat later. I hope it'll be something cool, like a sugar bug or something. Nothing like a regurgitation bug. Because bleh."

"Are you referencing *The Fly*?" he asked, incredulous. "Lemme see this bite."

He clicked on the flashlight and leaned over her. She stared up at him, big eyes wide with curled lashes that seemed to touch her eyebrows. Her hair lay around her head, and he imagined this was what she'd look like every morning when she woke. Beautiful and refreshed, ravished, and curious? That was definitely the look she was giving him.

"Lemme see," he said, leaning over her with the flashlight.

She went rigid below him and grabbed his shoulder. "Matt?"

He tilted his head, noting her gaze locked on his mouth. Did she want to kiss him again? "After all that talk about regurgitating bugs, not sure I'm in the mood to give kissing another shot, darlin'. At least for a few minutes."

"What's happening?" She fisted his shirt and pulled him closer, her voice rising with hysteria. "Why can't I hear out of this ear? Everything you're saying is supremely muffled." She pulled him closer. "Matt. Please."

"What the fuck?"

"Oh, my God," she said, panting now. "I can

barely hear you."

Pulling away from her fisted grasp, he lifted the flashlight to the side of her head. He couldn't see anything in particular, but a bit of blood trickled out her ear. Trying to peer inside her small canal was hopeless. He turned the light to the rest of the tree, attempting to find any bugs, spiders, or scorpions, anything that could have bitten her. They needed to find whatever it was, just in case.

Unfortunately, he unearthed nothing lying or walking around. "Shit."

"Of all the ridiculous things to happen. I mean really, this entire what—week?—has been nothing but extremely weird. W—E—I—R—D. Weird."

Matt turned to Juliette, eyeing her and not even a little bit wondering if she'd lost her mind. Or maybe whatever had bitten her had some venom and it was making her loopy because she'd been rambling since she woke up and he couldn't for the life of himself figure out how to get her to stop for just a minute. "Well," he said under his breath, thinking of how he'd gotten her to be quiet earlier. The kiss hadn't been a good idea.

She'd felt too soft beneath him, tasted too sweet. All things he should not be feeling about a suspect in one of his investigations.

"What are you thinking?" she asked. "Why is your face like that? Why are you making that face?"

He scoffed, allowing a surprised laugh to escape. As much as she rambled and attacked him with questions, she was also kind of amazing in a cute, little, psycho type of way.

"Agent Gonzalez," she said, artistically mimicking the same tone his ma used when he'd get caught with his hand in the cookie jar. Literally.

He winced and held his hand up, palm facing her.

"Slow down for a second."

"*Imma* need you to speak up. In case you forgot," she said and gestured to her ear in a wild fashion. "I cannot hear you that well."

His lips twitched.

Her eyes narrowed, and a threat of violence rolled over her expression.

He allowed the smile to escape and shook his head, then nodded toward the end of the log. Amazingly, she hadn't freaked out in the past few minutes, a far difference from when they'd first entered. "We need to try to get some more distance between us and the bad guys. You up for a walk?" He tried to speak slower, not necessarily louder, as he didn't have an idea if anyone were still out there. As it was, he could hear the sounds of the forest raging on around them, a likely sign they were alone.

Juliette looked toward the exit, and her shoulders stiffened as if she just remembered where they were. *Yeah, sweetheart, we're still lying in an abandoned tree.*

She scuttled her way down, and in her movements, came precariously close to unmanning him. He grunted and shifted in the nick of time as her elbow landed on his inner thigh, then her shoulder on his knee. Several painful expressions and minutes later, he rose outside the log to an awakening forest.

Fog crept in tendrils along the ground, weaving in and around trees and bushes. Farther away, squirrels scampered across the exposed land. And the sky above was quickly turning from gray to a light blue.

A plus with that sky. No clouds.

The dancing fog coasted along the forest's floor, and the sun's rays speared through thick leaves. Dew coated the surface of the foliage around them, enough to have him grabbing a heavy leaf and curling it under the droppings of others.

"Come here for a second, Scaggs," he said, loud enough to make sure she heard. She stepped up next to him.

"What are you doing?" she asked, and yes, her hearing definitely wasn't what it should be as she was speaking pretty loudly.

He pursed his lips in a shushing motion, then checked their surroundings again.

"Sorry," she said, this time softer. "What are you doing, though?" She gestured to the leaf he held with water about halfway full. The leaf was about two of his palms wide, and the amount of liquid he'd been able to gather wasn't necessarily enough to keep them hydrated for the day, but hopefully, it'd be a good start.

It was also better than nothing.

"Here." He lifted the leaf to her mouth. "Drink some."

She cut a glance up at him and obeyed, taking a tentative drink, then another longer gulp once she realized it was water. Her eyelashes curled up against her brows, the length long enough to make most women envious and craving a trip to the salon for a pair of fake lashes. With Juliette so close, her gaze holding his, and her expression so trusting, it didn't take long for him to become entrapped in the moment.

She cupped one hand beneath his and pulled the leaf away. "Matt," she said, her voice intimate and soft. "You drink the rest."

He blinked, and the moment was gone. Probably for the best, too, because they needed to be on their way. And no matter where they were or what they had gone through, she was still the subject of his investigation.

He'd do well to keep reminding himself of that.

He made quick work of gathering some water for

himself, the rifle, and the backpack, then they set on their way.

What must have been two, maybe three, hours later, they crested a steep mountain top. The weather had changed with cool winds pushing against their weakened bodies with a steady force. The sun, though high in the sky, still cast strong rays as if it were a kid with a magnifying glass and a dark curiosity about ants. His Jell-O legs felt as if they wanted to crumple at any moment.

At least he could see what was around them now that they reached the top. He paused and looked around, pressing his hands into his aching lower back while he tried to bend this way and that, working out the kinks.

The mountains seemed to go on for miles upon miles. As far as the eye could see. Ranges spread to the north, east, south, and west. There wasn't a speck of civilization, but there was a whole lot of trees and beautiful waterfalls.

"Wow," Juliette whispered beside him.

He took in her profile and searched for any additional impacts other than the loss of hearing in one ear. She swayed under the push of wind but stayed on her feet.

Tendrils of her hair had escaped whatever knot she'd put it up in. He watched those pieces dance around her head and brush softly over her shoulders and the fine slope of her neck. The sun kissed against her skin like a lover's caress, and an urge rose within him to dip down and taste her. Place his lips against her warm shoulder, take in the scent of sun of woman.

He bit off a harsh groan and looked away to get himself under control. His vision spun, and the world around him tilted. Dehydration would knock them both on their asses before the day was over. Combined with his injuries and whatever had bitten Juliette, they might find themselves in a precarious position before the sun set.

Her freak-out from earlier seemed to have abated. He didn't have a clue what had stung or had bitten her, nor did he have enough medical knowledge to understand what could be going on. All he could hope for was that the hearing loss would only be temporary.

"How are you feeling?" he asked, then winced as she turned tired eyes his way. She looked just as awful as he felt. There was no way they could crest up another mountain, but the only way from here was into the canyons. They had to keep moving.

She shook her head, mouth turned in a deep frown. "I still can't hear out of that ear. And I'm so tired, hungry, and thirsty."

He nodded, mouth grim, and took another look around, trying to find some natural trails that could help lead them somewhere. Hopefully away from where they'd been. Leading her forward, with a tap on her arm, he set them down a lightly used trail. It curved sharply into the shade of a canyon. Fortunately, they navigated this during the day because he could only imagine just how nicely those jagged and sharp peaks would feel on their already battered bodies. There was no doubt they would have toppled right into those rocks had they tried to navigate this path at night.

Gravel crunched under their feet, crows and that funky bone-sounding bird called to one another over their heads, and the sun disappeared behind the mountain slowly as they forged forward.

Growls, snarls, and grunts far off in the distance reminded him every so often they were not the predators in this range. Something far deadlier would find them unless they found shelter before nightfall. Going a whole day without fresh water or food would take its toll, too. Their already weak bodies would slow down even more.

They stopped every so often to take quick breaks, but he pushed them at a backbreaking pace, one allowing for cautious steps but one that already dared death. They had to find a place to sleep safely for the night, had to find some more food and water. There was no way they would last another day out in this heat.

The air wrapped around him as if it were a blanket, something he didn't need. As it was, the farther they pushed into the canyon, the more the feeling of being closed inside a crypt came over his skin. He kept checking the shadows, looking over his shoulder.

Something out there watched them. Waited for the right time to strike.

He could feel it.

He pushed them harder, moved them farther into the deep recesses of the canyon. Before long, a more distinct trail began to take shape. He followed along, noting man's imprint. A footprint next to a bush, the strike of a stick alongside. Small things his pops had taught him back when they used to go hunting.

He'd love to tell Juliette about it, sure she'd enjoy another story. But at this point, even she seemed to pick up on the feeling of them being watched. Her gaze kept catching his. While she'd been a trooper up until now, he could also tell her steps moved more into a drunken state—a sign she was about to go down or whatever had bitten her was finally rearing its head.

Up ahead, a bush had been cut through enough to allow a body to pass, but it still held enough growth to keep the trail somewhat hidden. He stopped for a moment and tried to think through what they needed to do. If they were where he thought, then there was a chance there could be marijuana farmers ahead. This region of the Copper Canyons had heaps of activity. While they needed to get to shelter and get some food and fresh water, he didn't want to risk getting them into another situation like the one they'd just escaped.

Juliette grabbed his arm, leaning heavily into him. Her pert breasts brushed against his chest. Something he tried like hell to ignore. She panted as if they'd been running for miles. He frowned. "You're well beyond dehydrated, Jules."

"I don't feel so good," she whispered, her hand catching his hip to hold steady.

She stumbled into him, and they both almost went down. Not good. Even he was fading.

They needed to find water fast.

His body waved a bit as a heavy wind came through. Juliette looked up at him, her eyes weary and battered. She had dark smudges beneath her sunken eyes. Her dry lips were cracked.

He couldn't help what he did next. Wanted to blame it on the lack of water, the pain in his body, and the very likelihood he had an infection raging through him. But he leaned down and kissed her parched lips. A chaste one, but he held her gaze the entire time and let her see him making the decision himself.

Breath fluttered over his mouth, and she swayed again.

It was the sway that pushed him ahead. He grabbed her hand and led them through the brush—directly into the path of four men with weapons.

Chapter Eleven

Alarms blared in his head and Matt stepped forward, blocking Juliette's body with his as four men dressed in what looked like a cross between traditional native garb wrapped around their waists, some sort of tan or ivory color, and simple western wear shorts. These two pieces were held up by a braided band of bright, powerful colors that stood out against the lighter linen. Each man wore a sleeveless shirt in a pattern reminiscent of old running shorts. They had on no shoes, and in their hands, they held knives at the ready. Longish, darkened blades better served for chopping meat in the kitchen than to fight off an attack.

The rifle strapped over his back felt as useless as a paperweight on a lazy summer day.

Matt's mind raced with knowledge of the area, trying to figure out who they were.

Juliette's hand grasped the back of his shirt, and she swayed into him, causing him to shuffle his feet slightly. *Shit.* His stomach clenched with uncertainty. They all stared at one another for what seemed like countless minutes.

The grip on his shirt started to tremble. "Matt," she said, the word overly loud in the endless silence.

All four men jumped forward as if they'd practice the synchronized movement. Some loud bark came from the one on his right.

Matt winced and held his hands in the air, hoping the universal sign of being unarmed worked here. His brain raced for information, trying to think back on all those classes they'd been required to take at the academy.

Understanding the cultural history of this area,

the people and customs, the crime and political agendas, all of it was important when it came to their criminal investigations and *who* they were dealing with.

He knew of the marijuana farms nearby, practically teeming through the area. If one came across those and entered without an escort, their head was more than likely removed from their body. It was a prominent market here, one booming as the demand rose in other parts of the world. There were other drug trades closer to the southern border and coasts in Mexico, but they were nowhere near these areas.

These men had to be from a local native tribe, one he should be familiar with.

"No, wait," he said, inching up as the tip of a knife pressed under his chin. He felt the area echo with his thundering pulse, just waiting for the moment it would pierce his skin. That action, he had no doubt would happen with one wrong move. Especially with the look in this man's dark eyes. One that spoke of Matt encroaching on their land. This guy was protecting his family. Rightfully so.

He understood. Boy, did he ever. He'd once had to protect his family, too. It was why he did the job he did. Protecting the weaker society, those who had no strength against such a powerful addiction.

"Matt," Juliette whimpered, pressing the length of her body to his. It only made the tip of that knife bear harder against his neck. Dammit. It wasn't like he could tell her to back off. He had a feeling she was on the verge of going down for good. Visions of her collapsing against him, the move pushing his neck onto the knife, ran through his head.

Whelp, guess that would be the end of that.
Internally, he winced.
A guy with light-brown hair to his left, wearing a

blue and white checkered shirt, barked something at Juliette, causing her to stiffen against him even more.

"Stop," she said.

The guy yelled something again and stomped his foot.

"Stop!" she screamed, the sound piercing his head.

Matt lifted his eyes to the heavens and tried to think of a way out of this, a way to de-escalate the situation. He waved his hands in the air again, wanting to draw attention away from a quickly panicking Juliette. He carefully swallowed against the blade.

"Hey, hey," he said, drawing everyone's attention to him. Away from the hysterical-screaming-at-armed-natives-half-deaf woman at his back. He wanted to cry—legit just wanted to break down like a baby and cry for his ma. Could this pseudo-vacation trip to Mexico get any worse?

"Hey," he said, returning his gaze to the guy who stood at his front. "We mean no harm." He tried to speak the words slowly. They probably didn't understand. They were definitely natives to the land. And now that his brain was catching up, he guessed part of the Tarahumara tribe, one known for running long distances without breaking a sweat. If that was the case, there was no way they were escaping. No way they'd outrun them, even if they wanted to.

He really needed their assistance.

This tribe was *supposed* to be friendly.

"We were taken. By some bad guys. We need your help." He said each word with a measured calmness, imploring they were not a threat. How one did that, he didn't know. But he was damn well trying.

"Look," he said and started to lower his hands slowly. He eyed the guy watching him. Not wanting to make any sudden moves, he kept his tone low and calm.

Then he breathed slightly easier as the guy stepped back. "Look," he said again and grabbed the bottom of his dirt- and blood-stained shirt. He lifted it unhurried, past the nicks and stab wounds on his stomach. Past the electric burns beneath his chest. And just over his almost-cut-off nipple on the right side. He shifted a little, needing to draw the shirt up past Juliette's grasp. She must have been paying attention because it didn't take too much of a tug for the shirt to slide over his left chest. Right over where his badge was tattooed on his skin. The DEA crest and his badge number, something he and a few on his team at the academy had done after one night drunk on the town before they all parted ways to their individual assigned offices.

Juliette's hold on him shifted until both of her hands settled at his hips. He felt her weight hit a second later. But he had to ignore her and the very alarming possibility that she was moments away from collapsing.

He held the guy's gaze but tapped the badge. Then said, "Help. Help us. Please."

The native man stepped forward to look at the tattoo, then his gaze strayed to all the marks made during the torture session before he turned and said something to another tribal man. That guy promptly turned and started running in another direction.

Matt shook his head, wondering where the guy went. But at the same time, it enthralled him at how light on his feet the guy moved. To run so free, almost like you were a piece of nature, was a gift he'd love to have. He watched the guy until his attention pulled back to the one who wore a bright orange and yellow shirt.

"We help," the guy said. "We help."

Thank God.

****

No more than an hour after the guy took off did he return. He came with another man, this one a bit more modernized, wearing a white t-shirt with some kind of blackbird in flight and a pair of tan cargo shorts. They were on horseback, one brown horse and one black.

Matt had been forced to hand over the rifle, something he hadn't been too keen on doing but also something he hadn't had a choice in.

Juliette leaned heavily on him, her feet tapping out a dance that spoke of how difficult it was for her to remain standing.

The new guy was atop the black horse and stopped in front of them with a soft command. "Hello. My name is Sam. I hear you all have had quite the adventure so far."

Relief unlike anything Matt had felt before rushed through him. A feeling so swift his legs almost gave out. "You speak English."

The guy gave a small smile. "I do. Spent five years stateside at university studying." Sam shifted in his seat and tried to peer around him at Juliette. "Wanna tell me what you're doing out this way with hardly the shirts on your backs?"

Matt rubbed at the burning skin of his nape. The sun pounded relentlessly. With the lack of water and his injuries, he didn't know how long he would remain on his feet. There were a lot of things he didn't know right now, such as the ability to trust these people. Yeah, the Tarahumara were known to be a peaceful, extremely isolated tribe that existed off trade between their different communities. They didn't get involved in politics or drugs and kept to themselves outside the occasional recruitment to run for sport in different countries.

Because that was all they did—they ran everywhere. So this guy being on horseback was a bit of a surprise. These others having basic weapons as the knives they held gave a bit more to that surprise.

Matt debated all of this silently for a few moments, unsure how to proceed or what to relay. The last thing they wanted was to end up back where they started. There was no way they'd survive that. But he highly doubted they'd last through the night on their own, too.

"Relax," Sam said. "We want to help. Toko," he said with a nod at the guy who'd inspected his wounds and crest, "mentioned some of the injuries he saw on you. Said you were a protector, a policeman."

Explaining the difference between a police officer and a federal agent was not a conversation he wanted to get into right then. "That's right. We were being held against our will until sometime yesterday? I-I don't really have a way to track the time. Everything seems to be running together."

Sam nodded. "And your friend? Is she injured like you?"

Matt swallowed against the dryness in his mouth. "No, but she can't hear out of one ear. And I think she might be sick, ill. She was … she was bitten or stung. Something in her ear."

Sam, his dark hair shining bright under the sun's rays, frowned. Lines bracketed his mouth. "Was she stung inside the ear?"

Matt shrugged and rubbed at the back of his head as a dull throb pulsed there. Dehydration was giving him some serious warnings. "We don't know. She just woke up like this. We were hiding in a tunnel." He shook his head. "I mean in a log. And there was blood coming out of her ear. But we couldn't see. Look," he said and staggered as a wave of dizziness crept. "We need water. I don't know how long it's been since we've taken in any fluids. And I know we're strangers here."

Juliette's grip on his waist slackened as her body leaned heavily against his. "Juliette," he called, pulling on her arm. She slid to the side and would have gone down had he not caught her.

"I don't feel good."

Her face was ashen, her eyes unfocused. He looked up at Sam, urgency pounding through him. "We don't want to cause any trouble. Please. Help us."

Sam eyed them both before nodding. He rambled off something to the other tribesmen before returning his attention to Matt. "I hope you can ride horseback. It's a long walk to camp, and I doubt either of you would make it on foot."

"Last time I rode a horse was during summer camp as a kid. But at this point, I'll try anything to get us where we need to go." He reached under Juliette's body and grunted as he stood, his feet almost coming out from under him. He tap-danced his balance back. It seemed as if the world moved entirely too fast around him.

She wasn't heavy. Curvy, yes. Solid. Strong. Hell, he didn't know of a single female besides her who would have hung in there through all this.

She protested and pushed against his shoulder. The movement shouldn't have jarred him as it did. But he stumbled, his feet finding it hard to catch their balance. Apparently his body knew he'd reached help and was raising a white flag in surrender. He stumbled backward again. Sam shouted something he couldn't understand. Alarmed tones went up around him before he felt strong hands steady him.

Sam was beside him a moment later. "You're going to fall. Give her over, my friend. Let us help you."

Instinctively, Matt's arms tightened. He didn't know these men. And Juliette was his to look after. His charge. His.

He shook his head, trying to clear out the cobwebs. She wasn't *his* in that sense. That wasn't what he meant.

"You're about to topple over," Sam said. "She won't come to harm. I want to make sure you get on that horse without falling off. If you can hold yourself up there, I'll give her back to you. Otherwise, I'll have her ride on my horse. You're safe here, friend."

Matt stared into Sam's dark-brown eyes, searching for any hint of deception or threat. Having Juliette in his arms meant he could keep an eye on her, but he needed to get his act together and make sure he could stay on the horse. It wouldn't do either of them any good if he couldn't. And if he had to prove it by giving Juliette over, getting on that horse, and staying on said horse, then dammit, that was what he'd do.

He pressed his lips together and nodded at Sam, who held his arms out and took Juliette. With a deep breath, he gave one last look at her before turning and forcing one leg in front of the other. Heaving out a heavy grunt, he pulled himself up on the brown horse, feeling all kinds of inexperienced as he did. His head spun for a few seconds but eventually righted itself.

Sam stared at him with a grim look, then barked something at one of the tribesmen. The guy wearing the orange jersey came running over and handed up a canteen. Matt took it and released the cap.

"It's water, but it's most likely also filled with *tesguino*. Kind of like a beer. Drink."

Tesguino, definitely a beer for their tribe. Matt raised his eyebrows at the tribesman who looked pretty steady on his feet. The guy gave him a crooked grin. He didn't have an option at this point. With a quick sniff that told him there definitely was more than water in there, he tossed his head back and drank deeply.

Surprisingly, it went down easier than beer back in the States and was almost refreshing with a hint of lime.

"Slow, friend. Do not drink too much. You'll get sick."

Much as he hated to admit it, Sam was right. Matt drew the canteen away from his mouth and felt slightly better. His head didn't spin as much, and with every passing second, his vision cleared more.

He passed the canteen back to the orange jersey guy with a nod of thanks, then immediately turned to Sam. "I'll take her now."

A small smile lifted the other man's mouth before he nodded and passed Juliette up into his arms. Matt sighed in relief at the feel of her, then promptly ignored that feeling. He settled her head against his shoulder, her legs over his lap, and the cushion of her ass between his legs. Her breaths were steady and deep. He didn't want to wake her just yet, so he let her sleep.

Sam had returned to his horse and came up beside him. "There's a healer back home. We'll be able to have someone look at her there and figure out what's going on with both of you. It's a little over thirty minutes of a ride on horse. Think you can manage?"

Matt tightened his grip on Juliette and grabbed the reins. "I'll make sure of it."

Sometime later, they were still atop their horses and meandering through windy trails thick with brush and trees. The horses lumbered along and shifted with the elevation changes. Every so often, Sam turned back with a worried expression and another offer to take Juliette.

He didn't know why he felt a sudden need to keep her close, but after the hell they'd been through, there was no way he'd place her care or safety in anybody else's arms.

It seemed as though they were making their way through a strengthening wind tunnel. Gusts battered him, causing his legs to tighten on the saddle. His entire weary body screamed in protest, and his arms shook with the force it took to keep Juliette with him.

The horses trudged ahead, and Matt kept his grip firmly around her sleeping body. His other hand clung to the reins, which he'd wrapped around his wrist multiple times. It wasn't a fail-safe, but if he toppled, then at least he'd slow their fall.

Fortunately, Sam pushed ahead and didn't say much else. Just a few snippets about what to expect of their community and the people they'd come across. He asked a few questions too, which was understandable. Juliette and he were outsiders, potential threats coming into a community known for its secrecy, amongst other things. Those other things specifically included running.

Juliette shifted against his chest, then curled her hand into a fist, grabbing a wad of his shirt. She mumbled in her sleep, something about hot chocolate and her mama, causing him to smile. If they survived this place, and that was a big *if*, then he definitely knew a place in the city to grab some hot cocoa. He'd take her.

He took quick stolen glimpses of her sleeping face. On one hand, those glances made him fill kind of skeevy, almost like a pervert, as if he didn't have the right to look at her. Maybe it was what had almost happened, the threat of what could have been. The ghost of a rape that fortunately didn't happen.

He didn't want to be lumped into the same category of filth as those men. Especially when he could now see what he hadn't before, back at the airport.

Juliette had an innate sense of goodness and

innocence about her, a beauty that surely could make most men and women stop and stare. Her dark curls had exploded out of whatever knot she'd tied them up in and sat in a rioted mess around her head. Rather than make her look out of sorts, it was endearing seeing her so free of bounds. The soft curve of her cheeks and jaw had slackened in sleep, and the lushness of her mouth pursed as something distasteful likely happened in her dream.

He remembered what her mouth felt like under his. The sweet taste of her. The softness of her body as he settled.

He wanted to kiss her again.

"How is she doing?" Sam asked, drawing Matt's attention.

He shrugged, fighting off the heat in his face from being caught staring at her. "She's still sleeping. But she's moving, mumbling, so there's that. Who knows what is really going on with her. Between the hearing loss and the fainting, I'm worried her injuries are more extensive than we originally thought. Or whatever stung her is causing some sort of reaction."

Sam waved a hand as if dismissing the danger. "It is most likely the exhaustion from the heat and sun, or her water levels."

Matt cocked his head. "Her what? Oh, you mean she's dehydrated."

Sam nodded. "Yes. The healer will most likely be able to help with both. The hearing and her water levels. Just watch," he said with a smile. "Your wife will be just fine in no time."

"Oh, she's not my…"

Sam raised an eyebrow, then cleared his throat. "If you don't mind me saying so, my friend, for the next however long you stay with us in our community, your lady there is your wife."

Matt frowned, a bit of an alarm ringing down his spine. He stiffened as all sorts of debauched thoughts ran through his head. They'd just left one situation. If he'd gotten them into another, he doubted they'd survive it. With Sam's ominous words, it sounded like they were walking into another.

It didn't make sense, though. He'd never heard of the Tarahumara being violent.

"Look," Matt said as the trail thinned and shadows peeked out from the tree line. Tiny little forms soon replaced those shadows. Children. They must be getting close to camp. "I really appreciate the help you've offered, but I'd rather not put Juliette, put either of us in one more dangerous situation." He drew up on the reins as Sam stopped his horse and faced him.

The other guy laughed, the sound thick and hearty. "You and your friend have nothing to fear from us. What I meant when I suggested she be your wife while you're here is if she is not, the two of you will not be able to stay together. It's against our culture, outsider or not. And I'm sure you want to keep an eye on each other." Something in the other guy's gaze twinkled at those words, but Matt ignored the gleam and the warmth in his stomach at the thought of Juliette being *his*.

"But more so," Sam said with a gentle smile, "your friend is beautiful. Both of you are. The people here don't get out often, but if word spreads that the two of you are unattached, it'll get kind of crazy for you very quickly. Understand?"

Did he comprehend they were hundreds of miles from any other city? That they needed these people to help them? Despite possibly being "fresh meat" and Sam was giving him a way out of that?

"Yes, I understand," he said. And he did. He nodded to a newcomer who had stepped up quietly. A middle-aged woman with long black hair that hung along her back until it hit her waist. She had several braids coming from the crown of her head, and each of those was wrapped with a different color string. She wore a blue and green muumuu and sandals and bore a striking resemblance to the man on a black horse.

"Mami," Sam said, speaking to the lady. "I'd like for you to meet my friend, Matt, and his wife, Juliette."

Matt decided not to correct him. He'd decided to keep her close.

"They need our help."

Chapter Twelve

Time moved as if she was in another dimension. Juliette felt like a fog surrounded her head, thick with a shell that couldn't be penetrated. She struggled, trying to rise to consciousness, but the fog pushed in harder, luring her back with a promise of peaceful sleep. She tried to bat the tendrils away, but they held her under. So, she slept some more.

Sometime later, she felt her consciousness rise again. Half-tempted to fall back into slumber, she shifted, pulling herself closer to a heavy warmth. In the back of her mind, a light warning pushed at her—a little buzzing noise telling her she needed to wake. But she was so comfortable, so warm and safe.

She eased closer to the warmth and felt the softness, not quite like her Tempur-Pedic back home. She'd saved up for that baby and didn't regret a single day of living off ramen noodles to afford it. Her bed was as soft as the clouds sometimes looked from her backyard: big, fluffy, and like a pillow of cotton air.

This bed felt rigid, almost as if it needed some more fluff. Her head rested on something hard, not quite comfortable, but not entirely uncomfortable either.

Another shift in position had her wrapping an arm and tossing a leg over that warmth. She made an effort to get closer and cuddled her face into the heat. The slight softness of whatever she lay on got momentarily harder before going soft again. Strange.

Something brushed hair away from her face. Her hair. Ugh, it must look like a rat's nest. Always did when she woke up from a long nap.

How long had she been out?

She couldn't recall. Couldn't quite remember when she'd fallen asleep or where she'd lain down.

With a sudden jolt, it all came rushing back, and she snapped her eyes open. Right next to her face lay sun-kissed bare skin dusted with dark-brown hair. She stared, seeing hints of other colors in the chest hair, because that was definitely what she lay on. A chest. One riddled with marks and wounds from what she remembered was one heck of a torture session. She stared at those blemishes on his skin and wanted to will them away.

Oddly enough, she couldn't quite get her head to catch up and tell her to move. Instead, she stared, fascinated by the red and blond hair laced within the deep chestnut, almost like whoever had created this body couldn't decide on one color.

"Juliette," murmured a deep, albeit sleepy-sounding voice. A voice that sounded vaguely familiar.

She tilted her head back and found the very handsome face of Agent Matt Gonzalez. Her stomach flipped at the intimacy of their position, but still, she couldn't seem to move. Didn't necessarily want to just yet. "Hi. Where are we?"

"You're safe. How are you feeling?"

"Feeling? Fine. I, I don't remember. Did we escape? Did they find us?" She tightened her arms around him.

"*They* didn't find us. We ran across someone else. The Tarahumara tribe. They're friendly, and we've had some time to rest and recoup. Last time you were awake, you looked pretty pale and were in a lot of pain. We've had a friend taking care of you since. How's your ear feeling?"

She took a moment to take stock and found she could hear. "Surprisingly fine. I can hear you, obviously." Her cheeks heated.

"Are you able to sit up for a bit?"

"I'm sorry, I was lying on you. I-I didn't realize who you… When I…"

"Calm down." He brushed a palm over her hair, his concerned gaze studying her. "It's okay. I'm worried about you. Let me know if you start feeling sick or faint, or have any pain, okay?"

She remembered bits and pieces of it now that she thought back. Someone groaning in pain. Others speaking in hushed tones. The continuous warmth.

"Have you been here the entire time?" she asked.

He bit his bottom lip, and she couldn't help but notice straight white teeth pushing into the plump flesh. Her attention turned to fascination.

"Jules," he said, and she lifted what must have been a dreamy gaze up to him. He shifted, tightening his arms around her and bringing her closer.

"Jesus, Jules," he said roughly.

"I remember dreaming about you," she said.

His expression softened. "What did you dream about?"

She shifted her attention to his mouth again. "Kissing you, apparently."

He bit that bottom lip again, only this time, it looked to be a nibble. She really wanted to take over. She didn't know where this intense feeling came from, only knew it existed. And she wanted to give in to it.

"What would you do if I kissed you right now?" he asked.

Her gaze jumped up to his before moving to his mouth again. She could become addicted to this. The intimacy of talking with only inches between them. His heat. His attention.

"Probably kiss you back," she said.

"Tell me," he urged. "Tell me what you'd do."

"You want to hear me say it?"

He nodded.

She wondered about what he asked, but then gave in to it, a slight thrill running through her.

"I'd touch my mouth to yours. My lips would probably tingle a bit, but if I pressed against yours more, those tingles would give me pleasure."

"More," he said roughly.

She licked her lips and went on. "I'd want…" She hesitated, unused to saying the things coming to her mind. But curious, too. About how much this affected her. Just saying these things. Thinking them.

"Jules," he said, the word like a warning. "I want details. Tell me."

She took a deep breath. "I'd want to bite your lips as you did to your lower one earlier. To see if it felt like what I imagined. Soft and plush. And I wonder if it'd make you groan as I did."

He let off a harsh curse under his breath. "And then?"

"Then I'd open my mouth and hope you'd open yours too, because I'd want to taste you."

Breath punched out from him, parting his lips.

"And once I'd satisfied myself with the taste of you," she continued, on a roll now, feeling a deep heat in her stomach. "I'd want to touch my chest to yours because my nipples would be begging for the contact." She knew they would be because they were now. They wanted to be pressed into him harder.

He swallowed thickly. "And?" he asked, his voice guttural.

"And as I pressed them into you, I'd probably be the one to groan because the pleasure would be almost overwhelming, my hard nipples against your chest. And since you are shirtless, I'd wonder what it'd feel like to have my bare flesh—"

She didn't get anything else out because he rolled them both until she lay on her back, and then he kissed her.

And it went wild.

His mouth opened over hers, and without waiting, she met him, wrapping her tongue around his until she felt as if they'd never part. The kiss went on and on, his arms wrapped around her until she was pressed to the length of him. He didn't try anything else, only kissed her deep. So intensely and thoroughly, she felt as if she were in a fog when he lifted his head sometime later.

"What was that?" she asked, her voice breathless.

He stared down at her and licked his lips. "I shouldn't have done that. And I'm sorry, but I couldn't resist any longer."

The fog started to clear at his words. "Matt."

He shook his head and pulled back. Immediately, the loss of warmth hit her like a shock. Really, she was getting a little tired of the back and forth with him. She couldn't get a read on exactly what went on in his head.

"You kissed me. There's nothing wrong with that," she said.

He looked back at her as he sat on the side of the bed, his expression incredulous. "I didn't say there was something wrong with it, per se. I just shouldn't have done it."

"Why?"

"You're the subject in my investigation, Jules. It's against the rules. Do I want to kiss you?" He motioned to the bed with a palm raised to the sky. "I think it's pretty obvious. But should I?" He shook his head again and stood.

She sighed, wondering how the mood had changed so much in the span of only a few minutes.

"How long have I been sleeping?"

"A little over two days."

Well, that explained the need pushing at her bladder. An urgent one, she might add. Colorful tapestries hung on bare red brick walls. One wooden door seemed to be the only way in and out of the room. Her face heated. Ridiculous after everything they had been through. But she really had to go, and this was human nature, after all. "Is there a bathroom close by?"

He nodded, studying her. The vanity within made her wonder what she looked like. Worrying over it was silly after what they'd been through and ended up where they were, but she couldn't help it. *Ugh.* Probably the last thing he even wanted to be bothered with, her fretting. Over her looks, their kiss, any of it.

She shook her head and slowly rose from the bed, silently calling herself ten kinds of fool. She needed to get a grip. They both needed to find a way home. This entire situation was a nightmare she wouldn't have ever thought she could dream up.

She stood on slightly unsteady feet, noting somewhat late she was barefoot. Her body grew steadier after a few seconds. Some good news at last.

"How are you feeling?" he asked, tone back to professional and removed. Nothing like it'd been before they kissed … again.

She wanted to get a rise out of him, wanted some emotion, but pushed that urge aside.

He stood near the door and had pulled on a light-blue t-shirt. Also barefoot. His concerned gaze traveled over her body, and her stupid brain noted the scan was clinical only. No heat. No flirtatious looks. No nothing.

She sighed, annoyed with herself. *Again. Get a grip, Juliette.*

"Are you okay?" He stepped forward. "They gave you something during the small moments you came awake, but I'm not sure how much good it would have done. This tribe is very off the grid and their methods are not modern at all."

She raised a hand, shook her head, and moved toward him instead. "I'm fine. Feel better than I did before. Whatever they gave me did the trick." She would not and did not mention their kiss. If he didn't want to talk about it, wanted to ignore it, fine. That was F—I—N—E fine with her.

Read: it isn't actually fine, but that's what I'm going with. I'll just be annoyed with him until the end of time.

As she neared, he popped open the door and gestured her outside before he followed behind. A long dirt-packed hall decorated with rugs and potted plants lined the walkway. Matt nodded for her to follow the path.

"They gave you what looked like a bunch of herbs and their, ummm." Matt seemed to search for a word before he finished with, "An alcohol of a sort. I don't understand how it works, only that it does. And it's used as a way for them to trade for goods. It's what their entire community works for."

"Interesting," she said. "Whatever it was, I feel as close to normal as I guess I could, all things considering. And you…" She trailed off, unsure of how to voice this, the words to use without giving herself away. "You look good, too. Better." She cleared her throat to cover her discomfort.

The path led to another door, this one looking heavier than before. Steps made of the same wood were before, looking to rise from a lower ground level to just flush with the earth. An entirely new way of building things, but it seemed to keep the temperature at bay. A heat that slammed into her face with a shocking amount of humidity as she pushed open the door.

"The bathroom is just across the way," Matt said, gesturing to a circular hut about ten meters away. She didn't ask any questions and booked it over as quickly as she could.

A few minutes later, and with a teary release of business complete, she stepped back out of the hut.

Wood and brick cabins dotted the area, built slightly into the ground. Many had long tunnels coming from where a front door would be, and all were packed with a heavy clay, most likely to keep the heat and humidity down. Trails wove from one cabin to another, and people moved around them in colorful clothing, carrying baskets full of fresh veggies and fruits, faces with hesitant smiles.

Matt waited under the shade of what looked like a tall weeping willow, leaning against it as if he had not one care in the world. He had a piece of some sort of sugar cane in his mouth, but his gaze was on her. Perusing her body from her toes to the top of her head in a slow path. One she could swear felt like a physical caress.

Despite the heat, she shivered and joined him. He reached out with a quick hand and pulled her closer until the side of her body touched his. His hand settled on her waist, and her spine went straight. "What's happening?" she asked.

"Relax," he responded, his gaze still on her. This close, she found the lines of strain around his eyes peculiar. She hadn't seen them before, but then again, there'd been a lot going on. Shadows darkened his face, too, as if he had slept little. And here she'd been conked out without a care in the world. She had no idea how he was recovering or even if he'd received care for his wounds. Earlier, she'd been too engulfed in their kiss to pay attention to much else.

"Matt," she said, turning to him more fully. This aligned their bodies in a way that seemed natural. As if they'd been made to fit. She shook her head to discard those thoughts. Not a path he obviously needed her to go down right now.

He pulled the sugar cane from his mouth and wound both arms around her, pulling her closer until they were pressed hips to chest. "How are you feeling?" he asked before she could tell him to knock it off, this game he seemed to be playing with her feelings.

"Fine, I guess? No headache. I can hear. I feel like I could use some time at a spa, but nothing pressing."

One of his large hands traveled back down her spine and settled on her hip. It was a very proprietary move. The squeeze he gave there a warning.

Her head spun for an entirely different reason now. The scent of earth and man filled her senses. His body was a magnet for heat against her, his touch a caress she wanted more of, like an addict who'd gone on for too long without.

"Please," she whispered low.

"Jules," he responded in the same tone.

"Please stop playing games with me, Matt. My feelings aren't a toy for you."

He stiffened momentarily, eyes studying hers. Something seemed to wage in his head, a war he didn't share, but that was okay. If he wanted to keep his thoughts, then she couldn't do anything about that. But she also couldn't keep up with him and whatever he was doing with this back-and-forth bit between them.

That hand on her hip traveled up to wrap around her back until the tips of his fingers settled against the side of her breast.

She sucked in a breath. He tossed the sugar cane away and turned them until her back pressed to the tree, then leaned into her with a hand cupping the side of her face. A very smooth move, one that had her legs turning to jelly beneath her body. She would have gone down had she not been in Matt's firm hold.

"What?" she asked, voice breathless. Against her breastbone, her heart pounded out a heavy beat.

"I'm not trying to play games," he said, leaning toward her until his face was only inches away. His gaze bounced between her eyes and mouth. Was he going to kiss her again? Did she want him to? But what he had said back in that room…

"In order to make sure we're kept together here so we can look out for one another, we have to pretend we're married."

With that bit of news, he leaned down until his mouth hovered at the corner of hers. A spiced scent filled her lungs, dark and smoky, as if he'd been out by a firepit too long. She labored to pull in a steady breath.

His next words were spoken against her skin there, and with each movement, his lips brushed in a caress against her. "The Tarahumara culture forbids unmarried couples to sleep in the same room before they are married. And while I'm sorry we're lying to them by playing it this way, both Sam and I thought it would be best for you and me to pretend."

She couldn't help it, she shifted her face until she was closer to his mouth, where they'd only have to move millimeters before they'd kiss again. His touch, his kisses, and even his words were like a drug to her. One she wanted more of.

She came up on her toes to better align her mouth with his, then shoved her hands in the long length of his hair.

His eyes flared.

She licked her lips, which meant she licked his, too. Dark pupils bled over with ink.

"Not all married couples would be so affectionate," she said in challenge. It was true. And this was something they needed to get straight. Something she wanted honesty about.

He shoved one leg between her thighs, then leaned further into her. "You're right. So let me give it to you straight now."

A bolt of alarm ran through her.

The hand at her face curled around her neck in an act so sensual and erotic, she felt a thrill ricochet through her belly and straight between her legs. The pulse hammering at her chest had moved south. Way south.

She gave a slight moan at the hold, and Matt's eyes flared.

"Fuck," he muttered, then leaned down and bit her lower lip in what seemed like a reprimand.

She gasped and wanted to ask him to do it again, but he spoke.

"I can't remember ever being so attracted to someone before you, Juliette. But you and me? We can't happen. It goes against everything I've been trained on. And agents getting mixed up with subjects in their investigations often find themselves in a world of career-ending trouble."

"You have to stop touching me then," she said, hating his words. Wanting to find some way to give in to this need thrumming through her body. As it was, she arched into his touch and bit her own lower lip to keep the moan that wanted to rise out of her mouth at bay.

"Jesus," he said, watching her. His eyes darkened. His gaze was tortured. Good.

"You're causing this," she said. "Stop touching

me, and maybe it'll go away."

Or not. Definitely not.

"I can't," he said, then stared at her mouth again. He let her see his hunger, and it was a beautiful thing. Ravaging his face with a need she wanted to feel.

He leaned closer, his aim intent on finding her lips in the bright of the day. A decision that could very well lead to more. Especially with that bed not too far away.

"Matt," called a voice not hers.

He froze before pulling back and turning to the newcomer.

"Sam," he said, voice back to normal as if nothing had just happened or been about to happen.

Meanwhile, her entire body was a flame that needed dousing, and the only way to cool it off would be a really cold shower or the stroking of hands by the very man standing next to her. She wanted to scream out her frustration. Wanted to run far away from this scene. But they were stuck in Mexico, and they needed each other to get home.

"The sun will be set in about an hour, so if you all want to clean up, it might be best to head down to the springs soon. That way, it won't be too hot," Sam said, breaking into her thoughts.

"A shower sounds heavenly."

Sam turned to her and smiled, his eyes wrinkling up at the corners. "It's not a shower as such, but hot springs that feed water down from the mountain to us. There are a few around, which is why our ancestors chose here. Typically, families can mark off the areas for privacy, and I can tell you how to do that yourself for you two."

Juliette's eyes widened as Sam nodded.

"Yes, you two should go there together.

Separately might cause too many questions. I'll get you both a modern change of clothing, then we can clean the ones you wear now so they will be ready for you when you leave."

"When do you think that'll be?" Matt asked.

Sam turned back to him. "About one more day. Then we must get you on the road. I am sorry, my friend."

Matt held up a hand. "No need to apologize. We've been here for as long as we should. We're both recovered enough to continue on with our travels. I appreciate all the help you and your mom have offered so far. So, thank you, Sam. Do not fret."

"I must protect my tribe."

"Absolutely," Matt responded. "I understand."

"Good. I'll direct you to the springs and bring you a change of clothes and some soap. If you stay longer than the sun is in the sky, don't worry, there is a lighted path back. Just follow it until you reach the hut again. We'll gather for dinner under the stars a bit later tonight."

Dinner under the stars sounded wonderful. Her stomach grumbled, but it had been nothing she noticed until now. If she were being honest, she'd pass on dinner for a dip in these springs Sam kept talking about.

With one last nod, Matt took her hand, and they followed Sam to his hut to grab the soap and a change of clothes.

****

Matt stepped out of the cabin a little later to find the sun had begun to set. The sky grew darker with light blues and purple, pink centering as a focus for the backdrop.

Desert sunsets were always his favorite, and this one was no different. Back when he went through the

Federal Law Enforcement training, he'd spent some time in New Mexico, even traveled a few weekends to Arizona. There was something to be said about sunsets on the western side of the US. They often had taken his breath away. And for some reason, the sunsets on the east coast were no different but it was something the bustling city of New York often overlooked. This one was no different from the beauty he'd seen back then in training.

He stood for a moment, transfixed in the natural beauty of the world, before he felt Juliette join him.

Without a word, they set off for the canyon springs.

Tall tikis lined the walkway Sam pointed out. Trees filled in the area, creating a tropical lushness. The walkway was surprisingly clear. He figured this far from a modern society, there'd be wildlife scampering about, walkways burdened by nature, but that wasn't the case here. It seemed there was a lot about the Tarahumara tribe many overlooked or simply did not know.

They walked for about five minutes before the trail curved sharply to the left and opened to a vista overlooking a few mountain ranges. With the setting sun, the sky had turned a deep orange with interspersed purple clouds making their lazy way through the skyline.

He paused, wanting to take in the sheer beauty of the day's final moments.

He didn't know how long he stood there before the sound of water being disturbed invaded his senses.

Juliette had knelt next to what looked like a natural spring, fresh water falling in a lazy way from a higher elevation. The tribe must have reinforced this spring because heavier rocks lined the area into a makeshift hot tub. Combined with the heated water coming down the range, water warm from the day's sun rays, the scene was entirely too inviting to the senses.

He was impressed. Not just with this, but with their very simple yet effective way of life. The love of people, of their community, really showed through their actions.

He had to make sure they didn't disturb it for too much longer.

They had to get going, anyway. There was no way around that. If they stayed, danger was sure to follow.

"That sunset was something else," Juliette said, flicking her hand free of the water she tested. "And this water feels like heaven. How do you want to do this?" She looked at him, then the spring.

How did he—right. Neither of them had bathing suits, and if they were married, as they said, surely the tribe expected them to take care of their needs together instead of apart. He cleared his throat.

"You can go ahead and get in." He rubbed the back of his neck, feeling all kinds of awkward. "I'll just turn around and give you some privacy. When you're done, I'll jump in quickly. Shouldn't take but a few minutes."

He gave her his back without waiting for a response. And even though he wasn't looking, his ears strained to hear something, anything. The drop of a piece of clothing. The rustle of her moving.

But nothing came besides the chirp of frogs farther down the mountain. The humidity in the air dropped with each minute, but his body dampened with perspiration.

"Why don't you join me?" she asked, her voice soft behind him. A temptation he could not—*could not*—give in to.

"Jesus," he muttered under his breath, then let his

head fall back so he could look at the sky. His body ached. Those assholes back at that makeshift prison or holding area, whatever it'd been, had really done a number on him. He'd had a few scars before—living the life he did and having the brothers he had, there was no escaping it. But now he had some wicked-looking cuts that would scar his body for the rest of his life.

Not to mention what he saw when he closed his eyes each night. The insidious words whispered in his ear.

How had he ended up in the middle of some Mexico desert, thousands of miles from home, with someone who was supposed to be his suspect in a drug trafficking investigation? A woman who had a look and air of naivety about her but seemed stronger than he did at the moment. At least emotionally.

"Matt?" Juliette asked, her voice inquiring and holding a touch of hesitancy. How could he tell? He didn't quite understand it. But he'd always been able to read more in a tone of voice than anyone else. Hers said she wanted to invite him close but was apprehensive about being rejected, about this new change in their relationship.

Maybe he'd been playing tug of war with his own attraction to her. He'd be blind not to find her beautiful. Stupid not to see how brave she was. And an idiot if he couldn't point out her smarts. She was just about the perfect woman in his mind, a full package he would have described had someone asked him to give details on his forever woman.

Cheesy as that thought may be, it was the truth.

Except, and this was a big one: for the reasoning on how they'd come into each other's lives. Did he feel like she was involved in whatever her brother had gotten her mixed up in?

He closed his eyes against the brilliance of the beautiful, unfiltered night sky. One that showed the colors of the Milky Way, the bright steadiness of the planets millions of miles away, and the twinkle of stars light years away. A whole vast space that gave him a sense of realization in just how small, how petty his current problems seemed.

He didn't know if she was involved or not. But goddamn, he couldn't deny this connection he felt toward her.

And wasn't that the crux of a big conundrum he had?

He let out a deep sigh and righted his head, focused over the dark shadows in the canyons before them. "Not sure it's such a good idea, Jules." The nickname popped out days before, and now that he used it, he couldn't stop. Short and sweet, yet hell on the gut when consumed.

His lips quirked.

She sighed, and the aggravated sound was closer than she'd been before. During his musings, she must have moved near because her palm landed on his upper back, another on his hip. He stilled, and every one of his muscles locked up tight. It didn't take his brain long to realize this was the first time she'd initiated physical contact with him.

"Matt," she whispered, then after a few silent seconds, stepped firmer against him. Her hands followed the movement, the one at his hip curving around to his stomach. The other coming over the top of his arm—a slight squeeze of his bicep—before sliding under to his chest.

She pressed close, fitting every single one of her curves, and at this moment, they were so, so dangerous, to his back. Warm air puffed through the t-shirt to wash over his skin. He gulped, the sound loud in their cocoon of privacy.

"Juliette," he whispered, laying his hands over hers. She flattened her palms, then started roving slowly. Taking her time in discovery.

Behind him, she rubbed her face against his back but didn't move away.

He shuddered under her perusal. Everywhere she touched, his body tingled. The scrape of a fingernail across exposed skin. The softness of her touch over a bruise. His body ignited. He was trying to fight it, and he knew he needed to be the stronger one here. This wouldn't be good for either of them. But he also craved her skin against his. Wanted her to touch him, to remind him he was more than some animal to be used for information.

As if she heard him, her hand at his stomach slipped beneath his shirt and landed skin to skin.

He sucked in a sharp breath, but she shuddered now.

"Take this off," she whispered, almost as if she were scared to break some moment they were having. He felt her fear and let it feed his, but instead of doing the right thing and pushing her away, he followed her orders and whipped his shirt over his head.

Dropped it at his feet.

Then he turned to her.

Chapter Thirteen

Perfection.

Juliette stared at Matt's body, her hands hovering, unsure where to begin. She wanted to take everything in at once, explore the canvas that was his skin, then move on to feeling his honed muscles because both were wonderful masterpieces.

He obviously liked his ink. Colorful drawings covered his skin, from the base of his neck, down across his shoulders and arms, sliding in a beautiful sweep of art down his stomach, and disappearing beneath the waistband of his shorts.

She spied a clock and a rabbit, tribal designs and his crest, numerous other pieces she'd love to study.

A sudden grip in her hair, and her head was yanked back. He came within inches of her face, his darkened eyes holding her captive.

"What game are you playing, Jules?" he asked. His voice sounded as if it'd been scraped over rocks.

She frowned, confusion bringing her brows down. "Game?" she asked. "I-I wasn't. Why would you think that?"

Keeping her head tugged back, he brought the other up to cup her jaw. His grip was firm, but she had an innate sense that if she asked for him to release her, he would.

"We've been kidnapped," he said, studying her.

She swallowed, and the sound was loud in the silence following his words. She didn't understand. "I know that."

"We've had to run for our lives," he stressed.

She blinked against the sudden stinging in her eyes. She knew this. Why was he saying it? "I know," she answered him, this time more forcefully.

"You were bit by only God knows what," he snapped. "And we had to hole up and shelter with a secret tribe who takes their privacy so seriously that not much is known about them."

"Why are you doing this?" she asked, still fighting against the sting in her eyes.

"I don't even know how we're going to survive this. How we're going to get help, especially in a country known for being run and patrolled by some shady outfits."

"Matt," she whispered. Something was happening here. She just didn't know what. He had been gentle with her, even while questioning back at the airport, so why was he giving the third degree now? Why remind her of the nightmare they were in?

"We're going to have to make a run for it. And trust me, we will be running, so those roadrunner moves you used a few days ago? You better prepare yourself to use them again."

She gripped the wrist holding her jaw, which caused him to tighten, then relax his hold, but he didn't let go.

"And even then," he said, dropping his gaze to her mouth. He still continued to study her, but it was almost like he talked to himself now. "Even then, I have no idea how I'm going to get us across the border. By now, I'm sure we have the *federales* and border patrol searching for us."

He adjusted his grip and used one finger to draw the plump bottom lip of hers down. His breath fanned over her face.

"I'm doubting we'll even survive this."

Her breath caught, and his gaze jumped back up to hers as if he realized he had her apt attention.

"I'm going to do everything in my power to make sure we do, but I am struggling, Juliette."

She licked her lips, and his gaze snagged on the movement before lifting to her eyes again.

"I'm struggling in more than one way."

She understood him then. "I know," she said, this time softer.

"Get in the tub."

She tightened her grip on his wrist and hip. "Join me. Please."

He closed his eyes as if it pained him to hear those words. Or pained him to make a decision—she didn't know. She wasn't asking for anything too crazy, but she did want to take some time to discover him.

"Matt," she said and waited for his eyes to open before continuing. "Why not take this opportunity? We obviously have chemistry. And even you made a point to say there's a really good chance we may not make it. So why not..." She bit her lip. "Unless..."

She released him and tried to step back, but his grip stayed firm. Her arms fell to her sides. "I'm such an idiot," she said. "So sorry. I didn't even think. There's someone at home, isn't there?"

He frowned, but then the expression cleared. He pulled her closer, releasing her jaw and wrapping his arm around her waist. "There's no one at home," he said. "But this is still a bad idea. I've already explained to you why, but fuck if I can anymore. Just—"

Then he kissed her.

His lips pressed to hers, and heat engulfed where they touched. She rose to her tippy toes, tilted her head, and opened her mouth under his. He took advantage as if he'd been waiting for the right time to strike. His tongue dived in and curled around hers. Tugged. Played.

There was a sweet taste on his lips, almost as if

he'd had some sort of fruit for lunch. Maybe it was the sugar cane from earlier. She wanted to get lost in the taste of him, in the feel of his body and mouth pressed to hers. He moved closer, arching her body into his more, and his grip on her hair tightened. It was the most erotic kiss she'd had in her life. The earlier kisses had been nothing but child's play.

This one was all-encompassing, driving a deep need from within her core. Building up as if reaching for a crescendo. Her stomach swam with heat. The area between her legs pulsed.

His mouth tasted of male and spice, surrounding her senses until all she knew, all she could feel, was him.

The grip on her hair tugged her this way and that, adjusting her to what he wanted. He'd be a man who'd take absolute control in bed. This kiss left no doubt. She'd be at his mercy.

And she wanted to go willingly.

That thought caused her to moan deep in her throat. He answered with one of his own, then gripped her jaw again and pulled back, staring at her with hooded eyes.

"Fuck."

He could say that again.

"You really need to get in that pool, Jules."

She opened her mouth again to ask if he'd join her.

"I'll come in after you."

He made a point of releasing her, finger by finger, hand by hand, as if he struggled to let go. But he gave her his back. *Ever the gentleman*, she thought, amused.

She quickly stripped down to her bra and panties and debated removing those too. They needed to be washed, but if she removed them, she'd be completely bare. It was a huge jump in expectations of what may or may not happen. She didn't want to assume, but she also wanted to make sure she got clean, as with the panties and bra. If she didn't take this opportunity now, it may not present itself again. They'd be wet afterward, but she could just wear the shorts and t-shirt they'd provided until the morning.

Hopefully, everything would be dry by then.

Decision made, she quickly got into the pool, removed her bra and panties, and began to lather them up with the soap they'd been given. The scents of coconut and lavender rose from the cube, refreshing and delightful.

She turned her back to Matt in order to give him the same privacy as he did her. "I'm ready. Just going to clean these up a bit if you want to join."

****

If he wanted to join.

Did he?

A million times, *yes*. But one glaringly *no*, pointed out by the obvious. This was no vacation, and she was supposed to be under his protection. Not under *him*.

He highly doubted it'd get to that point out here, anyway. He wouldn't let it. And there was no denying the truth of what she spoke: they did have some amazing chemistry. If they were captured again tomorrow, would he regret not acting on tonight?

He tilted his head back to the bright night stars and blew out a heavy breath, then unsnapped his shorts and pushed them over his hips. His boxers came next, and—hands over his junk, because he was modest, after all—he quickly spun around and entered the pool. She'd kept her word and gave him privacy, keeping her back to him.

He settled in, finding a notch of rock where he

could lean back and keep an eye on her, as well as the path leading to the village. That'd be the direction someone would approach from. Behind and at the sides were the deep drops of canyon cliffs.

While his blood still pumped hot from their kiss earlier, his skin had cooled. The hot water spring changed that and wrapped his body within a warm cocoon of comfort. He leaned his head back with a small moan and let his eyelids drop so only a sliver of vision got through. Then, he just relaxed as much as he could, some thousands of miles from home.

Water sloshed and rolled against him with soft waves, lulling him into a deeper contentment. Jules moved around, humming beneath her breath, and from the sounds of it, most likely washing her hair, her body.

A soft breath pushed out.

Dripping water.

Rushing like rainfall.

Whispering secrets.

"The soap is amazing, if you're interested."

He peeked one eye open. Her cheeks were pink from the hot water, her curly dark hair wet and heavy down her back. Pulled from her face, it brought out her olive skin tone and sharp cheekbones, the lush curve of her mouth and chin, each of which looked entirely too bitable under the moonlight.

He sat up, ignoring his thoughts, and held out his hand. The soap hit it a moment later, and he made quick work of washing the dirt, grime, blood, and sweat from his skin. He hissed when hitting open wounds and wondered how sanitary this could be. But he was clean, and that was important. An infection could get real serious real fast when you were hundreds of miles from a modern hospital.

Dropping beneath the water one more time to

rinse his hair, he rose again and pushed back the strands, then retook his seat against the warm rocks.

No sooner did he settle did she speak. "I want to kiss you again."

He rubbed the scruff of his jawline and eyed her across the spring. "Do you say everything on your mind or only enough to push me?"

Her lips curved in a small, teasing smile. "Have you ever known someone from New York City to hold back?"

He grinned and dropped his head back, then closed his eyes again. "How about you tell me a little about yourself instead?"

She snorted, the sound entirely unfeminine. His smile grew.

"You probably know more about me than I do, including my credit score.

He made a noncommittal movement with his mouth. Like *maybe I do, maybe I don't.*

She scoffed this time. "I never thought I'd go into banking. Found myself working in an audit function before I knew it. Always thought those bankers really didn't work much. Lived their nine-to-five lives with a nooner on Wednesdays, drinks after work on Fridays."

"Charming." Water moved against him in lulling waves.

She sighed. "I was pretty naïve about that side of the world. Turns out they work some serious hours. And now that I'm embedded deep, I find myself lost. Almost don't recognize who I used to be or who I've become. One of the two."

He opened his eyes at that, the conversation going dark pretty damn quick. "Who did you used to be?"

"An interior design dropout. The girl who took wood shop for fun in high school and enjoyed it so much she used to ask the teacher if she could hang there during lunch period and after school. My brother used to have to come looking for me, make sure I ate lunch. I was more concerned with building things, beautiful pieces of woodwork or functional pieces of furniture, than I was about getting a manicure or dating the jock of the high school football team."

He tried to picture a younger Juliette, someone free and artistic, like the one she described. The image his mind brought up was so at odds with the pictures of who'd he'd learn was Juliette Scaglione. The one in a manilla case file back in his car at the airport. One wearing prim and stiff black suits. Hair pulled into a tight bun. Makeup minimal but on point.

Not a woman who liked to get dirty, someone who ran like an animal through the forest, who kissed a stranger in a dark, hollowed-out tree trunk, who coaxed Federal Agents into hot springs, not wearing a scrap of clothing. Who may have trafficked drugs across the border.

He winced.

"What just went through your head?" she asked.

He shook his. "I'm having a hard time resolving the differences between what I know of you and who you've explained yourself to be once upon a time."

"And it was bad enough to cause you to look like you'd stepped on a big ole fat rusty nail?"

He laughed but sobered before he said, "I'm still stuck on you being a possible drug trafficker, Juliette."

She scowled but sat straighter and stared at him solidly for a good few seconds before saying, "Those aren't my drugs."

He sighed, not wanting to get into this. Here. Now. He laid his head back against the rock and closed his eyes again. "But you can't deny they were in your bag."

Silence followed, except for the slow ripple of water pushing against him. He felt her move closer. It made him doubt that he'd ever be able to be alone in a room with her and not know where she was. There was this connection he could no longer deny, like invisible strings linking them.

She settled next to him, and he turned his head toward her and opened his eyes. She had hers on him. "I don't know how those drugs got in my bag. Honestly, Matt."

She seemed so earnest. But he'd learned to listen to his gut, and unfortunately, he kept going back and forth on this one.

"I hate that you think the worst of me with this," she said.

He pursed his lips, not liking that either. "I—I don't." He sat up and ran his hands through his hair again, pushing the drying threads away from his face. The unruly strands would be a frizz of a mess here in a few hours. He took his birth mother's curls from her side of the family. Everything else from his sperm donor.

Pushing an even darker story out of his mind, he turned toward her and cupped her jaw again. "I don't think you're the worst. But I'm struggling to understand how you got into the position you did, especially knowing what I've figured out in such a short time." He shook his head. "I'm not talking about what I found out on paper or from my analysts working the case. But what I've found out myself."

She licked her lips, her attention on him with such an eager innocence he wondered if she'd hold the same look as she took his cock in her mouth. He bit off a curse.

"What have you figured out?" she asked.

He thought about his answer before responding. "You're brave but incredibly headstrong, some would probably say dangerously so."

"Dangerously?" she asked.

He gave her a droll look. "You did try to take on two armed guards while protecting me from harm, and don't get me started on coaxing a strange man into what is practically a hot tub in the middle of the wilderness."

The side of her mouth kicked up.

"You're also smart and funny. You've managed to keep up with my sense of humor, and not many can. And you don't complain, no matter what's thrown at you. You just deal with it and push forward."

Her face changed to one of confusion.

"Juliette—we were chased by gunmen through the forest, running up and down hills and climbing mountains. Then, when we needed to hide, you went inside a hollowed tree despite being what amounts to deathly scared of closed spaces, and handled it like a champ."

Her eyes cast down, and if he didn't know any better, he could have sworn her cheeks grew darker. "I did what anyone would have done, especially knowing what the result would have been on the other side."

He tilted her face up a bit more so he could have her attention again, then dropped his hand. "I get your point, but I also don't agree with it. I think the only reason we got out of the woods alive, well, we're technically still in them, but the only reason we're alive is because you pushed through and did what was needed."

She dropped her attention to his mouth, then back up to his eyes. "So did you."

They held each other's gazes in the silence of the night. Something swelled inside him that had nothing to do with attraction. Sure, he felt tons of that. But instead, this was similar to the feeling he had when he thought of his niece, his ma, and Charlie back home. Oddly, like affection, a protectiveness. One that confused the shit out of him, but one he also really wanted to embrace.

This brave, beautiful woman had managed to burrow her way under his skin and set up shop. He couldn't pinpoint exactly when it happened, but he also couldn't deny it.

"Matt," she said, her voice rough with a similar longing he could hear.

"I know," he responded, then cupped the sides of her face, leaned forward, and kissed her, unable to fight the urge anymore.

Her mouth immediately opened beneath his, and a moan escaped. He captured it and thrust his tongue deep inside, then twirled around hers. She scooted forward until she straddled his lap.

Her breasts pressed against his chest, the lushness of them unmistakable. He groaned deep in his chest and wrapped his arms around her, cradling one large palm against the back of her head to hold her. She wrapped her arms around his neck and pressed even closer.

There was no space between their upper torsos or mouths. It was as if he was drowning in the taste of her while unable to get enough. He'd never felt this kind of need before. This *want* for more.

As if she read his mind, she gasped, "More," then lined her hips up to his.

Both of his hands shot out and landed on her hips, stilling her. He dropped his head back and swallowed hard. "God," he punched out. The feel of her, so hot and wicked. Just right there. He could take her if he wanted. Could end this suffering for them both. Ease this building need. And finally, finally, he'd know.

"Matt," she groaned against his neck, licking and sucking at the skin. Her hips tried to move, but his grip held firm. Twin peaks of hardness shifted against his chest, and the feel of her, the sound of her, and the scent of her almost sent him over the edge. Almost told him to fuck it and just let go.

Instead, he ground his teeth together until his jaw hurt and tried to breathe through the haze of desire. His entire body tingled with the rush, from the roots of his hair, down his spine, and to his toes, which curled as Jules licked a long path up his neck. Then she lined up her mouth with his and stared into his eyes.

"Pretty," he thought and said out loud, staring into the deep color of her gaze. Her lids were heavy with want, seductive as hell.

"Matthew," she whined-slashed-moaned. And that was a jolt. He hadn't had anyone call him that since he'd been a kid. He didn't prefer his long name. But he found the sound of it in the manner she spoke—he liked it a bit too much.

She bit at his lower lip as if she knew him distracted. "Matt," she said again, this time with a grumble.

It would be so easy to give in. So fucking easy.

As if she knew his decision, she sighed and loosened her arms from around his neck. "Why?" she asked.

He gave her a quick squeeze on her hips. "There are a few reasons." She raised an impertinent brow. *Cute*, he thought. "No condom, for starters."

Her lips twisted to the side.

"And second," he said with a heavy breath, knowing the next words would probably ruin this chemistry between them. "I'm supposed to be taking you into custody in connection with a drug trafficking investigation."

"Ugh!" she shouted to the sky, then smacked the water. "Please tell me you still don't think I'm involved in that."

"Juliette—" he started, only to be cut off.

"I'm sitting naked on your lap."

He swallowed, that lone action challenging. "Kind of hard to miss it."

She narrowed her eyes. "Speaking of hard." She rolled her hips toward him.

They both hissed out a heavy breath. "Jules," he said, fighting the urge to just go on. "Fuck!"

She stopped moving and sat back again, her mouth cast in an adorable, yet resigned frown. "Fine."

Uh-oh. Any man over the age of five knew it was anything but fine when a woman said that.

"I keep saying that word around you, but fine. You make me feel like a leacher, pushing myself on you. I'm sorry, Matt. It's obvious you don't want this."

Well, hell, now he just felt like shit. She sounded and looked so dejected. "Jules." He stilled her as she went to move off his lap. Probably not the best move, but he honestly didn't want to let her go. Didn't want this moment, deep in the forest and under a canopy of dazzling stars, to end just yet. "I think it's pretty clear I want you. As much as I'd like to be able to do it, it's just impossible for a man to hide their desire, especially when naked as I am."

She looked down, almost as if she were trying to avoid his eyes. Had he hurt her feelings unintentionally?

"I didn't mean for any of this to get to this point. I'm sorry," he apologized. "I am attracted to you. Not going to deny that. I'm fighting against the urge to slide inside you right now, drive so deep inside that neither of us would know where one ended, and the other began.

My imagination is going *wild*," he said, stressing that last word, "thinking how hot, wet, and tight you would feel wrapped around my dick."

Her eyes popped wide and met his. Good. He had her attention now.

"But this isn't the time for that," he said, his voice gentle as he pushed back a strand of hair falling to her face. "I wish it could be. I wish it was that easy for us. But it's not. And it's something I'd rather not do for the first time in my life in this position we've found ourselves in. Do you understand?"

She stared blankly at him for a few seconds before comprehension dawned, as if a shadow cleared from her face. "Wait, are you saying?"

He squeezed her hips again. Just once, thankful he didn't have to go any further and say the actual words. "Yes."

Her mouth worked as if she were a fish out of water. Adorable. "How? I mean? I know how. But ... how?" Her face screwed up, and he tried not to laugh. "You're hot. Sexy. Stunning." She took a deep breath and settled soft eyes on him. "I don't understand how someone who looks as amazing as you do and is in a great job, that forgive me for saying, has some pretty macho men running it, is still a virgin."

She said that last as if the word were a secret and it caused him to grin. "Are you calling me soft?" he teased.

Her back went straight. "Never."

He laughed. "I'm just poking fun. I understand what you're saying. Honestly, it's never come up with the guys. And when we're working out in the field, it's pretty intense. I just, it's never been a topic that's brought up."

"But how?" she asked again, this time with a

sense of wonder.

"Oh, to hear everything going through your head right now." He shrugged. "The how is I was a pretty dorky teenager. Didn't really bulk up until a few years ago, then I was too focused on making my career and a name for myself that I never really thought it was something I had to do."

"Do you want to?" she blurted, then slapped a hand over her mouth.

He laughed again, tossing his head back. "Of course, I want to." He pulled her close to him again and dropped his voice while he stared at her mouth, wondering if he could get away with kissing her. "Do you feel how much I want to?" he asked in the intimacy of their cocoon.

She nodded and bit her lip. Then wound her arms around his neck. This brought her flush to him. Such a temptation.

"Of course, I want to," he said again. "But for now, I'd really like to kiss you." He squeezed his arms around her waist, drawing one hand up the length of her spine. Water drops tinkled as he broke the surface. "Are you able to control yourself enough to allow me to kiss and discover you properly?"

The side of her mouth kicked up, and she leaned forward before nodding, her lips brushing against his with each movement. "Yeah, I suppose I could do that."

He didn't make them wait for a second more.

"You kiss pretty well for a virgin," she said into his mouth.

If he were being honest, it was her tongue causing him to lose himself. His head spun under their lazy, yet heated and deep kiss. "Your mouth is going to get you in trouble one of these days," he teased in response. He deepened their kiss and tangled his tongue around hers.

She tasted sweet, and the thought made him wonder if she'd taste sweeter elsewhere. His arms tightened around her back. The tips of his fingers pressed against the sides of her breasts.

He moaned into another kiss. "Juliette."

She tightened her hold, too. "I know. Don't stop. Please."

As if he could.

Chapter Fourteen

The next morning, Juliette walked beside Matt as they followed Sam along a well-used trail. The sun had barely crested the sky, but the day promised to be a scorcher.

They'd had breakfast with Sam early that morning, and all of them had agreed it was time to move on.

She'd tried to throw her hair in a bun, feeling the humidity calling this morning, but several tendrils had already escaped, both because of the lack of a proper hair tie to keep her hair up and a lack of products.

With such heavy, thick hair, it was only a matter of time before it escaped its confines and ended up as a wild nest for birds around her head.

Meanwhile, Matt looked cool, calm, and collected. He'd braided his hair this morning, then tied it back with a colorful string given to him by one of the sweet young girls back at the tribe. The little girl, no older than ten, had blushed as he smiled in thanks, then proceeded to braid his hair as he ate on. As if it were the most normal thing for him to do—allowing a young child to fuss over him.

It had caused her heart to thump with joy at how easy he was around children. Something she did not need to think about.

Something she failed in thinking and obsessing over.

She shook her thoughts away and refocused on following the men along the trail.

Matt's long strides kept pace with Sam as if they were taking a leisurely walk to the store and not one through a wild jungle to find a car that had been procured for them in an assist to helping them escape this jungle.

And that was one thing, how much the tribe was helping them. Amazing that this place existed, that these people did. Despite how they'd come to be in this situation, it was a place she wouldn't forget anytime soon.

Nor would she ever be able to adequately express her gratitude.

There was no way Matt and she would have survived without their help—without their continued help.

And... Her cheeks heated as she took another look at Matt. Last night had changed something between them. Brought them closer than they'd been before. She hoped he felt it too because it was something she couldn't deny anymore. Her heart had opened toward him, especially after their talk and the kisses from last night.

That was all they'd done, too. Just kiss. But they were so deep and thoroughly done that she didn't think she'd ever been touched in the same way.

He'd kept to only the kissing, maybe with a few stolen touches here and there. She'd felt him hot, hard, and ready to take her. She'd wanted him so bad, but she respected his wishes and didn't want to push him to do anything more.

To say she'd been surprised he was a virgin was an understatement. She still couldn't quite believe it. The man was entirely too good-looking. Too good of a kisser. But he'd been earnest and open about it, so she'd have to trust him at this point.

Trust. That was something that didn't come easy, but she could see herself doing it with Matt. The hope she felt made her heart clench. Hope that he was a good guy. That he wouldn't hurt her. That maybe, just maybe, they'd have a chance to grow this budding relationship because she really, really, *really* wanted to.

She smiled at that thought, feeling like a giddy teenager. He turned back to her and held out a hand, caught her gaze, and helped her over a fallen log on the path. One brow rose at her expression and surely the blush on her cheeks because she could still feel the heat in them. He squeezed her hand but didn't let go, following Sam close behind.

They all walked on in silence for a bit. Around them, the forest chirped its joyful songs, some bringing with it the sounds of home. Others, like the rattling bone sound, were new to her ears. What she couldn't hear was the sound of humanity existing, of cars honking and speeding by. Of people talking or screaming at one another, calling out a greeting in passing. Of trains and subways. Life.

What must it be like to live with such utter silence yet so much noise? A different kind of life, she supposed. One filled with nature and learning how to survive off the land. Not necessarily a way for her, but an interesting one all the same.

The three of them rounded a sharp corner of trees, then came out on an unpaved road. Sam held back a bit and waited for them to walk side-by-side before they continued on the one-lane road.

Sam cleared his throat. "If you don't mind me saying," he said and gestured toward them, "you two look as if the creator above would have matched you himself."

Her hand spasmed in Matt's, but he held firm.

"What do you mean?" Matt asked.

Sam twisted his lips in thought, then went on. "You have a certain way about both of you that looks like... How do you say, two mates of animals finding each other after so long. Moving in sync. You … complement each other."

Did they? Juliette focused on how they moved now, even alongside each other. Their hands clasped between them. They were walking in step with one another, less than a foot of space between them, but she hadn't noticed anything else.

But if she had to explain how her hand in his felt, she supposed it felt as natural to her as if she held her own.

"Anyway," Sam said, "just a thought I wanted to share. Right around this corner, we should come up on the car. I'm told the keys will be under the mat on the driver's side. If you continue traveling along this road, then cut over to follow the sun's path once you reach the town of *Chihuahua*. From there, you'll need to get a map to figure out your route home. There are travel documents and some cash, identification in the car." He bit his lip, then stopped and turned to them, his expression grave.

"Try your best to avoid drawing attention. Your presence here has not gone unnoticed, and many are looking for you. Others would use your location as a means for them to get ahead, if you understand what I'm saying."

Matt nodded, and a sense of urgency pushed at Juliette. Did she understand that someone would sell them out in order to benefit themselves? Yes, she did. No matter where one went, greed was a driving force. She didn't want to think about ending up where they'd started here.

She shuddered, and Matt squeezed her hand, pulling her close to his side. "I'm not going to let them take us again, Jules."

She leaned into him and nodded. She didn't want

to argue about it now, but they had a long road ahead and were in a place they didn't know. There was no way he could make that kind of promise, especially if they traveled on the main highways. Surely, there'd be traffic blocks.

"Stay off the highway," Sam said, as if reading her mind. "And try to avoid border checkpoints. Sometimes the good guys aren't always what they appear."

"What does that mean?" she asked, and both men faced her. That question may have come out a little higher-pitched than she wanted.

"It means there's a lot of corruption that occurs in certain areas. Not all are bad. But there's a lot still there. If you follow the sun's direction, avoid the local cops, and don't draw attention, getting to the border should be easy enough."

Matt nodded. "I'm thinking we'll have about fifteen to seventeen hours of a drive ahead of us. I'm aiming for the eastern border. Maybe cross near Laredo, Texas."

"Are you sure we should leave?" she asked, feeling the panic rise in her body. She understood she acted very unrealistic right now, but the thought of traveling on their own, of putting her trust in Matt to make the right decisions to keep them safe, when they were safe now. She didn't know if she could do it.

"Jules," the man in question said, turning to her. "We can't stay here. We'll be fine. Trust me."

She looked into his eyes. Her entire body was strung tight. "I don't know if I can," she whispered.

He studied her, probably hearing what she really said. Could he blame her? After everything? Even after what he'd told her about her still being the subject of his "investigation?"

"You don't have a choice, unfortunately."

With those blunt words, he turned back to Sam. The expression on his face, the way he held her tight but tense, spoke volumes. It was like he was disappointed in her. She didn't want that, but she couldn't help the way she felt, especially the urge building within her that something was going to happen. Something bad.

In short order, Sam guided them the rest of the way to a two-door red Honda Civic that had seen better days. There was a stash of granola bars and water in the back, along with the gun they'd taken from their prison. She didn't know when they'd lost it, but her nerves settled a fraction at the sight of it.

She'd never been into guns, but having one nearby made her feel as if there was some control of her own destiny.

They drove in silence for a bit, and Matt kept switching radio stations, trying to hear the news. She asked him if he understood any of what was being said, but he could only pick up a few words here and there.

After a while of nothing but trees and mountains, she grew tired, lulled to a calmness by the shifting of the car. She kicked the seat back some and closed her eyes.

What felt like only moments later, the car's speed changed, jolting her out of a light slumber.

"What's going on?" she asked, seeing buildings rise around them. Long gone was the forest filled with lush trees and waterfalls. Only brown fields and half-dead trees seemed to survive here among buildings and houses.

He reached over and squeezed her knee. "We've reached *Chihuahua*. I think if we stay on the outskirts of town, we should be good to go. But I need to stop and get a map. When we do, you need to stay inside the car. Watch the parking lot for anyone following us. Can you do that?"

She looked at him sharply.

"I don't think anyone is," he said, glancing at the rearview mirror. "But I can't be sure. I need your eyes."

She decided to get snippy, still a little stung regarding being the subject of his investigation. "I can do that. But what makes you think I won't just run off when your back is turned?"

He cut her a look as he pulled into a gas station that looked to have seen better days. That look had been disgruntled, knowing, while at the same time, bothered by her asking that.

"I already know the answer to this question and the one you asked, but I'll ask mine anyway." He pulled to the side of the station and backed into a parking spot under a bare-looking tree that provided minimal shade. It afforded her the view of the entire parking lot, of cars coming in from both ways, while at the same time allowing her not to have to watch the rear, seeing as the tree backed into a tall wooden fence.

He pulled up on the emergency brake and turned to her, one arm leaning on the back of her chair. His gaze seemed to pin her to her seat. "Are you going to run?"

She swallowed under the full attention of Agent Gonzales, because that was who he was right now. Long gone was the playful yet serious Matt. She lifted her chin, unwilling to let him intimidate her. "You don't scare me. So stop with the glare."

"Answer the question, Jules."

Would she run when he turned his back? Obviously not. She wasn't stupid. There was nowhere for her to go. The safest place she could be was with him, regardless of her smarted emotions. But she was tired of him using that constant excuse of her possibly being a subject in his investigation to push her away. Just when she thought he would finally be honest with her, when that was what he'd been requiring of her up to now, he'd toss up that proverbial hand and take three steps back.

Frustration. Hurt. Annoyance.

Those were all her middle names now.

"What if I do?" she asked. "What could you possibly do down here? Your position gets you nothing." She wasn't trying to be a brat, but she was kind of proud of herself with that line. And her voice. It didn't even shake. Inside, though, the insides of her body were quivering.

Not with fear. But anticipation.

What would he do with that challenge?

He studied her for a moment, then two. His whiskey gaze bounced between her eyes, roamed over her face, and snagged on her mouth before coming back up. Then his hand darted out before she saw him move and wrapped around her chin and jaw, holding her in place. The move wasn't painful, but it caused interesting warm and tingly feelings to occur low in her stomach.

"You run, Juliette," he said low. "I'll find you."

"So certain of yourself?" she asked, her voice breathless.

He must have heard how this affected her, his hold, the proprietary grip in his voice. As if he damn well knew she wasn't going anywhere, for the side of his mouth kicked up in a grin. She'd seen this look before, back at the airport before everything had changed in their worlds. A glimpse of this playful man beneath the hardened agent. The look transformed his entire being and made his handsome face breathtaking.

He released her chin, a pleased look on his features before he leaned down and placed a chaste kiss on her mouth. "I am," he said against her lips. "You want to play, Juliette. All you have to do is say the word."

With that parting shot, he got out of the car and walked into the gas station. He moved with a lazy kind of swagger. Completely different from how she'd seen him move as they escaped the prison. A sudden clarity washed over—Matt had different skins he used, depending on what he needed to be. He could change in and out of them as if he were breathing. She'd never thought to adjust to her environment and was fascinated with the way he did it.

So caught up in watching him move, she almost missed the attendant pulling out her phone. The young woman with long, dark hair stood behind the counter and watched Matt roam the aisles. Then her gaze bounced out and made contact with Juliette. Back to Matt. On and on.

Tension crept up her neck as this continued until she sat straight up in the seat. Outside, the sun pulsed in waves against the windshield, quickly heating the inside of the car.

Sweat gathered at her nape and temples.

Matt walked up to the counter and dropped a pile of items there, then pulled something from his pocket. She guessed the local currency, but she wasn't sure where he would have gotten it from.

Just as Matt took the bag and turned from the counter to head outside, the lady picked up a cell phone, pointed it to Matt as if she were taking a picture, then to Juliette for the same.

"Shit," she muttered, then looked around the parking lot quickly.

No new cars, no one standing around.

She turned back to the woman who had her eyes on the back of Matt, who was now walking toward the car, and the phone at her ear.

"Shit, shit, shit," Juliette chanted, urging Matt to walk faster.

He was only a short distance away, but his entire demeanor had changed. There was a look of warning on his face, and he communicated something she couldn't figure out.

Seconds later, he opened the door.

"I think she took your picture."

"She definitely took my picture. Yours, too," he said, tossing the bag filled with snacks and water in her lap. He folded in and started the car before the door had shut.

Within seconds, they were peeling out of the parking lot and down the road. "Pull out that map, yeah? We need to get on the right track to get to Texas, but I don't want to pull over and become sitting ducks."

She rustled through the bag and opened the map, unfolding it until it lay across her lap.

"We need to avoid highways and try to stay on back roads, so anything with a box marker for the highway, let's shy from. Can you get me to something that may keep us a little more hidden but on our way east?"

She scanned the map for a few seconds, trying to get her bearings, then looked up to find where they were.

"We're right off of Highway 16 heading toward *Delicias*."

"Okay." She turned the map until she was fairly positive they were moving in the right direction. "We should be good to go for a bit longer on this road. About five miles up, take the first exit."

"Got it," he responded, his gaze jumping from the road to the rearview mirror.

She turned in her seat to see if she could pinpoint anyone following them, but all she saw were a few cars a block or so behind them. Nothing that stood out.

The Civic accelerated and changed lanes. She

turned back in her seat. "Do you think we're being followed?"

His lips thinned. "Not sure. But I really hope not."

She chanced a glance at the passenger mirror now, her stomach turning over.

Chapter Fifteen

A few hours later, Matt pulled into another gas station, this one on the outskirts of some mountain town called *Saltillo*. He turned off the car and faced Juliette. "I'm going to go pay in cash. Can you keep an eye out again?"

She bit her lip, wiggled in her seat, and looked around.

"What's wrong?" he asked.

"I need to use the restroom. All that water," she said, pointing to the stash of water and snacks he'd gotten at their last stop.

He searched for a sign for the bathroom and contemplated asking her to wait until they pulled over on the side of the road. They were in the mountains, and there was no doubt they'd be able to find something off the beaten path, but if they were here and a bathroom available, then maybe it wasn't such a bad idea to try and knock it out now.

"Okay, let's go in together. I'll wait for you to come out before doing anything else."

She grabbed the door handle, then tossed him a sharp look. "I'm not going to run off in the middle of the forest in Mexico, Matt."

Confused at her words, it took him a moment for them to sink in. "That's not why I'm waiting for you."

"Then why?"

"Because I'm trying to keep you safe, Juliette. But perhaps if escape is on your mind, then maybe we need to have a chat."

She pushed open the door and got out of the car. "Nope." She popped the *p*. "We do not need to have another one of your chats."

He joined her but didn't respond. Instead, he focused on their surroundings and the older man inside the gas station.

In short order, they found out there was a bathroom inside, which Juliette used. He'd wait. He got them some gas with the remaining funds they had, then they went back out and filled the car up before driving away.

Not another soul drove by, nor did the attendant pay them any attention.

Good news, at least. Hopefully, it'd continue for the remaining part of the trip. He wasn't counting on it, though because the area at the bottom of this mountain and surrounding the border would grow more populated. They'd get noticed and surely there were more people who'd be on the lookout at checkpoints.

Not that he was planning on using said checkpoints. No, he planned to cross the river itself. A dangerous venture, but one they had no choice to do.

"When we come out of these mountains, we're going to need to move quickly. Can you take a look and see if there are ways to stay on the outskirts of any major towns or cities?"

Juliette grabbed the map, nodding. "What border checkpoint are we heading for?"

"Laredo or Del Rio, though I'm thinking we may need to swim across."

The map slammed down on her lap with a jolt. "What?"

He glanced over at her before turning his attention back to the road. "You can swim, can't you?"

"Well, yeah. I mean, I'm not the best swimmer, but I can hold my own. I just, I don't know how I feel about crossing an enormous river. Why can't we cross at a border checkpoint?"

"You heard Sam," he said, his voice gentle yet firm. "What he said was true. We can't cross at a border. I don't want to risk it. Hopefully, we'll run into a patrol on the other side instead."

"I don't understand all of this," she said, shaking out the map again. "I don't understand why the corruption can't be flushed out in this country and even our own. It's like everyone turns a blind eye to it and it never gets addressed."

"Unfortunately," he agreed.

She found them a route and relayed a few directions but kept the map on her lap as they moved along. The silence between them was comfortable, and he found himself liking it. For the most part, the women he'd gone out with always had to fill in the quiet with chatter. Sometimes saying things that made absolutely no sense. And while things had been tense between him and Juliette, he'd grown extremely comfortable with her.

Almost at ease, in a sense.

Sure, his attraction to her was proving problematic, but outside of that, he had no issues being in her company even when there was nothing to say.

"For all the corruption of this country, there sure are some beautiful parts of it," she said. Her face was turned to the sun setting over the flat horizon of farmland.

"That it is. Would you consider yourself a city girl by heart?" he asked.

"No, I wouldn't call myself that. Though, I've only ever lived in New York. The times we'd gone camping or up to Vermont to see the changing leaves in the fall, I've felt more at peace than in my own home. Figured I'd eventually move up that way."

"Just like that?" he asked, curious to uncover more. Wanting to understand her, to know her. An addiction, he realized. She could quickly become his drug of choice.

"Well, I worried before about my brother wanting to stay close to the city. But now..."

"I'm sorry you had to see that, Jules."

"I hope one day I understand why he was involved in this. But I'd rather not talk about that now. Do you have another story?"

The side of his mouth quirked. "Like in the tree?"

She shuddered beside him. "Ugh, don't remind me of the tree. If I never see the inside of a tree again, it'll be too soon."

He laughed and saw a sign up ahead of a festival honoring *La Llorona*. "Have you ever heard of the story of *La Llorona*, its origin?"

"La who?" she asked.

He smiled and settled back, getting in gear to tell this story. "*La Llorona* translates to 'The Crier,' which fits this ghost or spirit or whatever you want to call her. She is known for being part banshee, part horse, part woman, and part creepy. Each of those being equal parts, of course."

"Of course," she echoed.

He tossed her a smile. "*La Llorona* haunts the riverbanks of the Rio Grande..." He trailed off, immediately recognizing this might not be the best story to tell with where they headed. "Actually, on second thought."

"Oh, no, don't stop. You've poked my curiosity button. You have to go on now."

He hedged. "You understand this is just an old folklore tale, right? A superstition?"

"Now you have me really curious," she said, turning to face him, one leg bent up on the seat. "I'm a grown woman. Just tell me the story already."

He let out a deep breath. "Fine. Don't say I didn't warn you. We will be crossing the Rio Grande and if you start freaking out on me…"

"This story can't be *that* bad."

He shrugged. "Anyhow, you asked for it. Okay, so she searches the riverbanks of the Rio Grande, continuously looking for her two children. You see, legend has it she stabbed those two children and threw them into the river after her boyfriend, who was extremely wealthy and good-looking, told her he didn't want to marry her because of them."

She gasped, the sound outraged and shocked. "How awful!"

He nodded. "After she killed them, she went back to her lover's home, still covered in the blood of her children, to show him her dedication and tell him she wanted to be with him."

Juliette let out a sound of disgust, and he couldn't help but smile. While the story was horrifying, albeit a folklore, her reactions were entirely too cute.

He reached over and took her hand in his, kissed the back of it, then went on. "Needless to say, any sane person would be horrified at her actions and this man, despite his values, was no different. He immediately ended their relationship."

"What happened then?"

A check engine light popped on in the car's dash and he took note but continued. "Well, the story splits here, depending on which part of the country you live in. Some say she stabbed herself then drowned in the river as well, so she could be with her children. But others say justice was served and an angry mob found her and threw her in the river just as she had her children. But both stories end with a heartbroken woman who died and whose soul was so grief-stricken that she came back to look for her children. There have been reports of people hearing a wailing sound coming from the river."

"Creepy," Juliette sang.

He nodded. "Definitely. Others have been a bit more dramatic and have even reported seeing a woman wearing a nightgown covered in blood. This has been pretty common over the years, and every single one of those reports has stated the head of what appears to be a woman is not human. But that of a horse."

"Okay, I take back my earlier statement. *That* is creepy."

"They say it's her punishment for her unforgivable sins, the head of a horse as her own. Local towns and cities on both sides of the border still warn people about veering near the river at night, saying *La Llorona* will force you to stay with her and keep her company."

"Not to interrupt, but you're going to want to take this exit," she said quietly, then when he did, she went on. "That's it?"

"Kind of," he hedged.

"Oh, don't stop on my account now. Please go on."

"Well, many have reported when they cross the river, and mind you, many of these are immigrants coming into America half in a daze with dehydration and sleep deprivation, so who knows if it's true."

"Yes?"

"Well, they say they've felt the hands of *La Llorona* try to pull them under as they swam across."

"Get out of here!"

"Yep."

She shuddered. "Can you imagine? Ugh. Okay, that entire story is creepy with a capital C."

The vehicle jolted forward with a short revving of

the engine.

"What's going on?" she asked.

"I think this car has reached its limit," he responded. "We're going to have to try to make it on foot across the farmland ahead."

She peered out the window. "Um, the sun is going down, and we have no flashlights. How are we going to find our way to where we need to go?"

"Study the map while you can, Jules."

The car jolted again. He turned off to a dirt road and sped up, trying to get as must distance as they could while they had the car.

Headlights flashed in the rearview mirror several miles back. He kept his eyes on the road but occasionally checked to see if it'd follow them along the dirt path. They bounced over potholes and dips in the road. The car definitely was on its last leg as it quaked so hard he thought the axle would snap.

Just as the sun dipped below the horizon, the car sputtered out and died.

"Shit," Jules said.

Matt kept his eyes on the rearview mirror, watching with dread as the vehicle pulled off onto the road behind them.

"We're going to have to make a run for it," he said. "I think we're being followed."

"What?" she exclaimed, turning in her seat to look out the back window. "For how long?"

"I don't know," he responded. "Gather everything you can. We need to be quick."

They both got out of the car to the surrounding darkness. Crickets chirped in the distance and coyotes called out their song. Farther off, probably five to ten or so miles, light filled the horizon. He suspected it was the US Air Force base just over the border, and that was what they'd use as a pinpoint for their direction. He told Juliette as much.

"What?" she asked, her voice breathless. He frowned.

"Wait. I don't think I can, I can't … breathe. The air isn't here."

"Shit." He rounded the car and moved toward the outline of her. For someone as claustrophobic as she was, the sudden darkness could seem suffocating.

"Jules," he said, crowding her against the warmth of the still-cooling metal car. The day had definitely been a scorcher, and they both probably reeked to high heaven. "I know this is scary, but we only have a few more hours to go. You can do this. Deep breaths now. Focus on taking air into your lungs. There is plenty of it."

Her wide, frightened eyes rolled around, taking in every inch of the darkness surrounding them. For someone who was claustrophobic, to be stuck out here had to be a certain kind of special hell.

"Hey," he said and leaned closer until it was only his face she could see. His lips brushed hers with every word he spoke, every breath he took. "I won't let anything happen to you. Give me your eyes, gorgeous."

Her hands gripped wildly at his waist, and she visibly tried to control her breathing, taking it one step at a time, reining in the fear and instead focusing on him.

After a few moments, she seemed to be drawing in air easier. "I don't know what I would do without you, Matt," she said, her voice shaking.

He fully leaned into her body, making sure she knew he was here with her completely. "Same, Juliette." He placed a gentle kiss on her plump lips. "We need to drink what's left of the water and be on our way. Are you up for that?"

She tilted her head toward his mouth, her intent

clear even before she voiced her want. "I guess I could be with a little motivation."

He grinned before he dropped down and covered her mouth with his.

A shock vibrated through him. One similar to what had happened last night. It was as if two ends of a magnet had been trying to connect for years, and with each touch of their lips, the connection was completed.

The jolt of contact rolled through his mouth and down his spine, then hit with some serious heat in his belly and caused his cock to grow in his pants. A frustrating outcome here in the desert where he could do nothing about it, but one he couldn't control.

She twined her tongue around his, meeting him stroke for stroke, lick for lick, and kiss for kiss. Their heads moved this way and that, their mouths unwilling to separate.

Out of some uncontrollable instinct, he reached down and palmed the lush curve of her breast. She gasped into his mouth, and he pushed his tongue and hips deeper, squeezed her breast, and then caressed it under his palm.

Juliette moaned and hitched a leg over his hip, angling hers toward him.

"Jesus," he groaned, rolling his hips back and forth, matching her movement.

It only took one kiss. One touch. And they ignited. Every. Damn. Time.

"Matt," she said, letting her head fall back to the top of the car. The call of insects around them rose as the heat in his belly expanded. As her breaths labored in crescendo. He could feel her orgasm hovering right there, as was his. If they didn't slow down, there was surely to be a mess in his pants soon.

He licked a path of salt up her neck, then lifted

his gaze and froze.

Headlights closed in on them in the distance, and the more he stared, the more it looked as though they were coming in his direction. How quickly she made him lose his head.

Jules bit the skin at his neck, and he jumped into action. "Someone is coming," he said, pulling away from the temptation of her body. "We need to make a run for it."

"What?" She looked over her shoulder and he caught the widening of her eyes before she turned back and waited, expectant for his direction.

He gauged the distance they would need to go before reaching the border. He only hoped they were in the right place to cross. It was a gamble, especially with the continued on-and-off work with the fence that separated the two countries. And even worse, they were going to have to try to cross the river at night, a treacherous task.

He scanned the dark horizon and eyed the light in the sky. That was where they wanted to get to.

They had to make it. Being captured again was a sure death sentence for them both.

With one last scan of the surrounding area, he clasped her hand and pulled her away from the car. "We have to make a run for it," he said, picking up his steps and moving toward the south end of the lights.

"Do you even know where we are?" she asked.

He nodded toward the light in the sky, though with how dark it'd quickly become, there was no way she could see him. "I'm hoping that light in the sky is a military base or city. We're heading toward the south end of it. So, whatever happens, just keep that part of the sky in your sights and keep moving toward it."

A grumbling growl sounded off in the distance,

eerily similar to a mountain lion. Closer yet came the chirping of the yaps from a pack of coyotes. If the rapidly approaching headlights from the cars bearing down on them didn't catch up, then surely the wildlife would.

Juliette squeezed his hand and obviously tried to turn toward both sounds because her progress slowed.

"Focus," he snapped, pulling her along and trying to listen. Shit, was that running water so soon?

The ground was uneven, and he kept tripping over large boulders, but he pushed forward. The car's headlights grew closer, and voices yelling out to each other became louder.

The sound of rushing water also grew in volume until he could no longer deny it. He prayed to whoever was listening while at the same time felt his gut take a tumble. Trying to cross this river at night was going to be extremely dangerous.

The light became clearer, and he could see the faint outlines of tall fencing in the distance. It had to be a base or airport. He'd only seen that kind of fencing around restrictive areas. If it was what he suspected, then he had a feeling they were just south of Acuna.

He pulled Juliette against a tree, definitely hearing the roar of rushing water moving past only feet away. It was a dark kiss of death standing between them and freedom, safety, his family.

"Jules," he said, feeling his heart pump hard in his chest. He clasped his hands around her head, holding her close to his own. "We're going to have to swim across the Rio Grande."

"What?" she shrieked, her voice high-pitched and shaking. She tried to pull away, but he held her close and dropped his forehead to hers.

"We have no choice. If we stay here, we'll surely

be found. If not by one of them then by the wildlife. I know you're scared, but we can do this. We *have* to do this. Don't ask me to leave you here. I won't do it. And if we both stay, we'll be dead within days."

Her little hands fisted in his shirt and pulled him closer. "I lied earlier. I'm not entirely confident in my swimming abilities."

He huffed out a little laugh. "If you swim like you run, we'll be fine. Just keep kicking. Remember what I said and aim for the south side of those lights."

"Oh, God," she moaned. "I don't know if I can do this."

He kissed her, hard and fast. "We have to. You will do this. You are strong enough to get this far. You only need to push a bit more."

An audible gulp sounded before she nodded.

"Good girl," he said.

****

Good girl.

Was that what she was?

Stranded in the middle of the forest-slash-desert of Mexico. About to cross one of the most dangerous rivers in the world to get to the safety of the United States with a federal agent of the same country. While a bunch of bad guys *and* animals—because no, she wasn't deaf, she could hear them in the night—hunting them.

What kind of good girl ended up in this position?

She pulled off her shoes, using the laces to tie around one of her ankles and hoping they stayed put. There was nothing to do with her hair since she'd lost the tie long ago.

She searched carefully for a few seconds and found the faint outline of Matt doing the same as her, then she turned back toward where the river must surely be, though all she could hear was the roaring.

Tears pricked her eyes, and helplessness clung to her. She let it ride her in a wave, following behind Matt, her hand securely held by his. "Just a few more seconds, Jules," she told herself, allowing a moment's pity.

It rose in a crescendo, bearing down on her with the force of a giant's step where she almost felt as if she were being crushed by it. She sniffed, tried to draw in air, and then found herself wrapped in Matt's warm arms. His hand on the back of her head, his chest vibrating with soothing sounds.

He stepped back, pulling her until her feet hit liquid. She drew in a slight breath at the cold water and took the scent of moss into her lungs. Held the air, then let it out slowly. Drew in a stronger breath next. And kept repeating it as they moved further and further into the water.

The river pushed at their legs with a fierce growl. Then they were at waist level and Matt pulled back from her. She tilted her head up and felt his whispered promise against her lips before he kissed her, deep and thorough.

Their mouths clashed together, moving this way and that, as if they had all the time in the world. It could have gone on forever but was over too soon. He pulled back, took her hand in his, and pushed away from the safety of land.

A jolt of power ripped their grip apart, and she got caught in the river's current. Her scream filled her head and the air as she was pulled under into the darkness. She kicked hard and rose above the surface, sputtering for oxygen and taking in entirely too much water. Panic rose in her chest like a geyser. She couldn't seem to breathe before getting pulled under again. Sharp rocks slammed into her hip, or she slammed into them. She couldn't tell and couldn't get her bearings. Darkness was all around her.

As if she were a tumbleweed in a strong desert storm, she was thrown around without a care. The violence of the river took her breath away again and again, stole her sight and hearing until she had the very real feel of being tugged.

As if someone had a grip on her ankle.

La Llorona.

Oh, God. Was it true? The sound of crying filled her head. Or was that her screams?

She tried to push toward the surface of the river, tried to reach for air, and felt the beckoning peace, the promise of no more suffering.

She was so stinking tired.

She had no one waiting for her, so what harm would it do?

Darkness pushed against her. Her lungs tightened, begging for air. A dozen images went through her mind.

"Fight!"

She thought she heard Matt's deep timber and she blinked against the suffering cloud of peace.

"Kick!"

She kicked against the ground. Slipped against the slimy bottom. Tried again.

"Jules!"

Was that him? Could his promise be sweeter than this peace? She kicked again and felt another tug on her ankle.

She tried to push away from the feeling and then realized her shoes were pulling with the current. The same ones wrapped around the very ankle she felt the tugging. She blindly ripped at the laces until the weight yanking her down went away. Then she kicked with all her might, put everything into it, and broke the surface of the water.

She had enough of a mind left to focus on the

light in the distance. She didn't know north from south, but she stared at it and kicked toward the other side of the river with all her might.

Her arms felt like jelly and her head was so heavy, but she pushed toward the promise of land. The promise of Matt, his kisses, and his arms. The promise of goodness in her life, of a man who was meant to be hers.

She felt possessive enough to use that urge to get her closer and closer to the light until her knees scraped against sharp rocks, jolting her out of the mindset of only swimming, only kicking. She rose on her hands and knees, pushing closer to land, coughing and hacking up dirty water. Her lungs burned and her body ached. Her vision swam with dizziness, and she collapsed on the shore, sand pushing into her mouth before all went black.

Chapter Sixteen

Between one moment and the next, it seemed as though the river had come to life and fell from the sky in sheets of rain. At first, he'd thought he was still in the Rio Grande before his hands had found purchase on sand and rocks.

Matt coughed up what seemed like a never-ending supply of water out of his lungs, then tried to draw in fresh air and get his bearings. The absolute darkness made sense now, especially if the cloud coverage blocked out any light from the stars and moon.

He fell to his back, then immediately rolled to his side. The rain falling on his face kept tossing him back into that river, and he needed to take some time to calm his head and body, get his wits about himself, and find Juliette.

Juliette.

An urgency pushed at his chest. The current had been an angry beast and ripped his grip from her. He'd never felt so humbled by the strength of nature. It was like he had absolutely no control over what would happen and the river wanted him to know that.

Lesson learned.

One he hoped he'd never have to repeat.

He staggered to his feet, still coughing out the remnants of water from his burning lungs. He looked around but could barely see a few feet in front of him. The only things that seemed to help were the sporadic flashes of light from the storm above. Not a good thing to be out in the desert during a lightning storm, but it wasn't like they had a choice.

They hadn't had a choice through any of this.

He hobbled around, cursing a bit when his bare

feet found sharp rocks. But he kept looking. He couldn't give up. And he hoped she'd made it out of the river.

"Jules," he called, then stopped and listened to hear if she'd answer back.

Nothing.

"Juliette," he called again, looking both up and down stream on the banks of the river.

For all he knew, he moved away from her. This entire situation was twelve shades of fucked up.

"Jules!" he shouted. A flash of light cut across his back, illuminating the area in front of him.

A rush of relief and then worry filled his chest at the sight of Juliette lying face-down only a few feet out of the river. In fact, it looked as though she hadn't made it fully ashore before collapsing.

Doors of a vehicle slammed behind him, but he paid no mind and made a mad dash for her.

Shouts filled the air and more lights as he fell to his knees and rolled her to her back. He frantically searched for a pulse, breathing, but his own heart beat so fast he couldn't tell what was what.

"Freeze!" a deep voice said at his back.

"Help her," Matt responded, still searching for that pulse. Water poured from his head, hitting her in the face, and he frantically tried to shield her from the rain. He couldn't tell if she breathed.

"Let us see," another urged.

"Sir," a female voice called.

All of them sounded distinctly American, so at least he knew they'd made it over. A border patrol, most likely.

"Force him back," another said, and before he could react, before he could fight his way to stay at Juliette's side, two sets of arms grabbed each of his and yanked him back. With his energy depleted from their journey, the lack of substance, the sleep deprivation, the torture, and their battle to cross this beast of a river, he was no match for their strength.

Helplessly, he watched as a male and female fell to their knees around her, blocking his view. The truck's headlights they'd been in, which he saw now, illuminated every moment of dread.

Another vehicle pulled up and cast headlights over them, but still, Matt urged Juliette to wake. Some movement, anything.

One minute, two... What seemed like endless time later. His heart galloped against his chest, begging to be set free.

Then, a cough and movement from Juliette. Relief hit him with such force, he fell back into the two bodies holding him.

"Thank God," he said.

"Hold him there," one of them said, then a flashlight beamed on his face.

"Mind telling me what's going on?" the guy asked.

"I'm a federal agent with the United States Drug Enforcement Agency, and I was kidnapped..." He searched for time and tried to count it out in his head but couldn't be sure. "Some time ago. I'm with the New York field office. You can verify my identity by contacting my Supervising Agent in Charge, Joseph Henninger."

Things moved quickly after that. In short order, both he and Juliette were separated and taken back to some sort of holding facility office while they called Henninger to verify who he was. He'd been asked to give a quick debrief on all that had happened in the past week and a half. They'd also had someone with some fancy medical credentials come down and check him out. He'd been told the same would happen with Juliette, when asked.

The conversation with his supervisor, who'd been on speaker phone, had been a surprise when he was told of the amount of time that had passed since they'd been taken. There were a lot of questions asked, and he tried his best to answer what he could, leaving out a few details of their ordeal. A lot of people were listening to what he said, which included several border patrol agents. He did it for a reason, something that had been instinctive. He didn't want Juliette in a holding cell overnight. He wanted her close so he could watch over her.

The border patrol didn't need to know she was a subject of his investigation. They only needed the basics and for now, he wanted to keep it to himself. Keep her to himself.

A pot-bellied man named Bill walked back into the room he'd been held in and nodded to Scott, the agent who'd been hanging out with him while they completed the verification of his identity.

"He checks out," Bill said and sat back in his chair with a groan. "Your department seems eager to hear from you again, but I told 'em we're giving you all the hospitality Texas has to offer."

Matt sat forward and clasped his hands between his knees to keep them from shaking. He wanted to check on Juliette, then get a shower. In that order. He'd follow up with his office later. They knew he was safe, and that was all that mattered. "I appreciate the assist. Where did you take Juliette? I'd like to make contact with her, check in."

Bill eyed him over his white mug as he took a sip of what had to be room-temperature coffee. It was hard to get a read on the supervising agent. "Any reason you didn't just come up on the checkpoint instead of going across the river?" he asked instead of answering his question.

Matt shook his head. "Not the way we've been trained. I was hoping to run into a patrol and obviously overshot where I was in the scheme of things. We don't hit up the checkpoints as, no offense, sometimes those aren't the most secure, especially when you're on the run from what looks like a violent cartel."

Bill's lips thinned with displeasure. Yeah, what Matt said was tough, but it was also the truth. All three of them knew US federal employees got paid by the cartel. It was why there was such a high turnover in border patrol units—well, the corruption and from what they'd seen the cartel do to people at the border—and it was why Juliette and he had been kidnapped. Someone at JFK had dropped the ball.

"I'm not sure I like what you're saying, Agent Gonzalez."

Matt shrugged. "I don't like it either, Bill." He made a point of using his first name. This wasn't a pissing match, and he did not need to get into one. "But we both know it's the truth. Now," he said and stood from the couch. "I'd really like to check in on Juliette and get some sleep. I can arrange everything else if you'd just point me to a phone so I can contact my office."

Bill stood with him and looked like he wanted to say more, and Matt was thankful he held his tongue. "Follow me."

****

Juliette stared out over the vast darkness of the night in front of the hotel, unseeing anything—it was pitch black, after all—but in her mind's eye, everything that had occurred in the past few days replayed. The running from their captors, the time spent with the

Tarahumara tribe, their trek across Mexico, and finally their daring escape over the Rio Grande River.

She shivered, remembering the cut of cold water across her skin, the power of nature showing her just how insignificant she truly was.

Wrapping her arms tighter around herself, she turned from the window and grabbed the gray crew sweatshirt she'd been given upon arriving at the hotel. She'd relayed all she'd known to the nice agent who'd taken her statement at the station before dropping her here. She hadn't known much, and fortunately, he hadn't pushed too hard.

Telling them she'd been with Matt when they'd been taken at JFK had been a bit of a trick. She hadn't wanted to tell them the exact reason she'd been with him. Something told her to keep that to herself. And apparently Matt hadn't said anything either because they made quick work of getting her set up at the hotel, a fresh set of clothing—grey sweatsuit, black t-shirt, basic bra, and panties—before leaving her be. She'd been told all she had to do was call the front desk if she needed anything, but they'd follow up with her later.

She'd still been a bit dazed by all that had occurred, so she didn't say anything. Just simply nodded. Then locked the door behind them and immediately jumped into the hot shower.

She hadn't been able to scrub hard enough, feeling as though she'd had layers upon layers of grime covering her skin. Eventually, her skin pruned, so she turned off the water, slathered herself in the hotel-provided lotion, brushed her teeth, and settled in to stare out at the darkness.

Her hotel room was pretty standard—a queen-size bed, a writing desk, a dresser, two end tables, and a bathroom. There was a door separating her from the room next door, but it was shut and locked. This room was her haven away from all the craziness and unknown of the outside. She felt as if she were in a completely different world. As if the goggles had been ripped away from her face and everything was cast in a different light.

A knock sounded, just three raps. She stiffened, eyeing the door, wondering who it was. It had to either be the agent or Matt. Surely anyone else would use the main door and not the one that separated the two.

"Jules," Matt called behind the door.

She let out a breath of relief, then crossed the room, feeling the soft fibers of carpet under her feet. The knob was cool to the touch, but she opened it as if it burned, then looked up, relief making her dizzy as she took in Matt.

He looked as disheveled as she felt when she'd first walked into the room. "Apparently, they had more questions to ask you," she murmured, looking at his tangled hair around his shoulders. Hers was braided and held back by a simple band.

Matt let out a rough laugh. "You could say that." He studied her face, dropped his perusal to take in the rest of her, then gave a slight nod, as if satisfied with what he saw. She wondered what that was.

"What happens now?" she asked.

He scrubbed a hand over his face and leaned against the door frame. "We wait. I need to make contact with my office. They'll give us tickets to get home, we'll get debriefed, and then we'll just"—he shrugged—"go on."

She frowned, not really liking that last bit.

"What's with the face?" he asked.

She wrapped her arms around herself again, uncertain about any of what she thought she'd felt from him. Now that they were back in civilization, away from danger, what would happen? "I don't know," she said instead of voicing her fears.

He gave her a bland look as if he could tell she lied. "Jules," he said.

"Ugh—fine." She moved away from the door. Didn't want to face him as she said this. If he didn't return her feelings or pitied her, then so be it. She'd learned nothing over the past few days if she didn't learn to just take in the moment, to just go for it. "I don't like the idea of *just* 'moving on.'" She looked out the window again. "I know we've only known each other for a few days, but I feel as if I've known you for so much longer." She could hear the yearning in her voice, the softness. Too late to dial it back, but at least she'd be able to truly say she gave this—whatever it was—her all before they returned to their lives.

"If just the *thought* of going on with life when we get back includes any part of you and I going our separate ways, then I'm sure I'm going to like it a lot less than I do now." She turned and met his eyes, letting him see everything cross her face: her want, her emotions … her need. "I don't want to move on and go my own way. I want to continue seeing you every day. I can't imagine my life going on without you in it."

Pressure clamped down on her chest. She took in a deep breath, then let it out with steady control, as if she were searching for some neutral ground.

He stared at her for a minute or so in silence. That silence made her uneasy, but she kept his gaze, refusing to back down.

Finally, he opened his mouth. "Juliette, I—I want that, too." He blew out a hard breath, puffing his cheeks with the movement, then settled his hands on his hips. He looked at the ground, pressed his lips together, and met her gaze again.

She let out a startled laugh. "Was saying those words that hard?"

"Yes," he said, then relayed no more.

She tossed her hands out, wondering what his deal was. He normally seemed so open, so willing to talk. But now that she'd done the majority of the conversation and let it all hang out, he suddenly became wordless.

"Listen here, big fella. You gotta give me something more. I don't understand."

He looked at her with an incredulous expression, eyes disbelieving, with a hint of frustration. "What don't you understand? I told you I wanted all that you wanted, too." Then he dropped his hands from his hips and took two steps toward her. He was only a few feet away, but she couldn't see anything else in the room but him. A plethora of emotions crossed his face, and he looked somewhat bewildered, and nervous?

"Juliette," he said again, "I really like you." His voice grew rough, like he scraped his vocal cords over sharp rocks. "I'm struggling with how this will work out on the other end, up in New York, especially with what my superiors will say. A suspect/agent relationship is rule number one of what *not* to do."

Her back went straight. "Do you—do you still believe I have something to do with those drugs?"

He pressed his lips together again, looking as if he were thinking over his answer. Her chest caved in with dread. She'd thought they'd moved past this. How could he still think that?

She held up a hand. "You know what? You don't even have to answer out loud. Your face says it all."

"Jules…"

"No." She turned away from him, back to the window, and wanted to hide her face. Surely, he'd see just how much it hurt that he didn't believe her. Despite all they'd been through, she didn't feel comfortable showing him what he could do to her. "God, I really thought we'd worked past this. I can't believe you'd still have doubt."

"I wished you'd take a moment and think about it from my point of view," he said, his voice less rough, but softer somehow. As if the turbulence of a journey over those rocks had smoothed out. "It is not that easy for me to just will away the product of circumstance in how we met. That history has already been forged, and it's something we're both going to have to deal with, even with this chemistry, even with this harsh"—he tossed the word out as if it were a baseball and he a pitcher in the major leagues—"need I have for you."

She turned, taking in the lines of strain on his face, the openness of which he held himself, imploring her to believe in him but helpless to change where each of them stood. She wanted to curse Jorge, but could she really? It was his actions that had put her in this situation, albeit a fucked-up one at that, but in the right spot at the right time to meet this amazing man.

She cupped a hand on one side of his cheek. The hard spikes of bristles from his beard scraped her palm. "I'm sorry."

He shook his head and dropped it to her shoulder, gathering her in his arms. "Don't apologize. This isn't either of our faults. It's just something we'll have to try to work through. We'll both have to ride it out."

She leaned back and squeezed both of his arms, trying her best not to let the little thrill that went through her belly at the feel of hard muscles show on her face. "What exactly will happen once we get back?"

He considered her for a moment. "I'll have to recuse myself from the investigation. Especially now that this is building between us. I'm sure my supervisor will love that."

He released her and stepped back, then ran a hand through his tangled hair. He made a face as it got caught, then gave up and pushed it away. "I need to shower, but I want to continue this conversation. You good if we put this on hold for a second?"

She nodded. "Of course, go do your thing."

He made quick work of leaving her room but kept the door between their areas open. She stared off in the direction he went, heard the shower turn on, then felt her face flame as she wondered what he would look like under running water. Her lips parted on an indistinct sound, imagining the rivulets running down and over his skin as if tendrils of water wanting to worship Matt Gonzalez.

With his longer hair, inked skin, and strong physic, he'd be something to explore, a god among all other men, standing under a waterfall of hot water.

She shivered, shaking herself out of that dreamland, then spied the clothes they had left for Matt. Since he'd been otherwise occupied, Border Patrol Agent McKinney had asked her to hand them off. She grabbed the pile, his colors darker gray compared to hers, then quickly darted into his room, intent on leaving the clothes on his bed. Just as she dropped them, the shower turned off. She turned to leave but caught the image of the shower door, Matt behind the frosted glass, watching her.

She froze, utterly transfixed.

Move! her mind screamed, but she couldn't. Didn't really want to. Wouldn't dare.

He wrapped big palms around the top of the shower, keeping his gaze on her. She could only make out the outline of his body, but there was no doubt he watched her.

Her imagination hadn't lied earlier. His dark hair fell over wide shoulders, which thinned to a trim waist before showcasing thick, strong thighs.

He opened the shower door, and her breathing sped before she slammed her eyes close. "I'm sorry," she said, unable to move. "I meant to drop off the clothes for you, but you, you finished. And the door…"

He chuckled lowly. "Are you really sorry, Juliette?" he taunted, sounding closer.

What did he mean? She frowned, but her ears strained to hear where he was. "I wasn't staring, I promise."

"Yes, you were," he said, his voice right next to her ear. She jumped, but his hands settled on her hips. He smelled of fresh water and soap, and underneath it all was the woodsy scent of man. His entirely.

Was he naked? She pictured what they must look like in her mind and felt her nipples tighten to little needy peaks.

"I wasn't, Matt, I swear," she said, slightly breathless.

He pulled her toward him until her hips met his. Something plush was between them. Her eyes opened in shock. A towel. He wore a towel. His hair had been pushed back from his face, looking as if he'd run his fingers through it. Water dripped down his chest, but his eyes had darkened considerably.

He looked every bit the god she'd imagined him to be. How could this man be even remotely attracted to her? How could he have gone this long in life without the experience of sinking between a woman's thighs?

Hers clenched.

"What were you just thinking about?" he asked, head cocked. One of his big palms moved slowly up her back, encouraging her closer. But his eyes were on her face, studying her, watching.

Could she tell him, really? No way. But it was about time she put on her big girl panties, per se, and be an adult here. He felt the chemistry between them, and if they were going to try to make things work, then maybe a bit of honesty needed to be introduced. She lifted her hands and lay them on his arms again, clenching her fingers once more.

That same thrill from earlier went through her belly, only this time it was much better seeing as she touched his skin directly. *Nice.*

"I was just thinking," she said, "how sexy you are. I'm amazed by the fact you look as you do, are as smart as you are, and as successful"—he lifted a brow—"yet haven't been with a woman." She cleared her throat. "Like that."

He promptly plucked out the hair tie holding the mass that was her curls and tossed it over her shoulder.

"Matt," she gasped, watching the tie sail to the other side of the room. Her hair loosened as his hands made quick work of releasing the braid. "My hair is an absolute mess."

He stared at what had to be a riot of curls around her face before meeting her eyes again. "Your hair is beautiful. As for me being a virgin—just because I am one doesn't mean I was a monk, Jules."

He threaded a hand in her tresses and pulled back slightly, arching her neck.

She gasped again, then watched as his eyes darkened until it seemed as if the pupils bled into his whiskey irises.

"Didn't you ever wonder what it would feel like?" Her voice shook.

He dipped his head and brushed his lips across her neck. Her toes curled.

"Do I ever wonder what it would feel like to push my cock inside of a woman's heat?" he asked.

Her breath jumped as he pushed her back into more of an arch. Her hips and chest touched him solidly, and against her stomach, she could feel just how affected he was by this conversation. She swallowed, and it sounded as hard as he felt.

"Yes," she answered.

"You." He looked up at her, pulling back so he could catch her gaze. "I wonder what it would feel like to sink inside of *you*."

Then he kissed her.

His hungry mouth almost overwhelmed her with how voraciously he conquered. But she didn't underestimate her own starvation for him, how she felt the gnawing ache deep inside her belly. She wrapped her arms around his neck and met his kiss with as much fervor as he dished out. Their mouths clashed this way and that, and her body inflamed into a ball of urgent need.

He lifted her with his arms around her waist and turned to press her against the wall. A hungry growl sounded. One she devoured with another swipe of her tongue.

She expected him to put a halt to this any minute because he'd made his intentions with her clear. He wanted to go slow. He didn't know how deep they should get entangled. If all they did was explore a bit tonight, she was more than on board with it.

"This needs to come off," he said, and without missing a beat, whipped her crew sweatshirt off over her head. His strong hands cupped her with such intimacy, then palmed both of her breasts with a firm squeeze.

He bit off a curse. "And this." He promptly removed her tee with the same urgency as the sweatshirt.

"Matt," she gasped and stared up at him. He hovered over her, breathing heavily and staring down with a dark concentration at her chest. The plain white bralette she wore seemed so out of place between them.

"I wish it were something of mine," she said, and he returned a brief, confused stare to her eyes.

"I'd wear something sexier than just a plain bralette. But obviously, my stuff was taken."

"This," he said and trailed fingers lightly over the curve of one breast, "is just as sexy as anything else you could wear, Jules. It's not the outfit that turns me on. It's you."

Her heart swelled at his words. "So unabashedly direct and honest."

He fingered one strap of her bra, then slowly started pulling it over her shoulder. But he held her gaze. "Would you rather me not tell you?"

She couldn't help but arch her back a bit. It offered her breasts up for him. Already, she could feel the loosening of the hold from the bra. "It's not that. I'm just not used to it."

He dropped the strap but left his hand over her arm. Then he switched his stance and went to the other side. Hooked a finger under that strap. "Been lied to a lot, have you?"

Under his attention, she could strive or drown. She couldn't tell which. Only that she'd be fine with either. This man, once he gave himself to a woman in bed, would take over completely. His demand for her full and utter attention would be a requirement. "I wouldn't say that." She gasped as he drew the strap down. "But I've never had a man be as direct as you are." She bit her lip. "I like it. I like knowing what you're thinking."

He released the strap. Her bralette only stayed up now because of the band. Her breasts heaved with each breath she took. Matt stared down at her, not holding back, letting her see his hunger and desire. "I want to touch you, Jules."

She swallowed again, then nodded. "Do it." She arched further. "I want that, too."

He went to the bed, retrieved his own black t-shirt sitting there, then tossed the remaining clothing to a chair in the corner. The front of the towel pitched out with his need. She stared unabashedly, then licked her lips.

"Take off your pants, please."

Her gaze jumped to his face, and she found him watching her with that same dark hunger he'd held since the moment he stepped from the shower. In his hands, he twisted that black tee. Curious about what he'd do, she did as asked and hooked her fingers in the band of the pants, then pushed them past her hips so they dropped to the floor. She stepped out and stood before him in a pair of plain white panties and the bralette hanging loosely from her frame.

Chapter Seventeen

A decadent dish waiting for him to devour.

That was exactly what Juliette looked like, standing in his hotel room some thousands of miles away from home.

Matt fought the urgency to rush this. He wanted to take his time and explore. Needed days to do everything he had ever fantasized about with this woman who drew out such a hunger he'd never felt before. But they only had these few scant hours alone before they'd be tossed back into the real world.

He'd make them count. There was no doubt in his mind they'd be contacted soon and told to report back to NYC. No doubt their tickets had already been purchased.

He'd probably be told to keep his distance from her until the investigation was complete. And even then, his job allowing their contact was a big maybe.

For now, he decided, she'd be his. He'd be a little selfish and take the time to discover every inch of Juliette Scaglione. It wasn't something someone with the utmost integrity would probably do, but he was done denying this draw. He was done being the nice guy who did the right things all the time.

At least, that was what he felt like.

He moved toward her, the tee in his hands readied, and lifted the cloth with a murmured, "Hold still, beautiful." The endearment did as he expected and intended, softening the features of her face. She held in place as he wrapped the cloth around her head, then tied it in the back.

He pressed his body to hers then, fitting the front of him to the back of her. Her breath kicked out in a nervous and heightened pitch. A smile disappeared before he kissed her lightly on the shoulder.

"Your smell makes my mouth water, Juliette." He dropped his towel.

She gasped and kept her back in contact with his chest, but now her breasts jutted out before her in offering. He intended to take that gift.

Now, he rested a hand over her stomach, the other on her hip, and guided her forward until her legs hit the bed. He reached around and pulled the comforter off. "Climb up. Just move straight forward until I tell you to stop."

Her hands found purchase against the white sheets. The warm, sun-kissed skin stood out starkly against the fabric. She briefly clenched the material before doing as he asked and crawled slowly on the mattress. One movement, two, three.

"Stop," he said, then rose onto the bed himself. He guided her until she lay on her side next to him. Then he placed one hand on her shoulder from behind and used the other to steer her body until it rested against his. From this angle, he had access to her entirely. Breasts jutting up in the air, hip pressed to him slightly, the ability to spread her legs easily. She lay before him, a feast he couldn't wait to indulge in. He told her as much.

"I want to touch you, too," she said.

"All in good time. For now," he said and kissed her on the swell of one breast, "let me. Please."

"O-okay," she said.

Unable to wait anymore, he dragged one side of her bra down until the dusty rose of a nipple came into view. The shade matched that of her lips when she chewed on them. A pleasant surprise. He pulled the cup some more until her entire breast popped free. Then he released the material that had held her, a full offering he intended to take.

And he did. He dipped his head and took her nipple in his mouth.

Jules cried out, back arching, hips pushing into him. Pleasure pulsed in his groin. He groaned at the feel of her so close to what pounded in a vicious demand for attention. His cock wept for her touch. Begged.

Soon, he promised and swirled his tongue around the pebbled peak. She tasted of coconut left in the sun on a warm beach, of spice he'd once associated with nights by a fireplace. He drew on her, plumped and teased, pushing her sensual cries higher and higher. They were music to his ears, and she was definitely sensitive to his touch.

Her heightened state made him briefly wonder if her ex had touched her so, with the attention due to give to someone as sexual as Juliette. She moved restlessly beside him, trying to get closer and closer until their hips were aligned and she was plastered right up against his chest.

He released her with a pop and stared down at the wet bud shining up at him.

"Matt," she said softly in question.

"You taste of cloves and cinnamon here," he said and touched the pad of his finger to the erect tip. She gasped and pressed her chest up as if to get more friction. "Reminds me of my favorite dish as a kid—the sweet potatoes my aunt used to bring for holiday dinners." He licked a path alongside her breast, then palmed her taut stomach. "They were more of a dessert than anything else."

Her breath skipped out as his hand began a downward journey. Without waiting or teasing, he slipped his hand beneath the band of her panties and found her legs closed. Whether that be from embarrassment, the position of how she lay, or the speed with which they were moving, he didn't know. But he wanted her with him, wanted her to go where he went. With this. With them together.

"Will you be as sweet, Jules?" He traced a finger back and forth over the top of her mound. "Open your legs for me, beautiful."

For only a moment, she didn't move. Then she spread her legs wide and shuddered.

He slid his hand down, and air punched out of her at his touch. "So wet," he murmured against the side of her breast. He dipped his hand to her opening, then came back up and circled her bundle of nerves.

Her scent rose from there, a sweet musk that made his head spin.

Jules cried out, arching her neck up, chest out, and hips splayed wide. He held her still with one hand on her shoulder and continued his onslaught, pumping two, then three fingers inside while using his thumb to apply a steady and coaxing touch on her clitoris.

She moved wildly beside him, chest heaving and body undulating. His name fell from her lips like a chant and had him swelling until he thought he'd burst.

He rotated his hips against hers, meeting her thrust for thrust, the thin cotton the only barrier between them. Heat engulfed his stomach, a promised pleasure pushing through his body until his scalp tingled.

It felt as if the hair on his body stood on end, as if his nerves were on fire.

For her.

"Matt," she said urgently. She reached back and held on to his bare hip. He hissed, wanting her touch lower. On his cock, stroking until they both reached their peak. "Please," she said, pulling him closer.

He continued with the pumping and swirling. Sounds of what he did filled the room. Her musk in his nose. The taste of her in his mouth. She surrounded him utterly, in all ways but one.

Despite holding off for so long, for reasons he could no longer remember, he wanted that connection, wanted to feel her squeezing him, coupled to him as closely as no one had ever been before.

"Jules," he said, then hooked his finger on the side of her panties and pulled them down. They slipped beneath the rounded curve of her plump ass. She stopped moving and turned her blindfolded face toward him.

"Matt?" she asked, and it was a question. Of consent, of whether he wanted this with her. Now. Here.

"Yes," he said, sure. He pulled the panties along her legs and tossed them aside.

She pushed the blindfold up and stared at him, the question still in her eyes, but there was a hunger on her face, too. One he didn't want to deny either of them anymore.

"I'm on birth control and clean. I just had a checkup last month and hadn't..." She trailed off, the rest of her sentence clear enough. She hadn't lain with her ex in what, a month? How he'd managed to not have her every night, every day, this sensual, sexy woman, Matt didn't know.

The guy was an idiot.

"Then it's settled." He lifted her leg back and over his hip.

"Like this?" she squeaked.

"Like this." He grabbed his rock-hard cock and lined them up. Her heat called to him. He met her gaze, wanting to see her face as he entered her. As he became someone he hadn't been only minutes ago. Then he started to slide in.

The feel of her made him want to weep.

Juliette's mouth dropped open, and her neck

arched, taking her eyes away. But he was okay with it because a ton of sensations had taken him over. The heat and grip of her body wrapped around his cock was intense, overwhelming. Pleasure zapped with each inch he pressed inside.

"God," she said, pushing her hips toward him.

Sensations took him over until he couldn't contain it anymore. He let the trapped groan free, then closed his mouth over her waiting nipple and pressed fully inside. Jules cried out, and he grunted in wonder. He paused, trying to breathe through the pleasure he'd never known before. Had he, he probably wouldn't have waited so long.

But that was a lie. For this moment, here with her, he felt as though it was complete. It was meant to be for both of them.

"Move, Matt. Please. Please, you need to move."

He released her breast, pressed a chaste kiss to her shoulder, then did as she asked. He withdrew until just the tip remained inside, and surged back in. Her freed breast bounced with the movement, drawing his attention. So he did it again. And again. Pressing in and out, feeling the heat suck and grip him tight.

Juliette cried out again, urging him on. He wrapped his arm around her waist and kept going, feeling the increasing pressure deep in his stomach wanting to unload with the impending orgasm.

He adjusted his hand and felt where they were connected, the slide of himself disappearing inside of her, then coming out slick and wet. He circled her bundle of nerves, then massaged it with the same rhythm as he pushed inside until he felt her body go taut.

She held herself for one moment, two, before crying out with a sensual pleasure, exploding around his cock. Milking him so strongly he couldn't hold back anymore. Pleasure took him, causing his vision to haze around the edges, and his orgasm hit him with the force of a semi-truck, bowing through his body until he thought he'd pass out. It went on for suspended moments, and he held her close, never wanting it to end.

Moments later, Juliette shifted in his arms, drawing his attention out of the awe-struck wonder. His cock slipped out of her, making them both groan. She shifted again, pushing closer to him. He smiled and kissed her shoulder, then leaned up and grabbed the blanket to toss it over them both.

She settled back into his arms with a sigh resembling contentment.

"Are you good?" he asked, wanting to be sure. This was a new area for him, one he had absolutely no experience with. The afterglow, pillow-talking time. His body felt languid unlike ever before. Tingles of pleasure still bumped over his skin, but in his mind, that thing ran about a million miles an hour with thoughts of what they'd just done, of how she felt, and of how soon they could do it again.

How this would affect who the two of them were going forward.

Obviously, it'd change everything.

She made a deep rumbling sound, and he laughed.

"Did you just purr?" he asked, amusement dancing through his veins.

Her body shook with silent laughter. "It's been a long time and that was fantastic."

He smiled and kissed her shoulder again. "I'm glad."

"You sure you haven't done that before?" she asked.

His hand roamed along the side of her hip and

down her leg, then back up again. "I think I would know if I'd done that before. What we just did was a first for me, Jules."

"Well, you were pretty confident in knowing what you wanted to do for someone who hadn't done that before."

He smiled at the back of her head. "I will repeat, I'm not a saint or a monk, gorgeous. What I wanted all just came naturally, and I went with it."

"Well then…" she said, but said no more.

He laughed.

She rolled to her back, big doe eyes looking up at him. "I'm glad we did that," she whispered.

He dropped his head until it was only inches above hers. "Me, too."

"I want to do it again," she said on a breath, her gaze on his mouth.

He grinned and dropped down to kiss her again, diving in deep with his tongue. Her arms wrapped around his shoulders, and he shifted until he was on top, his hips between her thighs. Heat and a calling wetness met his groin. His cock jumped in response, more than ready for the challenge.

He shifted, then sank inside her tightness without a warning. She gasped against his mouth, and he swallowed it down as he pushed both his cock and his tongue deeper inside.

She moaned, then sucked on his tongue, which almost caused his eyes to roll into the back of his head.

Twin peaks of hardness pressed against his chest, and her nails scratched along his spine. He drew his hips back and surged inside. The pressure of the movement caused him to break his mouth from hers with a gasp.

"Oh, God," she said, neck arching, teeth clenching. "Again," she begged.

He hooked one palm on the inside of her thigh and pushed it up and out, then sank even further inside her body with a grunt.

"Matt," she screamed.

He froze above her, then met her wide eyes. "Are you okay?" he asked, his heart pounding against his chest.

"Don't stop." She grabbed his ass.

He didn't have to be told twice. He dipped down at the tempting sight of a ripe pink nipple and took it inside his mouth as he surged inside Juliette again. His body moved automatically, as if it'd known all along how to do this. How to bring pleasure.

Back and forth. Back and forth. His hips rotated slowly at times, then faster as the pressure deep inside his gut promised an amazing ending.

Juliette's hazy gaze met his, her teeth biting down on her lower lip. "More," she rasped.

"Yes," he answered with a grunt, then moved faster, deeper.

Her hot channel clamped down on him as she cried out and scored his back with her nails.

He hissed and felt the pressure erupt inside of him. His eyes met hers and refused to close, but together, they cried out as their orgasms took over. Until he wrung every bit of pleasure from both of their bodies and collapsed on top of her, making sure to hold the majority of his weight with his arms.

He dropped his head to the pillow but found his face nested within the curve of her shoulder and neck. She smelled of soap and fresh air, and a scent entirely Juliette. He placed a soft kiss against her skin.

She ran her hands idly up and down the sides of his body, the languid movement causing him to fidget just a tad as she hit a sensitive spot.

"Let me up," she said quietly.

He shifted and fell to the side, then watched as she rolled out of the bed and shuffled to the bathroom. A whole lot of skin filled his vision, and moments later, when she returned, the view was even better.

He took his fill.

She laughed, jumping under the covers and sliding up to his side.

"I would apologize, but I can't. Your body is something I can't look away from, an authentic piece of art," he murmured, pulling her closer. Contentment settled into his muscles. He lay on his back, and Juliette had a leg tossed over his, her arm across his stomach.

She settled her head on his shoulder. "You have any more stories?"

He grinned. "I have plenty. What do you want to hear about?"

"How about your parents and how they came to adopt six of you? That's a pretty unusual story there, them being saints or not."

His smile softened as he thought about his parents. "The world would be a poor place without them in it. Ma worked in social services, and I'm sure you can imagine, being so close to the city, there was a lot of activity to keep her busy. Pops just loves her so much he could never say no. And even though he's maintained that excuse for years, I know he'd do everything in his power to help those weaker or in need. It's just his way. And Pops isn't one to get overly emotional."

"They both sound wonderful," Juliette said, her voice wistful.

"They are, one hundred percent. And when Ma started working on my case, I remember her talking to me all the time about the great life I would have as I got older. How she saw so much opportunity in my future. In those first few weeks," he said, his gaze on the ceiling but his mind caught in the past, "she would stay up with me throughout the night to make sure I wouldn't wake alone. She never left my side, even having other children she had to care for."

"How old were you?"

"Eight. Though I weighed as much as a toddler."

Juliette gasped against his side, her entire body going rigid.

"Relax," he said and soothed a hand down her spine.

"What happened?" A current of anger lay within that question.

He ran his hand down her spine again and kissed the top of her head. "I survived." Turning back to the ceiling, he answered her question. "But I was severely neglected. Kept in a closet for years. Given scraps of food, mouth taped shut at times, and beaten if I made too much noise when she had visitors over."

"Matt," she whispered and pushed closer to him. "I am so sorry."

"I didn't know how to use the bathroom, dress myself, or even speak in full sentences. I had no idea of what school was. Who friends were. Or that there was a life beyond that tiny, dark closet."

"Jesus," she said, clutching at his side.

"My adoptive parents and brothers taught me all of that in the first few weeks following my rescue. And not once did any of them make me feel stupid or inadequate."

"I'm sorry, but I don't understand how some people are allowed to have children while others fight for years to even get pregnant. The way you were treated, what you had to go through."

He turned to her and caught her gaze, then

palmed her cheek. "What I went through made me the man I am today. I had good people who eventually looked out for me, still do to this day. I survived. That's what should be taken away from this. Not the anger at what was done, at what my birth mother claimed was 'doing her best,' but at the fact that I survived that."

The phone rang next to the bed, and Juliette jumped in response.

"It still pisses me off," she said, a fire in her eyes.

He smiled and dropped to give her a brief kiss, then reached for the phone.

Chapter Eighteen

Matt tightened his grip around Juliette's palm as the plane touched down at JFK airport hours after that call from his partner. The world seemed so much different from a couple of weeks ago. A brighter, vividly blue sky. The Hudson River a contrasting gray. Landscapes and mansions in the rolling hills just outside the airport sparkling with wonder.

He'd never seen New York City through such eyes, ones that told him he should be grateful to live where he did and be able to experience it. That he was alive.

The sense of wonder was short-lived though because he recalled that conversation from this morning, the next steps he was to go through, and the concern for what his partner had meant by saying there was something he needed to see.

In short order, which was unusual, the plane pulled up to the gate. They unloaded, and he walked side-by-side with Juliette, following the signs for taxis and ground transportation.

"Are you sure you're going to be okay getting home?" he asked.

She smiled up at him and ran a caress along his arm, but didn't try to take his hand. It was as if she knew they had to be careful with who they were, especially since they most likely already had eyes on them. "I have a key hiding in the garden at my place. Some cash inside the house. I'll be fine. I just want to get a proper shower, some food in my stomach, sleep, then I'll call in to work and figure out what comes next."

They stepped outside, and he found, from the corner of his eye, Watson standing from a bench, but he made no move toward them. Matt led Jules across the street and dipped down to have a brief conversation with a waiting taxi driver, then turned back to her. She stared up at him expectantly, a question in her eyes.

He hated this. The uncertainty he saw there. The same he felt.

"Jules," he murmured and brushed a thumb across her cheekbone. That was a tell, one he was sure his partner had noted. It was too late, though, because of his feelings toward this woman and for what he'd have to answer for. He leaned down and placed a chaste kiss on her lips, then held her gaze. "I'll come to you after I'm done at the office."

She sent him a soft smile. "You sure you don't want a break from me? I wouldn't take it personally."

He kissed her again, this time longer, and gave a tug on her bottom lip. "I'll come to you after I'm done."

Breath stuttered out of her mouth, an enticing sound he wanted to hear again. "Okay."

He stepped back and opened the door of the cab to let her inside, then turned as the car drove off. It was a weird feeling, being separated after being together for so long. Even for the short time they'd been apart at the Border Patrol office, the distance hadn't seemed much. This felt as if something pivotal was about to change, as if there was a chance he wouldn't see her again.

A silly thought since he had both the means and the knowledge to find her, knew where she lived, where she worked.

Watson stepped up next to him and nudged his shoulder in greeting. "Good to see you back, man."

Matt turned and embraced him with a slap on the back. "Definitely not a trip I would recommend. One-star review on Yelp."

Watson laughed and nodded toward the parking

garage, where their government-issued SUV surely was.

"So, Juliette, huh?" Watson asked.

Matt settled in the passenger seat. "Yeah," he said quietly. "I tried to fight it. Really. But things were—are—just intense between us and…" He trailed off with a shrug, unable to explain it. He didn't have the words.

Watson sighed, pulling onto the highway, which surprisingly enough was clear for once. "That's not going to go over well."

Matt rubbed his temple. "Don't I know it." He adjusted himself in the seat. "Any idea what I'm walking into? Can you give me a heads-up?"

Watson glanced over before putting his focus back on the road. His lips thinned and disappeared. Only this time, Matt didn't find it so funny. "What is it?"

Watson held up a hand and sped up a little. "Like I said last night, this is something you're going to have to see for yourself."

Almost an hour later, Matt stood in a conference room, having come to his feet a minute earlier, and stared at the large TV screen before him. "This is bullshit," he said.

Henninger, the Supervising Agent in Charge, otherwise known as the SAC, drummed his fingers on the table. "Shut it down, Gonzalez. Sit back in your seat and run us through everything that happened, including anything Miss Scaglione told you."

Matt fought the impulse to storm out of the conference room, to go find Juliette, and demand answers. His mind couldn't believe what he saw. Didn't want to give the images credit. But the proof was right there. He stared disbelievingly at the screen.

"Gonzalez," Henninger barked.

"Matt," Watson said.

He closed his eyes and forced himself to bring it

all under a fierce control. Unable to see the screen, he turned from it. But the anger had sparked inside him. The emotion fueled his energy as if it were a living dragon gearing up for an intense battle.

She'd lied. She'd met his eyes numerous times and outright lied to his face.

"God, she's good. I'll give her that." He winced at the hurt in his voice. Neither man spoke up or called him out on it. They just waited.

He dropped his head between his shoulders, aching deep in his chest but welcoming the fury building. He couldn't believe it. Never been had so well. And she'd played such a beautiful part in all of it.

Taking a deep breath, he lifted his head and pushed the extra noise down, focused on what needed to be relayed, what needed to be done, and on conducting his duties in a manner appropriate for the Drug Enforcement Agency.

He took one more look at the screen, at the back of what was Juliette's head, her slim shoulders, and rounded ass. Standing next to her was a man who had been identified as Jimmy in the Cancun airport. At a video that had shown who she called her ex-boyfriend stuffing bags, the same bags into the suitcase he'd searched and found drugs in. All the while Juliette watched on. While Juliette cupped the side of Jimmy's face. While she bent down and kissed the guy just before she went to her plane.

The betrayal stung a path in his gut again.

He'd been had.

He turned back to SAC Henninger and began to tell his story.

****

Juliette pulled the white whistling teakettle from the stove and filled her mug with water. She'd come home to a not-so-nice-smelling house, ended up having to toss out nearly all the contents of her fridge and some apples she had on the counter, and then opened a bunch of the casement windows lining through the downstairs, as well as a bunch of windows upstairs to air it out.

Now, with the sun quickly sinking in the sky, the breeze flowing through the house was distinctly cooler and carried the scent of late-evening barbeques. Soon, she may need to grab a cardigan, but for now, she enjoyed the remaining hours that marked the end of summer.

Finished making the tea, she set the kettle aside and looked around to make sure everything else was in place. The soft vanilla sandalwood candle flickered by the sink, and the clean quartz counters gleamed under the setting sun.

It'd been therapeutic cleaning her place—not that it'd been a mess to begin with. Her aunt had always told and shown her the importance of clean floors and counters, but with the number of home improvement projects she normally had going on, sometimes those cleared spaces could get cluttered and messy.

Not tonight, though. The only project she had going on, at least one she prepped for, was the wainscotting she'd add to the far wall of her kitchen. She'd designed an area to hold coats, herbs, or whatever she wanted. It'd go about shoulder level, with some hooks to hang a plant, maybe some other knickknacks. Then this floor of her home would be complete and she could start on the second.

A knock sounded at the front door. After setting the mug on the counter, she grabbed a light-rose-colored sweater she'd brought down earlier, which had been tossed over the back of a chair and a half, then went to see who was there.

Behind three frosted glass panes on the top half of the door, she found Matt's handsome face. She smiled, thrilled he'd done as he said and come to her.

He didn't return her smile as she opened the front door.

"Nice place," he said, the words sounding like he meant anything but. She stepped back to let him in, then closed the door.

"Thanks. I bought it two years ago after it went into foreclosure with the previous owners."

He pursed his lips, crossed his arms, and looked around, brows going up, then down once he finished taking in the entirety of the open floor plan on the first floor. She knew what he saw but didn't think he'd react as he had. He appeared almost put off by it. His reaction almost seemed as if he'd physically slapped her.

What was going on?

Her house wasn't entirely huge by any means, but it was larger than most in this area. New York City was an expensive place to live unless you moved well outside the city limits, sometimes even in another state nearby. She'd ended up getting this place in Yonkers, a pretty established area outside the city limits.

It was an old colonial built in the 1940s, and there'd only been two owners prior. The last had been an older couple who'd let the house fall in disarray. She'd taken her love of woodworking and design and put all her free time into fixing up the place. So now, she had a nicely tended yard outside, with roses and hydrangeas lining the house. She'd also built window boxes for flowers and set one on the second-floor window, just outside her bedroom. The other outside the easement windows near her dining room.

One of her favorite activities involved watching hummingbirds drink from those flowers.

She'd also completely renovated the kitchen with last year's bonus, adding in all-new black stainless-steel appliances.

The house looked like it cost more than what it was worth. But that resulted from her hard work. Not because she bought it like that.

"Pleasant area, too," he said, dropping his hands to his hips and turning his attention to her. "Nice house, nice area. Paying for your *boyfriend's*"—he spat that word, and she took a sudden step back—"vacation to Mexico. All on a bank auditor's salary? In this region?" He sounded disbelieving, so much so she struggled to keep up.

"I don't think I care for the insinuation in your voice. What's going on?" she asked, confused. "What happened between the airport and now?"

He took a single step toward her, and as much as she hated it, as apprehensive as it was, she had a moment's fear rise up her spine. He looked furious.

"Where's Jimmy?" he asked.

She blinked, then tried to calm her racing heart. "What? I don't—I-I don't know. Why are you asking me?"

"Stop with the innocent act, Ms. Scaglione. I know."

That actually felt like he'd slapped her. "Ms. Scaglione," she murmured. "We're back to that. After everything?" Her face flushed. She looked around, wondering if she had entered another dimension. "You're not making any sense. How would I know where Jimmy is?"

He took another step toward her, and her back went straight, as if a rod had entered her spine. Matt wasn't looking at her with any of the normal softness, nor was he the quiet flirt out to play. This man was someone else entirely. He'd transformed completely into a pissed-off federal agent who needed to do his job. Her scalp tingled with unease.

He opened his mouth, but she got there before him. "I don't even want to know where Jimmy is. Why are you asking me this?"

He crowded her against the wall, pressing into her space in such a way that she felt both a thrill and fear roll through her. She couldn't help it. This was Matt. Being close to him, even this angry, would be nearly impossible not to be affected as she was. But at the same time, she could feel her walls going up at his line of questioning, at how he'd come to her tonight. She'd been through enough the past two weeks.

"I've seen the video. You can drop the sham."

She narrowed her eyes. "The video? What, like a sex one? How dare you?" she seethed, arms straight by her sides, hands balled into fists.

He pressed his body to hers, and against her stomach, she could feel the evidence of his desire. But his face told an entirely different story. "How dare I?" he asked, the words coming out dark and vibrating. He curled one hand around her throat in an erotic move that had her thighs clenching, body softening toward him. "How dare you," he whispered. "I trusted you."

He was so angry. So dark and menacing, but she couldn't help reaching for him. She hated the flinch he gave as her hands landed on his upper arms. "I don't know what you think I did, but I didn't do it."

"So quick to deny," he taunted, his attention moving to her mouth for a moment before coming back up to her eyes. "They showed me the video of you and Jimmy at the airport. I saw him putting things in your bag, saw you watch him, saw the two of you kiss"—he said this last with his mouth within centimeters of hers—

"before you got on the plane."

Stunned, she felt as if a bell rang through her head. "What?" she asked, voice shaking. "Jimmy didn't take me to the airport. My brother didn't even come with me. They were both sleeping off a bender."

He shook his head, brushing his lips against hers. No air separated their bodies, and it looked like soon there'd be none between their mouths. "Such a pretty little liar," he said, and her vision went red.

"Get away from me," she hissed and tried to push him. He didn't move an inch, which only pissed her off more.

"Tell me." He bit her lower lip.

She gasped but remained mute. This hurt. Not the bite, not the touching. But this line of questioning. His obvious refusal to believe her. She didn't know what he'd seen, but it had to be worthwhile for him to be acting like this. Something in the back of her mind made her pause, but she knew her own memory, knew she had no part in the setup she'd been placed in.

"Don't want to talk?" he asked. "Fine, I'm sure I can come up with other ways to get the truth out of you."

Before she could ask him what *that* meant, he slammed his mouth down on hers. The action so jolting she felt the taste of iron briefly before she lost herself in the feel of him against her.

****

Matt's body vibrated with a dozen different hungers. A hunger to do violence of the erotic kind. His face felt as red as his insides surely had to be at the thought that the beautiful Juliette Scaglione had deceived him. Had led him down this path of thinking her innocent in all of this. Had tricked him into believing she could be someone he'd go to and let out his day's burdens.

A hunger for sex, this unrelenting attraction for

her, slowly tore at him. This aching, gnawing *thing* that had been building for years in his gut wanted to be appeased, wanted him to sink between her lush thighs no matter how she'd deceived him. Lied to him. Tricked him.

He growled against her mouth, at the *hunger* that refused to be abated with such minimal contact.

She'd wrapped both her arms around his neck, pressed her breasts to his chest, and lifted onto her toes to meet him kiss for kiss. She moved her mouth over his with the same anger he had, the same he heard vibrate through her voice.

He grabbed her lush ass, groaning at the feel of her overflowing his palms, then she jumped up and wrapped her legs around his waist.

Her body surged against his, moving with a sensual grace that threatened to take him down.

How dare she be this perfect for him?

How dare she be so devious?

He shoved one hand in the long, wild mass of curls that was her hair, his other arm wrapping around her waist to hold her as he moved across the room. She sucked and pulled at his tongue in an action that nearly had him tripping over his feet and definitely had his eyes crossing.

The surrounding air smelled of a spicy vanilla, but she tasted sweeter against his tongue, and that only fueled his hurt, his anger that she'd done her best to dupe him.

He set her on the gleaming kitchen island and took only a second to lean back before ripping away the white ribbed tank top she wore. Next went her dark-green leggings as he peeled them down her legs, underwear included, and tossed them aside.

Both actions had been rough, but he took a

moment and inhaled a deep breath, pushed it out, and waited to see if she would object to this, to what they were about to do right here. Right now.

She said nothing. Neither of them did. Her wide-eyed gaze went over his shoulder to what he suspected were windows, then returned to him. He took her in and committed how she looked to memory. Lush lips pink and swollen from his kisses. Hair a riot of curls around her head. Perky breasts just begging for him to taste. A slim waist leading to hips that fit perfectly in his hands. Toned legs that seem to go on for miles. She sat before him, a goddess of desire, bared down to the flesh.

He stood before her, a man on the verge of tumbling over the edge. A man who was hurt and so damn angry with her.

He straightened from the counter. "Maybe we shouldn't do this."

She grabbed the front of his tee, then wrapped a leg around his hip and drew him back toward her. "Like hell." Then she yanked him down to her and kissed him.

From there, it went wild again. His shirt removed, his jeans unbuttoned. He barely had the wherewithal to take his service weapon and set it in the holster aside before returning to her.

Her hands pushed at his jeans, working to get them with his boxer briefs over his hips. But against his tongue, her hardened nipple wreaked havoc with his senses. The bud teased his tongue with both softness and strength. Much like the woman reaching into his boxers to grip his hard length.

He grunted against her skin as she found her mark, then began to pump. Her fist squeezed around him as if she'd been made to do just that.

It was so perfect between them. This was something he'd always hoped to find. Someone who matched his hunger, his energy. Who kept him on his feet and went head-to-head with him in conversation.

Anger rose in his chest, that hurt eating at him.

Damn her.

He tore his mouth away and knocked her hand from him. She sent up a quick protest, but he wrapped an arm around her waist and pulled her from the counter. His eyes threatened to cross at the feel of her body sliding along his, but he turned her to face away, then bent her forward so she leaned over the island.

He settled his hands on her hips and stared down at the lush perfection that was her ass. Pre-cum glistened at the tip of his cock, and his body shook with hunger and anger, the two emotions clamoring for control.

"Last chance, Juliette. Tell me if you want this."

She arched her back and pressed her hands out before her. "Yes," she hissed.

That was all he needed. He sank inside her channel, groaning at the feel of her heat and wetness gripping his cock. Goosebumps broke out across his skin, and tingles rode the length of his spine. He shivered.

Tangling one hand in her mass of hair, he held the other at her hip, keeping his hand between the bone and the counter, then he moved.

Each surge pulled him deeper, the walls of her core gripping him as if it didn't want to let him go. Juliette groaned under him, murmured things he couldn't understand. Her hands pressed against the counter above her head, trying to push her body back to him with each move.

As if she wanted more.

Damn her.

He went wild, pumping in and out, his vision spinning around him until he thought he'd topple over. Her sweet musk filled his lungs, and her groans demanded entrance at his ears.

She pushed her body up and turned her head to the side. "Matt," she gasped.

He struggled to stop, but did, then clamped his hand down on her hip and yanked her head back with his grip in her hair. "What?"

"I want to see you. Face you. Please."

With a curse, he pulled out, turned her abruptly in his arms, and picked her up. She wound those long legs around his waist and with one step, two, then three, he pushed her against the wall to their left and surged back inside her sweet body.

She cried out in pleasure and went to dip her head to kiss him.

No more. She would not fool him anymore.

He wrapped a palm around her neck and held her to the wall as he pumped his hips in and out of her.

She gasped and kept his eyes with her own. Her breasts bounced between them, but he couldn't look away.

"So beautiful," he grunted, wanting to take his frustration out on her.

Her eyes softened. "Matt."

He stopped moving, feeling the temptation of an orgasm hovering just there.

"Don't stop!" she cried out.

He leaned close until he was only an inch over her mouth. "Every time I look at you, my breath literally gets caught in my chest. Happened the first time I met you at that airport and continued right up to now, when I put you against this wall to fuck you. Damn you, Juliette."

She squeezed his shoulders. "Matt," she murmured.

"Damn you," he said again, then leaned in and

placed a single kiss against her lips. Saying goodbye. This was it. The end of them. He'd step away and let her do her thing after this. Another agent would have to take over.

The kiss lasted one second, then two.

As he leaned back, a question entered Juliette's eyes, but he didn't allow her to voice it before surging in again. He continued until they both cried out their pleasure with orgasms that seem to rip his soul from his body.

A minute, maybe two later, he found himself still holding her to the wall, his head on her shoulder, his arms around her waist.

Deep inside, he had another more abusive type of hunger, one that made him want to hurt her as she'd done him. He pulled out of her body, then made sure she was steady on her two legs. "Was it all a lie?" he asked as he pulled away. He winced as he shoved his semi-hard cock back inside, then buttoned his jeans.

She turned toward him, wrapping a blanket that'd been hanging on the back of the couch around her body. Even covered, even knowing what she'd done, he still wanted her. Wanted to remove that look of wary apprehension from her face. Kiss her and tell her they'd work through this.

But he was so damn *angry*.

She sighed, the sound cracking through his chest. "I haven't lied to you. I don't know how many times I have to tell you."

He swallowed, knowing his next words would inflict some damage. He wanted to hold them back, to take a moment to think, but it was like someone else had possessed him and he couldn't stop the words. Couldn't halt the harm surely to follow. Deep inside him, the man who'd been hurt by her actions and her continued refusal to tell him the truth, wanted to see her upset, like him, for just one second. So she could feel a fraction of the betrayal he did.

"Just answer me this one thing."

She held the blanket close to her chest and stared up at him expectantly as if she knew she was safe. That she could trust him to do her right. Long curls, wild from his hands, lay around her face and over her shoulders. He could have lived his entire life staring at her, at this look, knowing he did both. He put the trust on her face, the satisfaction there.

And he was about to shatter it all.

He grabbed his SIG and shoved the holster in the back of his pants.

"Do I need to go get tested?"

She blinked and drew her two little brows together. "What?"

"Did you lie about the birth control?"

Shock slammed into her features before she slowly hid it, then he watched as the shutters started coming down over her eyes.

"About being clean?" he asked, voice low, knowing this was it.

His end.

Hers.

Theirs.

He almost regretted it and the words he'd said.

Her chest caved before she looked away. "Get out." Her voice shook.

"Juliette," he called, wanting her eyes.

She closed what he sought and swayed as if she'd been hit. He took a step forward to catch her, and she took two steps back and pressed to the wall. The same wall he'd just fucked her against. Then she bent forward, her beautiful face ravaged by so much pain. He paused and started to wonder.

Had…?

"Get out!" she screamed just as tears filled her eyes and rolled down her face.

He grabbed his cell, slipped it into his pocket, then faced her again. "We haven't been using protection," he started, only for her to speak over him.

"God, what are you still doing here? Do you think I'm a fool? A slut?" she spat. "That I would sleep with a big, bad federal agent just to try to get my deadbeat boyfriend some free time to try to do only God knows what?" She took a step toward him, tears still tracking in rivulets down her cheeks. But she vibrated with something as she pointed to the door, one hand still gripping the blanket tightly to her chest. "Get out. Even if I were the fool, I wouldn't call you for anything. Leave. Now."

He cut a hand in a knifing motion between them. "You will let me know if you're pregnant."

She tossed her free hand in the air, then stomped over to the front door she'd been pointing at. Even pissed and betrayed as he was, he had to give it to her. She had a fantastic stomp in her anger. She opened the door, barely catching it before it slammed into the wall. "I know you don't believe me, or you're not listening, one of the two. But as I told you before, I am on birth control. I'd like you to leave." She wiped a hand over one cheek. He could see the wall going up between them, brick by brick. Second by second. "Please. Please leave."

She took a breath that shook, then looked away. The wall between them was complete.

He grabbed his keys, crossed the room, and then paused by the front door. There, he looked at her and tried to take in her features he hadn't seen before. The almond shape of her eyes. The high cheekbones. The soft curve of her jaw. Lips he had bitten until they swelled, as they did now. He wanted to memorize it all.

"Another agent will be in touch," he said quietly.

She didn't respond.

"Take care of yourself, Juliette."

Her eyes closed, and one tear tracked a lonely path where so many others had been.

He left, and the door clicked close behind him.

Chapter Nineteen

Matt floored his Cloudburst Gray IS 500 Lexus and sped down the Saw Mill Parkway without a destination in mind, his attention not on the road before him but on the scene that had played out at Juliette's. His gut churned with unease, making him feel as if acid was eating at his insides. His anger, too, seemed to have turned, almost as if the flame from the dragon that had been burning was suddenly snuffed out.

Now, he wondered and speculated. Had he done the right thing? Had he acted without thinking, putting his feelings before his mind? That was something Pops had always taught him and his brothers, to not let the heat of their feelings override their good sense, and it appeared he'd completely obliterated that rule.

But on the other hand, he'd seen the video proof with his own eyes. Watched as someone who looked very similar to Juliette leaned up and kissed Jimmy. Stand by him. Sure, she'd been facing away from the camera, but the hair matched her. The way the black leggings hugged that perfect plump ass…

Shit!

He crossed several lanes of traffic, thankful the highway seemed to be fairly light. His phone ringtone came over the speakers. He came to a jarring halt on the side of the road, dust kicking up around his sedan.

Juliette had been wearing deep-red leggings, a long white t-shirt, and a black zip-up hoodie when she landed at JFK that fateful day. He remembered taking her in, could still picture the vision of her in his mind as if it were just yesterday.

The ringer cut off, then started up again almost immediately.

"Fuck!" he exclaimed, slamming his hands on the steering wheel. He took a deep breath, then answered the phone with a push of a button on his steering wheel.

"Gonzalez here."

"Hey. It's Tommy down in computer crimes. Agent Watson asked me to touch base with you."

Matt dropped his head against the seat, a million thoughts racing through his mind. He'd acted without thought, said spiteful things, and treated her like crap, all because of some video evidence that could or could not be her. How was he going to work this out?

"Agent Gonzalez?" Tommy asked.

He shook his head. "Sorry, I'm here. What's up?"

Tommy cleared his throat. "Watson had asked me to take a look at this video pulled in from Cancun CUN airport. Make sure it hadn't been altered or falsified. I was going to run it through a forensic review and didn't do it before sending it up. There are a few different ways we can do this. Running it through FotoForensices. An InVid verification. Reviewing the code to ensure it hasn't been turned into a deep fake—"

"Jesus, Tom. You're speaking another language right now. Get to the point."

"This video isn't what it appears to be."

Matt's stomach flipped so hard he had to swallow rising bile. "What does that mean?"

"Well, Watson said it was supposed to account for a date about two weeks ago, correct?"

He stared ahead, unseeing anything before him. But in his mind, he saw Juliette's ravaged face from earlier. "Yes."

"Well, InVid analyzes the metadata to make sure the creation, thumbnails, and key frames all align. It also does a reverse search so we can check the clarity to ensure it came from a source. All the originals, location, date, thumbnails, are checked here."

"Tom, my man, we have to work on your delivery. Talk to me like I'm a first-grader, please. What does that mean?"

"This video was created two days ago."

His head rang as if a shot had been fired from his weapon inside his car. This video was created two days ago.

This video was created two days ago.

This video was created two days ago.

Like a loop in his head, the sentence kept repeating itself.

"Gonzalez," Tommy called.

"Fuck," he said, drawing the word out.

"Matt," Tommy called again, and the use of his first name was so out of place it pulled him back from his self-loathing.

"I'm here." He rubbed his eyes with a thumb and pointer finger.

"There's more. And as soon as Watson heard this, he dashed off to grab the SAC, said something about a team. But he wanted me to call and ask you to get to a Ms. Juliette Scaglione's house as soon as you could."

The hairs on his nape rose, and unease skittered along his spine. "What's going on?"

"Well, we're tracking incoming flights as per Watson's request, since you all had been taken. A few names on the list included yours and Ms. Scaglione, a Mr. Jorge Scaglione, and Jimmy Rubio. We also have an alert running for all known associates for certain cartels, just to make sure we're keeping track of these guys and seeing where they may or may not be heading. Sometimes it works, but as you know, a lot of the times these guys fly under different names—"

"Christ, Tommy," he interrupted. "Spit it out."

"Oh! Sorry. We got a hit a few hours ago for one Mr. Rubio and a Jose Robles, who is a known operative of the cartel."

Matt's heart pounded against his chest, as if it wanted to be let free. *Please don't say it, please don't say it...*

"They landed at JFK about two hours ago."

"Fuck!" He shifted to drive, looked over his shoulder, and sped back on the highway, then took the first exit to turn around.

"What can I do to help?" Tommy asked.

"I'm only a few minutes away from Juliette Scaglione's place. Call Watson and let him know I'm on my way. Notify local law enforcement and advise them a plainclothes agent will be on the scene. The last thing I want is for some trigger-happy patrolman to put a hole in me."

"Roger. Anything else?"

His mind scrambled to think of something he may need but was coming up empty. All he could think of was getting to Juliette. Making sure she was safe. "Not at this time. Call me if you hear anything else."

"You got it. And Agent Gonzalez?"

"Yeah?"

"Sorry about the mix-up. We should have figured this out before sending the video up to you all."

He wanted to shout and scream, strangle them for this blunder. If they had done their job at the right time, he wouldn't be rushing to Juliette's, hoping she was okay. He wouldn't have hurt her so. He shook his head. He'd done that all on his own—he couldn't blame it on anyone else.

The team had their own mix-up and it should have never happened. Instead of saying any of that now, instead of letting anger explode, he focused on his task at hand and said, "Mistakes happen. Let's make sure it doesn't again. Call me if you hear anything else." Then he hung up and sped down the highway.

Not thirty seconds went by before his phone rang. Thinking it was the analyst again, he answered while changing lanes. "Tommy, I don't have time for—"

"It's Watson. I take it you know what's going on?" Sirens sounded in the background on Don's side.

Matt slipped in between two cars as he tried to get around a slower-moving vehicle and lifted a hand in thanks as the driver blew his horn. "I'm on my way now. About ten minutes out. How the fuck did this happen?"

"You know how these things go. There are so many moving parts, sometimes things slip through. Listen, I need you to let us handle this. Give me everything you have, but let us go in first when we get there."

"Like hell," Matt said with a growl, all at once feeling extremely feral. Like a lion on the prowl to protect its own. He'd once watched an animal documentary about a lion's den under threat. Apparently, the den had sick and elderly with them. And there was something to be said about animals in the wild and the way the stronger of the pack had lain around those one would consider weaker.

As some hyenas had stalked the pack in attempts to separate one of the elder and sick pups, the entire den had reacted as if they'd practiced earlier, and not only protected the pack but also worked as a team. One lone lion stood off to the side, watching it all play out as if he'd directed it all.

That was who Matt related to at that moment. The lone lion waiting for someone to slip through the cracks so he could go to town and rip them to shreds.

"You are too close to the subject," Watson said,

sounding like he was trying to console Matt and take tempers down. His partner knew him well.

"You're failing, in case you're wondering," he said in response to the consoling. "And let's get something clear." He paused for a second as he cut across two lanes of traffic, then pushed the gas and sped past a handful of slower vehicles. "Jules is not a subject. If you know what I do, and I suspect you fucking do, seeing as you're calling me now, then you know the entire video was a scheme to throw us off. These people are smart, and for a moment, they were smarter *than us*." He stressed the last two words.

Watson cursed, then came back over the line. "You're at least fifteen or twenty ahead of us. We're coming from the city. Wait for us."

"I've got Tommy calling the locals."

"Not good enough. Wait for us," he urged, and with that last one, Matt could hear the worry. It was stupid, what he considered. He wanted to get to Juliette's, rush inside, and make sure she was okay. Neutralize any threat against her. Especially with thoughts of Jose in his head and the looks he'd given both of them the last time they were together. He wanted to spare Juliette any of that, any terror or pain. Any of this messed-up world they'd both found themselves in.

He'd trained for this scenario over and over with his office. How to breach houses smartly, how to take down infiltrators and cartel members safely. However, right now, he kept dismissing all of that and everything he knew because he only had one thought in mind.

The need to get to Juliette. To protect her from all of this.

The realization of his feelings hit him as if he'd been slapped. His foot slipped on the pedal a bit, slowing him down as he blinked at the windshield.

A couple of moments passed before he shook out of his stupor, then re-engaged in his pursuit to get to her.

"Matt," Watson said.

"Tell your driver to floor it," he said. "Call the locals and tell them to expect me. If anyone tries to slow me down or stop me from getting into that house, there will be some hell to pay."

"Now you sound like you've lost your mind. Think this shit through, man."

"I love her," he said, and a stunned silence came over the line. "So, you'll get me when I say absolutely no one is going to stop me."

"Shit," Watson said, "I'll call the locals."

"Thanks."

"Stay safe, brother. And be fucking smart."

Matt hung up. There was no need to respond. He had to get his head in the game. He had to save his girl.

****

Juliette stared at the guard and Jimmy. Of all the luck. She'd been a mess when Matt had left, feeling as if he'd taken a piece of her with him as he walked out the door. But the anger deep inside had refused to call him back. Refused to cower at yet another man who thought he could walk all over her and treat her as they wanted, not as she deserved.

She was better than that. Deserved more. So, she'd kept quiet even though all she'd wanted to do was run and put herself between Matt and his car.

No sooner than she'd closed the door, it seemed, did it reopen again. She'd turned, elated he'd come back. Ready to talk it through—after he apologized, of course—but her face fell as Jimmy, then Jose, walked into her house.

"Well, well, well, if I had known you'd give it to me on the kitchen island like a dirty girl, I would have stayed with you a bit longer," Jimmy said as a greeting.

She backed away from them both, wariness flooding her body. Her mind scrambled for purchase on things she'd be able to use to protect herself, ways to escape. There was no reason for either of them to be here together.

Together.

Her brows drew down. "All along, Jimmy?" she asked. "This whole thing was you?"

Jimmy shrugged and tossed Jose a wicked grin. "It's a good setup we have. Was going to work even better with the haul you were bringing in, but then you just had to go and get yourself caught. By a DEA agent, of all people."

Juliette hit the island, and a moment's jolt sent pain along her hip. She pushed it aside, then started creeping alongside the piece to put something between her and them, anything to slow them down or stop them from touching her. Too late, she realized she had boxed herself into her kitchen. Especially as one started coming from one side, the other the other way. They did this without speaking, as if they knew before they came in what to do.

Her heart pounded against her chest, as if it urged her to run. The look in Jose's eyes filled with a gleeful anticipation. Jimmy's held nothing but humor. As if he found this entire thing entertaining.

"Why are you doing this?" she asked him. "Why me? Why now? You could have just disappeared and did your own thing. We're not even together anymore."

He shrugged and looked over at Jose, who edged around the counter. Her pulse pounded in her ears. He was only a few feet from her now. There was no escape. No way for her to defend herself. She hadn't thought, like Matt had told her over and over to do, to look for a way to escape, a means to protect herself. All she'd done was panic and get herself backed into a corner.

"I was happy to let things go, but Jose here told me all about the fuss you two caused in Mexico. And you see, Jose has a hard time letting old grievances lie. He really wanted to come here and teach you how to play nice."

She thought she saw her chance and tried to speed past Jimmy, but he caught her around the waist and pulled her roughly up against his body, chest to chest.

"But now that I've seen you shacking up with a fed, I'm thinking I want to have some fun, too. What do you say, Jose?"

A meaty finger ran slowly along her jaw, then wrapped in her hair and gave a brutal yank until her neck bent in a painful arch. Tears burned the back of her eyes from the sudden jolt. Jose pushed against her, and she could feel the evidence of his excitement against her behind. "I'm sure we can think of something."

"No!"

Chapter Twenty

Matt pulled up to the curb several houses down the block from Juliette's, then scanned the area, looking for anything out of place. He tried to remember the cars that had been out here earlier but knew it was a useless endeavor. His emotions had been so heightened, he'd had tunnel vision. It would have wasted precious time getting to her with this exercise. Even if he saw something that seemed out of place, there was no telling if it belonged to Jimmy or not. And he would not sit here and run plates with local law enforcement when he could do a better job and creep up on her house to take stock of the situation. He had been trained in the art of remaining unseen. It was what Drug Enforcement Agency Agents did best. Blend in with their surroundings. Become a shadow one didn't know existed. Turn invisible, not in the literal sense.

He wished.

A couple of car doors slammed shut down the block, but he didn't pause. He had a feeling it was local law enforcement, and they'd take a bit longer in their consideration of plans to move in on the house.

Behind him, more car doors closed.

Definitely the locals. Seemed like they were surrounding the property and blocking off the neighborhood.

Without lingering, he made sure to take his tactical badge, also known as a tac badge, and set it around his neck. He didn't want to catch some trigger-happy patrolman's bullet, so this was the best he could do.

Slipping alongside the pine fence between Juliette's property and her next-door neighbor, he kept his attention on the windows and tried to remain unseen. With the sun setting, the shadows were allowing him to stay masked, but there was still enough light for him to stand out. He hoped some nosy neighbor didn't start making a ruckus.

Matt couldn't see anything going on in the living room from his vantage point, so he kept going, sliding around to the back. Lining the back part of her house were hydrangeas in every color. His mother would love it. When he was a child, she'd spent many a Saturday planting her own garden filled with roses and hydrangeas. Enough to make even Martha Stewart envious.

It seemed the only place he'd be able to see inside was the corner window, which he knew was over the kitchen sink or the back sliding door. He didn't want to make himself a target, and most times, people looked at doors before they did windows, so he chose the little window at the corner.

He popped around the corner quickly, then pulled back and pushed himself back against the wall of the house. His heart pounded with adrenaline, and his mind tried to catch up with what he'd seen.

Juliette had been in the embrace of a man. Someone tall and lanky. Had to be Jimmy. But he couldn't believe it. She'd been kissing him, arms on his shoulders, bodies pressed together, mouths touching.

He blinked several times, staring at the fence before him but still seeing the scene from inside.

Had he been completely duped? His chest pumped up and down twice, as if his body wanted to fight, wanted to roar out in anger.

Instead, he forced himself to calm, to take stock of what was going on around him. Deep breaths.

Focus.

The darkening shadows as the sun crept lower. A barking dog down the street. Someone in a car a few blocks over playing a song a little too loud. Birds flying in a perfect v-formation overhead.

Draw air into the lungs. Hold for a second. Let out. He repeated it a few more times before he braced to look again.

Turning, he grabbed the side of the house, the dark siding and wood frame warm beneath his palms. He poked his head around the corner and took a few more seconds to take stock. Juliette struggled in the arms of the man who he suspected was Jimmy, pushing against his shoulders, turning her head one way then the other as the man towered over her, trying to kiss her again.

Rage burned a hole in his gut. He wanted to rush in and push him off. The guy had about an entire foot and a half over her smaller frame.

He took a quick look around but didn't see anyone else. Didn't mean no one else was there. Jose had come into the country with Jimmy.

Matt's hands gripped the ledge, and he let the lethal anger build inside until it turned to a pure intent of focus.

He pushed back from the window and ducked. Went around to the sliding door and prayed it was unlocked. He'd hate to have to announce his arrival by breaking it, but at this point, he wasn't waiting for anyone else. He had to get in there.

Enough was enough.

She had been through enough.

He crouched low next to the door, tried the handle, and found it moved slightly. Great, it was unlocked.

He took just a few seconds to get his breathing under control and send up a silent prayer he wouldn't make his ma sad by getting shot. Wouldn't put Juliette through any more trauma by being unhelpful. He needed to be there for her, needed to put an end to this nonsense and constant state of her being in danger.

Once this was over, they were going to have a chat about where they sat in terms of a relationship. It was a conversation he knew he'd have to work for, and produce quite a bit of groveling, a huge apology, and give her nothing but honesty. But he had hopes for the outcome.

With that goal in mind, he drew his service weapon, checked to make sure the magazine was set, blew out a deep breath, and entered her house on quiet feet.

Jimmy had Juliette pushed against the wall she'd been working on. Her voice rose in anger and slight panic. She berated him, tried to push him away, but he kept at it. His back was to Matt, so he took the quick opportunity to look around. Not finding anyone but knowing that didn't guarantee they were alone, he crept up behind Jimmy, then slowly placed his gun at his temple.

"Don't even think about it," Matt warned as the guy went for his waist. Matt felt around the same area and came away with a gun holstered on his belt. "Step away from her. Follow the sound of my voice. Do not turn around."

Jimmy hesitated.

"Please," Matt whispered, his voice vibrating with anger. "Please try something. *Give me* a fucking reason."

Apparently, Jimmy heard the promise because he stepped back. Juliette darted away from the wall and moved farther into the kitchen. Matt didn't take his eyes off Jimmy. He couldn't take her in his arms as he wanted to, couldn't take stock to make sure she was okay. He had to take care of the threat standing before him, of the other he suspected was in the house. Somewhere.

"Jules," he said, keeping his weapon trained on Jimmy. "There are some cuffs in my back pocket. I need you to grab them and put them on this guy here."

She blew out a shaky breath right next to him, then he felt her tentative fingers on his t-shirt. He swallowed hard but didn't give in to his urge to take her in his arms. It was a damn hard fight with his instincts.

"I don't know how to do this." Her voice trembled and shook.

He tsked under his breath and remembered a conversation they'd had in the log of a tree thousands of miles away. "You mean to tell me you only watched *Chicago Fire* and not *Chicago PD*? We're going to have to change that."

Jimmy tensed before him.

"You forget, *hombre*," he seethed. "I have a gun in my hand that I'm just *itching*"—he stressed the last word—"to use. Spread your feet and put your hands on top of your head. Next hesitation will get you the promised kiss of what's loaded in the chamber. Try me."

Jimmy did as instructed.

Once the guy was in position, he walked Juliette quietly through the process of getting cuffs on him. Her body trembled while she did it, and he made a promise to himself to ensure he never saw her like this again. He would make sure of it.

Meanwhile, one ear was trained to the rest of the house, listening for any out-of-place noises. So far, he didn't hear anything, but he wouldn't let his guard down until he made sure.

As soon as the last cuff was in place, Matt quickly holstered his weapon, then walked up behind

Jimmy and knocked his knees out from under him, guiding the guy down with a hard thump to the floor. He pressed his face to the wood, then turned to Juliette to take her in. To pull her into his arms, if only for a second.

But her eyes widened at something over his shoulder. She opened her mouth to scream and shout. He didn't know what, but he didn't wait.

He dropped to a knee as he turned, pulled his weapon from its holster, and let out one round at the same time as another shot off. Matt's landed between the eyes of Jose. A Jose who had a gun pulled and aimed at where Matt had been standing. A Jose who promptly fell to his knees, then face-first to the floor. Dead where he had stood.

Matt wasn't sorry. Not even in the slightest. While that might make him just a little of the gray in between black and white when it came to the law, he couldn't help but look at the space where Jose stood and think about all they'd been put through.

Pain radiated from his right arm just as Juliette spoke up behind him.

"Matt, you've been shot."

He looked down at the hole in his shirt and the spreading of a red stain. "Shit."

Chapter Twenty-One

About an hour later, Matt hissed as the doc shot some local anesthetic into the area around his wound.

"Stop being a baby," his older brother, Dwayne, spoke up.

"It's only a *little* needle," Chris, his other brother, said with a wince.

Matt narrowed his eyes at the movement.

"And hey, compared to that big ole hole in your shoulder, it's nothing." Charlie spoke up next to him, where she leaned against the bed. She waggled her brows.

"I've seen bigger wounds on children who scrape their knees in Central Park," Jake said, standing next to Charlie.

He looked up at the doc, whose lips twitched with humor. "Can't you just kick them all out or something? Isn't this a violation of HIPPA?"

"Now you're really sounding like a child," Watson said from the corner. It was the first time his partner *had* said something since they'd left the scene.

And he got it. He broke a ton of department rules by going into that house alone. Getting shot on top of it would not make anyone happy. But Watson, he could tell, was taking some of the burden of this situation on his shoulders. He had been the one working with forensics from the beginning.

Matt would deal with him later and try to get Watson's confidence back up and take some of that load from him. He was sure he'd get shit from the guy for years to come, anyway. After all, Watson hadn't shown any reaction to Juliette holding his hand when he came into the house earlier. Nor had he blinked when she kissed him goodbye before he got in the ambulance.

He hadn't wanted to take a ride in that thing, but SAC Joseph Henninger pushed him to do so due to the bullet passing through his shoulder, so he went with a grumble or two.

He'd made one phone call to Dwayne about the same time, which led to his brothers and Charlie descending on the hospital.

He had no idea where Juliette was, and he wanted to know. But asking in front of his brothers was sure to begin a pretty wild line of questioning he wasn't ready to deal with.

"I still wanna hear about Mexico," Trent said from the other side of the room, and Matt groaned, tossing his head back on the pillow. He winced as pain shot through his shoulder.

"I'm going to have to ask you not to do that again," the doc murmured next to him before she grabbed a syringe. He looked away. No way was he going to watch them clean out the wound.

"You're looking a little pale there, buddy," Chris popped off.

"He looks a bit scruffy, too." A pause. "The DEA allow their agents to grow their hair wild and have beards? Man, must be nice," Mike, his other older brother, said.

Matt cut them both a glare. "Just because you chose the wrong uptight agency to work for doesn't mean you can cut on what I look like."

"Juliette seems to like his looks just fine," Watson said.

Matt cut wide eyes to him. "Traitor," he hissed. "You've been pretty mute this entire time and *that's* what you say?"

All at once, everyone in the room started asking

questions.

He looked at the doc, who was outright smiling. "Please, just knock me out."

Her pretty brown eyes glanced up at him before going back to work. "Sorry. A bunch of them flashed fancy badges at me. I would knock you out with the good drugs, but you seem to be doing just fine. Only a few more minutes, and we'll have you almost as good as new."

The door to the room opened, and in walked SAC Henninger, followed by Juliette.

Everyone went quiet. Matt sucked in a sharp breath as she froze at the door, taking in the crowd. She looked a little frazzled, understandably. Her hair had been pulled back into one of those loose styles most women did where they twist the hair around to create some sort of messy gig. She wore a large black hoodie, which hung down to her upper thighs. Forest-green leggings covered her legs. And on her feet were a pair of dark sneakers. She didn't have on a speck of makeup, so her face looked fresh and clean, but a heavy darkness sat under her eyes. One he didn't like and one he had a feeling he contributed to putting there.

Juliette's gaze met his, moved to his shoulder, then came back to his again. The second pass held some concern, but she didn't move from the doorway.

"You going to live?" Henninger asked, drawing his attention.

"He's going to be fine. Just a few stitches and he'll be back to new."

SAC Henninger nodded. "Your car is in the parking garage, second floor. Juliette here has the keys."

A few in the room sucked in surprised breaths at the sound of her name.

Matt almost groaned.

"I'm heading back to the office. Have some paperwork to complete." Joe's attention cut to Watson. "Which you're going to help with. Matt," he said, eyes coming back to him. "Take the week to recoup and get your shit together. We'll talk when you're back in the office."

Joe Henninger gave a two-fingered salute and left the room. Juliette shifted so she came inside, but stayed against the far wall, still watching him. He wanted her closer but didn't know how to ask for it. She looked uncomfortable as hell, too. Reasonably so. The room was filled with strangers and both of them had an intense scene, one right after another, over the past few hours.

"I'm going to head out with him. I'll be in touch. Glad you're okay, buddy," Watson said, then gave his own little wave to the room and left.

"Soooo," Charlie said as the door swooshed closed again. She rocked back and forth on her heels, looking like a kid about to go on their first roller coaster ride with her excitement. Her gaze bounced between Matt and Juliette, and if she rubbed her hands together in glee, he wouldn't be surprised.

He scowled.

Trent wrapped an arm around her shoulders and pulled her sharply against him. The FBI agent said something in her ear before both smiled.

His scowl grew.

The door opened again and bustling in came Ma and Pops. He turned a furious look to Dwayne, who simply rolled back on his heels and stared up at the ceiling.

"The fuck, D?"

"Language, Matthew Liam Gonzalez," his ma, Karen, said.

Someone laughed.

"Jesus," Matt said under his breath and dropped his head to the pillow. At this rate, he'd never get Juliette alone so he could talk and get a few things straight.

The pretty little doc finished taping up the wound, then stood and removed her gloves. She shot him an amused look of sympathy. "You're all set. I know you already said no to painkillers, but if it gets to be too much, just give us a call and I'll put something in. You should keep the dressing and area clean and dry. Try to keep your shoulder elevated. This will help reduce swelling. It may be sensitive, so if you find you need painkillers, don't try to be macho. Take them. And take your antibiotics to help kill off any infection."

He sat up and tossed his legs over the side of the bed. "Am I good to go?"

She nodded. "Give me just a few minutes to get your paperwork all done, then I'll send a nurse in with some discharge instructions. You shouldn't drive, but from what I understand, you have a ride…" The doc trailed off, her gaze going to Juliette for a moment before returning to him. "So I don't need to have someone call you a taxi. If you need anything else, though, don't hesitate to reach out."

As her attention went to Juliette, everyone else's eyes did, too. His parents included. Matt did an internal groan at the spark of interest that entered his mom's expression.

He studied Juliette for a second, needing to ensure she wasn't running for the hills. At least not yet. She looked uncomfortable, but also like she was intent on seeing this through. Whatever was going on in her head seemed locked behind a wall of black ice. Nothing escaped. No warmth, anger, or affection.

She had every right to her own thoughts, especially after what he put her through. But that didn't mean he liked it.

"How are you feeling, *hijo*?" his ma asked.

The doc bustled out of the room. He turned his attention back to his ma and allowed her to take his face in her warm hands. Even with him sitting on the hospital bed, she was a tiny little thing, only coming up to his shoulder. "I'm good. You didn't have to come all the way down here."

He closed his eyes as she bussed a kiss over his cheek, then his forehead. Such continued affection from them, something he still cherished, so he didn't push her away. Pops laid a hand on his good shoulder, gave a squeeze, then let go.

He couldn't ever remember his birth parents giving him such affection. Even the first time he'd been taken in Karen's arms had been a shock. He hadn't known how to react. Now, he soaked up the affection with ease.

"Why don't you come home for a few days, stay in your old room, and let me take care of you?"

"Ma, thank you, but I have some stuff I need to handle. I'll be fine. It's just a little hole. Through and through. Nothing to worry over."

"Nothing to—" she sputtered, then spoke a few choice words in Spanish under her breath that had both Matt and Pops raising their brows. "Don't you sit there and tell me this is nothing to worry over, Matthew Liam Gonzalez. I'm your mother. I'm going to worry over whether you're getting enough sleep and fiber in your diet until one of us dies. You're just going to have to let me fuss."

Matt smiled, recognized the stress lined around her eyes, and tried to defuse the situation. He pulled her close and kissed her cheek, then spoke low enough for her ears alone. He told her how much he loved her. What a great mother she was, and as nice as he could, to back off so he could have some time to deal with a certain lady in his life.

Her back went straight, and he swore her ears perked up. She sniffed and looked over at Juliette again, but then brushed a hand over his cheek. "Okay." She stepped back and into the arms, as if a gravitational force existed between them, of Pops.

"Okay, everyone out. Matt has this under control," Pops said. His voice held the same authority now as it did when they were teenagers and acting up. Even Charlie knew not to mess with that tone because she immediately pushed from the wall.

Trent led her to the door, tossing a smile over his shoulder to Matt.

Dwayne looked disappointed but mouthed a *later* his way and started moving toward the door, too.

Everyone filed out of the room in front of his parents, but no one said a word to Juliette, who stayed perched against the wall. She stared at the floor, not meeting anyone's gaze, including his.

****

Juliette listened to the last of Matt's family file out the door, then the soft *whoosh* as it shut. Her stomach made a similar whooshing feeling as everything caught up with her.

All of it—from the kidnapping to the escape through Mexico. Their time together in a small hotel in Texas to the scene they'd had earlier. The words he'd said to her. The ones she'd returned. And the topping of it all, the utter ugliness that was her life's drama bleeding into Matt's good one.

He was so fresh and good, full of integrity and honor. It was clear his family, partner, and even his boss adored and respected him. They'd all come to his side to wish him well after he'd been shot while dealing with her shit.

Because that was what her life had turned into—absolute shit.

She had no one to turn to. No family, no close friends, and she had fooled herself for a few days and thought she'd be able to build something strong with Matt, but their entire foundation had crumbled around them at the drop of a hat—or in this case, at the drop of some video he thought was her.

Joe Henninger had explained everything on their way to the hospital. He'd given her an iPad to watch the video, so she understood how Matt had thought differently, but that changed nothing. It didn't change the fact he was good and whole, working for the right side of the law. Working with the love of his family and friends behind him, whereas all she had was a dead brother and an ex-boyfriend who'd gotten her mixed up in something that remained a threat in her life. One she'd have to seriously think about in the near future.

"Juliette," Matt said. "Can you please look at me?"

She took a deep breath and braced for the impact of his dark gaze. Even from across the room, she grew dizzy as they connected. It was like this every time, it seemed, a jolt that sent the room spinning. Something that hadn't lessened even with everything they'd been through.

Walking away from him was going to hurt. She'd get used to the pain—it seemed to be the only constant in her life.

He went to open his mouth, but she jumped in before he could say anything. She inched her way toward the edge of a cliff, ready to jump off and fall into the deep end of despair and loneliness. "Your boss showed me the video. I completely get why you didn't believe me."

Matt's lips thinned, and he shifted toward her with a wince.

"Look." She held up her hands. "We don't have to do this. Seriously. Don't stress over it."

His eyes narrowed. A shadowy look shifted over his handsome face. "This?" he asked, and had she paid heed, she would have noted the dark undertone to that word. Instead, she was too focused in her own head with moving this along, cutting that cord quick to try to lessen the impact for them both.

"Yes. This. This talking it out and apologizing for whatever went wrong." She shook her hands out to the room, at a loss to explain it all. What she felt and what she really wanted to say. She tucked those same hands across her chest to keep them from reaching for him, which was what she really wanted to do. Her hands itched with being constrained. Her body ached for his touch. "We don't have to make this awkward. I don't even know why I'm here, but Joe insisted I come."

Matt's jaw tightened, and a tendon jumped in his face, but he blew out a breath. "He insisted you come here because he knew I'd want to see you were okay. Because he knows me and understands I'd want you close."

Why? She wanted to shout. She couldn't go down this path with him, the *what-if* it seemed to be gravitating toward. "I don't understand that, but fine. I'm here. Can I help do anything to get you to the car? Is there someone I need to talk to?" She turned to go out the door, ignoring the very real need to escape him. Using the excuse to find someone to help them out-process as her reason. She was simply operating on automatic at this point. She couldn't control her emotions around him, and he was too intense, too … everything.

"Stop," he said behind her, the word sounding like a gunshot.

She squeezed the handle of the door but didn't turn to face him again. "I need to go, Matt. Please."

A few seconds of silence passed. She thought he hadn't heard her soft plea, but then, "Why are you running from me?"

She closed her eyes and dropped her head to the door. Hopefully, no one came in the room right now because she was sure to end up with a mark on her face if they did. She thought over his question, debating on how to answer it or even if she had to say anything at all. She could go now, just simply drop his keys and find her own way home. But she knew he'd find her. They'd have this out one way or another. So maybe now was for the best—just cut the cord and get it done at once. If he didn't want to take her home after this conversation, if he were that guy who would leave her stranded, then so be it. She didn't think he was. Matt was too pure and good, which were the reasons she couldn't stay with him. But then again, her mind wasn't thinking straight.

"Jules…"

"It's driving me a little wild, or mad, one or the other—to be in the same room with you and have to deal with how you make me feel," she said.

"Look at me, please."

She faced him but didn't look at him. Instead, she kept her eyes closed. Childish it may be, but she just couldn't. "I can't. Just let me go, Matt."

He sighed. "I can't let you go. I don't even want to try. I want you to look at me so we can talk about earlier and about what's going through your head right now."

Opening her eyes, she took him in and felt that

same impacting jolt rock through her. His face seemed so earnest, as if he truly cared. He couldn't let her go? Didn't want to try? His words shook her. Didn't make sense. Couldn't make sense. He couldn't possibly... "Please don't do this." By *this*, she meant to drag things out.

He gave her a grim look, then shook his head and hopped off the bed, rising to his full height. Colors roamed over his exposed skin, touching as much of him as they could.

He reached for a t-shirt sitting atop a chair in the corner, then winced as he went to shake it out.

Without thinking, she crossed the room and took the material to help him. He stared down at her but didn't interrupt. Instead, she focused on her task and bunched the shirt up in anticipation of helping him put it on.

"I really hate that you keep using that word," he said.

She briefly met his eyes before lifting and sliding the shirt over his head. "Which one?"

"This," he said and pushed through his good arm. Then he settled that hand on her hip. She swallowed hard.

"We're not a *this*, Jules."

A thrill went through her stomach at his soft tone, the nickname, and his touch. The intimacy of them standing so close together.

"Take a deep breath and move slowly," she said, referring to his other arm. He did as instructed, a grimace on his handsome face, but he blew out a slow breath as he got his arm in. She was thankful the shirt had been so stretchy. She pulled it down to his hips, then let go.

He didn't let her move, though. The hand on her hip tightened. She looked up and got snared in his gaze.

"I'm sorry for what I said earlier." He shook his

head. "I wasn't thinking. I shouldn't have jumped to conclusions, and I broke every rule I've ever been taught by doing so. I made an ass out of myself and hurt you. It won't happen again."

She blinked, caught off guard. Jimmy had never apologized. Ever. Even when he was completely in the wrong.

That Matt had just done it with a sincerity in his expression and words, when he was such a proud man, one who wanted to control everything, shook her. It couldn't have been easy for him, but it loosened some of the coiled tension inside her gut.

"But we're not a *this*," he repeated, then wound the hand on her hip around to her back and pulled her close.

She set her hands on his chest and leaned back. "Matt."

"I've dated a lot of women," he said.

She stopped and stared, then really began to push away. "Not something I'm sure I want to hear about."

"If you'd listen for one stinkin' moment, Juliette, you'd find there's a lot you'd hear. But you're stuck in your own damn head and determined to push me away." He tightened his grip and shook her a little. A grimace pushed over his face, but resolution set in. "Stop and listen."

"Fine. What is it you want to say?" she asked, feeling helplessness rush in. If he wanted to have this out, then they just needed to get through it. She'd pick up the pieces later.

"I've dated a lot of women, but none of them have ever gotten as close as you have, not just in the physical sense, as I'm sure you know now." He gave her a pointed look. "But also, mentally, emotionally. I've told you things I've never told anyone else. I've felt vulnerable and comforted by you." He shook his head. "Again, something that I've never done with another woman. And yes, I've acted like an asshole, but I've apologized for that. Promised to not let it ever happen again, and I do not break promises." He stared at her expectantly, as if he wanted something, anything, from her.

She held out as long as she could. "What do you want from me?" she whispered.

He held her gaze. "You. Don't you get it now? I want you. I want us. Give us a shot. Do *this* with me and let's see what we become."

Her hands wrapped around his arms, squeezed, and she leaned in, wanting him to hear what she said. To really take it in. "You don't know how tempting that is."

He opened his mouth to say something, but she jumped in. This gorgeous, wonderful man could be hers if she let him. Let herself. "I'm the opposite of everything you are," she started.

His head drew back, and dark brows turned down into a V.

"You've seen the mess that is my life. The ugliness. I've got this stink all over me that will never wash away. And you're just so..." She faltered and looked anywhere but at his face, needing to find the right words. "You're so good, so wholesome. This perfect man."

He snorted at that, and she gave a little smile.

"I'm anything but perfect."

She squeezed his arms again. "But you could be perfect for me. If I was anyone different."

"I think that's a bullshit copout, if you want honesty."

"What?" she asked, startled.

"You giving me this excuse for why you can't do

this with me. You've never, not once, in all we've been through, and gorgeous, we've been through quite a bit, even in the short time we've been together. But you've never shown me an inkling of this so-called ugliness. This stink. Even when we were trapped in that dirty cell and fighting for our lives, your caring self, your heart bled through."

His words stole her breath. "Matt."

"I hate that you see yourself like that. And if you listened to anything I've said, listen to this: give me some time to prove you wrong."

She swallowed and stared up at him, hope a tiny kindle in her chest. Did he really think this of her? Could it work out between them? Could she hope for an ounce of happiness without the promise of failure?

"Give me a chance to show you what we could be. A chance to make us both happy with each other. Juliette, I swear to you, you will be safe with me. I will not hurt you. I'll take care with everything that happens between us. Give me a chance to show you I speak the truth."

"All right," the doctor said, pushing back into the room with papers in her hand. "Just take these to the front desk—" She paused and took them in. "Sorry," she said, sending them a sheepish smile. "Take these to the front desk and check out. Follow up with us or your primary care doctor in about two weeks. Sound good?"

Matt cleared his throat and loosened his arms. "Yes. Thanks, Doc."

She sent him a smile. "Anytime." Then she left the room again, all bustling ER energy. On to the next emergency, most likely.

Jules stared at his t-shirt-covered chest and felt him prepare to move, as if he wanted to get the night over with. As if he just wanted to move on from it all.

"We can finish talking about this later," he said, stepping back.

She moved into him immediately, and he froze. "No."

He sighed, the sound not one of defeat but one of resolution saying he wasn't giving up. "Jules…"

Apparently, he misunderstood. She looked up and met his pretty whiskey gaze. "I don't want to continue this later. Let's finish it now."

A muscle in his jaw pulsed.

"Yes," she said before she lost her nerve. "Let's give us a shot."

His body tensed at her words. "Fuck," he exploded under his breath. That sound and word moved through her as the tension left him.

Then he dipped with a grunt and lifted her in his arms.

"Matt," she shrieked. "Your shoulder!"

He set her down again but leaned in and kissed her silly. The room spun, and her body was a ball of heat when he finished, but the smile on his face was the only thing she saw. The only thing she could focus on.

Epilogue

Three weeks later...

"Matt, it's been a few weeks. If anyone was still after me, or you for that matter," she said with a cute little head twitch as she finished curling long ringlets in her hair. Her gaze met his in the mirror, a sparkle still shining through even though it had been, as she said, a few weeks.

A few weeks since they'd escaped their cartel kidnappers. A few weeks since he'd scaled the fence around her heart and started making his way closer to bringing said fence down entirely. Permanently. And a few weeks since he'd seen that spark in her eye grow brighter each day. He knew he was getting somewhere with her because of that glimmer. He'd work every day to keep it there, to keep her safe, and to make her the happiest she'd ever been.

Just like he promised her.

She didn't finish her earlier thought process and instead sent him a small smile through the reflection.

He pushed off the wall and came up behind her, moving her straightened, then curled hair again—he'd never understand why women did that—over her shoulder before dipping to kiss her neck.

"Matt," she mock-complained with a shiver.

"You look beautiful, Scaggs," he said, using an old nickname despite her complaints about it. She thought it made her sound as if she were some private detective in a rundown office. The way she explained it had him howling with laughter, especially when she started talking about the pot belly she pictured, the old coffee mug, and all.

His girl was hilarious. Had an active imagination.

"I'm not even wearing makeup," she complained with a huff.

"You don't need makeup," he responded, then settled his hands on her hips and squeezed.

"You always say that."

He met her gaze in the mirror again. "I'm hoping one day you'll hear me when I say just how beautiful you are without the makeup. I like you with it just fine, but your true beauty comes through, Jules, when you're wearing nothing at all."

She gasped. "You can't just go around saying things like that!"

He chuckled and bent to kiss her neck again. "I mean it. But not to stray too far from our earlier topic, I'm not asking you to move in with me because of the threat hanging over us both with Antonio Ruben Cardalas Gonzalez still being at large. We're together every day anyway, at one place or the other. It makes no sense for us to continue having two places when we're always together. I'm sure about us," he said. "I'm going to be sure about us years down the line, too."

Her face softened at his words, becoming yet another look of wonder. As if she didn't understand why he said the things he did but loved them all the same. If he could, he'd go back and shoot Jimmy, due to her low self-esteem when it came to relationships. He'd make it his mission in life to make her feel so secure with them that she'd never hold back.

"You don't think it's too soon?"

He turned her around and pulled her close again settling his arms around her waist, his face close to hers. "I don't, because I am sure about *this*, Juliette."

A troubled look brought down her brows. "You've only ever had sex with me. How can you be sure? Maybe you should—"

"Don't even finish that thought," he said, tightening one arm around to bring her closer. He brushed the back of his knuckles over her jaw. "I'm in love with you, Juliette Scaglione. That's why I'm sure. I suspect it happened in that hollowed-out tree back in Mexico. But I'm sure it was there the first time I sank inside you. I know I love you because I don't want to have sex with any other woman. I don't want to spend time getting to know anyone else. I want to build a home with *you* and eventually, build a family. If this is moving too fast for you, I'm sorry. But I want to be honest with you. We've been through too much together, and I've dedicated myself to not breaking a promise to you. So, I won't hold back now." He pulled her so close there was only a breath of air between their mouths. "Move in with me, please?"

Air skipped out of her and over his lips. He bit her lower lip lightly before laying a gentle kiss there. "Move in with me, Juliette."

"Matt…"

He kissed her, going full gusto. A kiss so deep, so slow and thorough that he felt it down to his toes. Her body was plastered to his, and her hands were in his hair as he pulled back. "Move in with me."

"Okay," she answered on an airy breath.

He smiled, and her eyes widened. "Wait."

He groaned.

"No, I still want to live together but," she said and bit her lip, looking suddenly unsure. "I've fixed up this house from being almost rundown. I—I—I have so many plans I still want to do to it. I've grown really attached to it."

His smile returned. "Are you asking me to move in with you, Juliette?"

"Well, yeah."

"I'm shocked. Don't you think it's too soon?" he teased.

She gaped and slapped his shoulder with a laugh, but he joined in with a chuckle and started walking her back toward the door leading to the master bedroom. "I'd love to move in with you, Juliette Scaglione. Thank you for asking so sweetly."

"What are you doing?" she asked, looking over her shoulder as they came up to the bed.

"Celebrating," he said.

"Your family is going to be here any minute for the barbeque."

"We'll be fast," he said before he pushed her onto the bed with a playful movement.

She bit her lip as he reached under her ruffled three-tier skirt so he could grab the panties beneath, then pulled them down her legs. He guided her legs apart and stepped between them. His gaze jumped to the skirt, which had ridden up to expose her, then back to her face.

"Put your hands behind your head, baby."

This was something else that had come out with a vengeance between them. He liked a little bit of dominance in bed, and Juliette seemed to get off on it. He caught the catch in her breath as she followed his command, but then she pulled them back out and grabbed his wrist on her leg.

"Wait a second. Can you come here?"

He squeezed her thighs. "I'm right here. What's wrong?"

She tugged on his wrist, and he got the hint. He leaned over until he braced himself over her face. "What's going on, beautiful?"

She smiled softly, then traced his lips with one finger, intent on getting whatever was going on in her head in order before she spoke. He allowed this too, because most times when she did this, what she ended up saying rocked his world.

Finally, after a few seconds, she took the sides of his face in her hands and held his gaze. "I love you, too."

His heart stuttered to a stop at her words, then sped. He swore the organ wanted to come out of his chest.

"Jules…"

"I love you, Matthew Liam Gonzalez."

Emotion surged inside. He kissed her quickly, then started fumbling with his belt and jeans. "We're going to go fast right now for the sake of people showing soon. But later tonight, gorgeous, when I'm so deep inside of you that neither of us knows where one begins and the other ends, I want you to say that again."

Her breath caught as he checked her readiness, then he leaned up. "Hands behind your head, gorgeous." She did as he asked, her eyes alight with anticipation and that wonderful sparkle he'd come to look for.

He pushed up her cream-colored tank top, then pulled down her bra so her full breasts popped free. Then he pushed inside of her and watched the sway of her tits with the movement. He met her pleasure-hazed eyes before he withdrew from her heat, then entered again, feeling a wave of euphoria ride up his spine.

She smiled and welcomed him inside her.

It was fast but no less amazing than any other time he'd fallen between her thighs.

****

Juliette arranged her skirt just as the doorbell chimed. "Shit," she said, mind on everything that needed to be done.

"Relax," Matt said with a grin. He entered the bathroom behind her and did a quick check in the mirror. "They are going to love you, just as I do." His eyes met hers in the reflection again, and her cheeks heated.

"I still need to do my makeup, the hamburger needs to be mixed, and the patties made, and I'm sure I'm missing something else." She dithered on under her breath, reaching for her makeup bag.

Instead, she found her hand in Matt's, and he pulled her from the room. Panic alighted in her veins. "Matt," she hissed. "My makeup."

He threw her a sweet smile over his shoulder that made her stomach flutter. "You're beautiful as you are. Come meet my family."

Her stomach twisted with unease at meeting them so bare. Maybe it was her and wanting to hide behind another shield, especially after baring her soul to Matt only a few minutes ago. But they'd talked through her "walls" as Matt liked to call them, and she'd promised to start opening those doors to allow him in. It was only fair to do the same with his family.

She blew out a breath, trying to steady her nerves, and let him lead her down the stairs.

A group of people stood there as Matt opened the door. Suddenly, they all swarmed in with hugs and kisses for Matt, handshakes and warm smiles, but eyes very curious of her.

There was Dwayne and his lovely girlfriend, Brooke. A man dressed impeccably even for a Saturday barbeque, wearing khaki pants and a nice button-up shirt. He pulled it off well without appearing as anything but genuine. His green eyes hypnotized her at first glance and if she hadn't just confessed her love for his brother, she would have had a serious new crush. Brooke was no less beautiful and stunning with long sandy red hair and bright blue eyes, and she was dressed just as elegant yet simple as Dwayne.

Brooke's daughter, who she learned was

extremely close to the family, having grown up around them and been coached by Dwayne with a few of the other brothers pitching in at times in softball. She had serious dark brown eyes, but her hair was the feature that stood out, falling in long rivulets down her back. Dwayne hovered at her side, a protective figure for this young woman, but there was something about Hailey that just drew her. Made her want to take the girl in her arms and hold her tight.

She didn't understand it but would have to remember to ask Matt about it later.

Chris, who immediately referred to himself as the older and better-looking brother, which had her laughing up a storm, and his very pregnant girlfriend, Samantha, came in next. Despite the humor, which she took as a way to defuse the awkwardness of meeting new people, he held himself with the quiet ease of a soldier who took in every detail around him. And his girlfriend shined by his side, her hair a dark and vibrant red, highlighted against the sun behind them.

"No Dumbass today?" Matt asked.

Juliette gasped. "Matt! What in the world?"

Chris laughed and shook his head. "My military working dog. He's retired now." He sent her a gentle smile. His words confirmed her whole soldier vibe. "We call him Dumbass, but only in an affectionate way. He's the goof of the group." He turned back to Matt. "But yes, he's at home. Had a rough past few days, so we figured he needed a bit of a break. Next time we meet up, I'll bring him. A smaller crowd may be a bit better anyhow."

"Sounds like a plan. Take Red here," Matt said with a teasing glint in his eye and a huge smile for Chris's girlfriend, "out back and get her something to drink. We'll see you out there in a few."

"These men," Sam said with a grin for her. The

gorgeous redhead rubbed her belly and blew out a heavy breath.

"You okay?" Juliette asked, taking a step toward her.

"I'm fine," Sam responded with a small wince. "Baby has been pretty active today. Seems to be rearranging all my internal organs and kicking up a storm."

Juliette's eyes widened at that mental image.

Samantha laughed. "It's not as violent as it sounds. I promise you."

"Uhhhh, I'll take your word for it."

"Jesus, Chris, take your girl out back. Get her a drink. Maybe rub her feet or something."

Samantha turned with doe eyes to Chris. "Rubbing my feet does sound divine," she said.

Chris laughed, then wrapped an arm around her neck and pulled her inside the house. "Your wish, Red."

A gorgeous, muscular, dark-haired man came in next. He looked like a darker version of Mark Wahlberg and she had to slow the putter of her heart at the sight. Little did Matt know, the former rapper turned actor was a childhood crush of hers.

"Jules," Matt said now, after a back-slapping hug with the Mark look-alike. "Meet one of my baby brothers, Jake Gonzalez."

Jake turned to her and gifted a fantastic lop-sided grin that made her stomach flutter. She couldn't help it and wouldn't trade Matt for anything in the world, but the man standing before her was sure to garner a few passing looks. "Pleasure to meet you, Jules."

"Hi," she breathed, feeling her stomach tumble again as he shook her hand.

He sent a grin to Matt.

"Jules," Matt called, drawing her attention.

"Wanna let go of Jake's hand?" He laughed through his words.

"Oh!" She dropped his hand with a jolt, then felt her face flame. Surely it was as red as the tomatoes that still needed to be cut on her counter. "I am so sorry. I don't—"

"All good," Jake responded with a laugh. "I imagine you've had quite the past few weeks."

If that was the excuse he wanted to give her, she'd take it.

An arm wrapped around her shoulders and pulled her up to the side of a lean and muscular body she knew well. "You could say that," Matt said next to her.

Whoopsie.

"Jake is a detective out of New York. From what I hear, congratulations are in order. You just made the homicide squad?"

Jake grinned.

"Nice. We'll have to catch up."

Jake nodded and moved into the house, then walked up to Don, who gave her a cautious smile. Luke, who referred to himself as the baby of the group, had her laughing. She learned he was a U.S. Marshal. Something about him had her wondering just how close he and Matt were. They both held a similar shadow.

Then Mike, a United States Secret Service Agent who caused her to blush—again!—when he teased her about the soft glow she sported.

Matt grabbed the last one with an arm around his neck and dragged him farther into the house. Trent and Charlie walked up to the front door then, both sending her more warm smiles before they entered.

"Is it a family business for everyone to go into law enforcement?" she asked.

Trent laughed as Charlie answered. "It would

seem so, right? And it's weird how they've all kind of done that, even not being related by blood."

Juliette closed the door and led them through the house. Her stomach was a knot of nerves with meeting so many new people. She'd never had a big family and typically kept to herself, so she felt a little overwhelmed with everyone but wanted to hide that feeling. Depending on how observant all these detectives and agents were would tell how good of a job she did.

"It really is. Thank you both for coming, by the way. I know Matt is looking forward to catching up. He mentioned you all were pretty close."

Charlie startled her by pulling her close. "I'm warning you now—everyone is in everyone else's business and there are no secrets, but we'll all be by your side no matter what. If Matt has attached himself to you, prepare to have us as family, too."

Juliette's heart skipped a beat at being so exposed, at having this wonderful group of people who were so important pounding at the walls around her heart. That they would refuse to be denied entry. Charlie's smile faltered, and she turned to her.

"Relax," she said, her voice softening. "We'll give you some time." Charlie grabbed her hands and squeezed. "I'm glad you're here for Matt," she whispered, then released her and stepped away.

Matt met her eyes across the yard, his filled with laughter. The smile slowly died out and concern entered its place as he continued to take her in. He sent her a questioning look, but she shook her head and raised a hand, then escaped to the kitchen to get started on the patties.

A little while later, as she set the meat on a plate, the sliding glass door opened and shut, then two familiar arms wrapped around her waist.

"Hey," Matt said.

The feeling of being overwhelmed had settled in her chest but now it fluttered again at the presence of him. This man who had grown to mean so much to her.

"Hey back," she responded.

His cheek brushed against hers before he kissed her neck, then settled in behind her while she continued with making the patties. "Can I ask what that look was about outside?"

She bit her lip. Of course, he would ask about it. He saw entirely too much and made it his business to get answers.

"It's just me being me," she responded, her voice subdued and quiet. "I'll work through it and be okay."

Matt stepped away before she felt gentle hands turning her. With her hands covered in raw hamburger, she held them away from his body but allowed him to tug her back.

"Did you miss our conversation earlier?" he asked, his tone holding an edge of impatience, yet still loving.

Her brows pulled down, not understanding what he referred to. "I'm not sure."

He squeezed her briefly. "Juliette, beautiful," he said, causing her breath to hitch. This man... "You and I are moving forward together. In case you missed it, let me repeat that. Together," he said with a pause and a firm look.

"We're a team and whatever is going on in your head, whatever your troubles are, I want to help. And vice versa."

She rolled her eyes. "How can I help you? All you've done so far is solve my problems, taken them on even though you didn't have to."

He dipped down until his eyes were level with

hers. The movement jolted her so much she froze. "They were *our* problems. And you've helped me more times than I can count."

"Like when?" she whispered.

His gaze bounced between hers. "Like in that cell after I'd been tortured," he whispered back. "When you'd protected me throughout that night, when I'd been completely vulnerable. When you've made me laugh. Talked me through things that were scary to you when you didn't realize they were just as scary to me." He brushed a stray curl behind her ear. "Teaching and allowing me to learn to be a better man for you by being patient as I worked through being an ass."

She tilted her head. "Matt."

He cupped both of her cheeks. "And showing me all of what there's to know in our bed."

Her breathing stuttered. "Matthew."

He smiled. "Talk to me, beautiful. Let me help."

She took a deep breath and mentally took down another layer of bricks, deciding to allow this man closer to her heart. "I'm scared."

He frowned. "Why?"

"I've never had a big family. Or people I could count on. Or even a boyfriend who I could depend on. And your family, they are all just so..."

"What?"

"They are wonderful. What if they don't like me? What if they realize I'm not the best person for you? To have a taste of all of this, then have it taken away?"

He smiled again and brought her closer. "Matt, my hands."

"Relax. I've got you."

She stared up at him.

"Do you understand what I'm saying?" he asked. "I am here for you. Let me show you just how wonderful life can be, Juliette."

"Just like that?" she asked.

He nodded.

"Huh."

He busted out laughing, dropping his head to kiss her quickly.

The door slid open on the heels of his echoing laughter, and they both turned to find Dwayne enter, his expression serious yet excited. "So," he said, drawing the word out. "Sam's water just broke."

Juliette's eyes widened, and she spun toward Dwayne. "Ohmygod," she blurted.

Matt laughed behind her again, the sound soaking into her for a moment.

"Chris is getting her ready to roll. Brooke and I are going to go with them because I doubt either is able to drive. We'll drop them at the hospital, then go get the go bag from their place."

"What do you need from us?" Matt asked.

Dwayne winced. "Sorry about your barbeque."

Juliette waved off the apology. "No need to apologize. This is exciting! A baby is coming."

Dwayne grinned. "Indeed." He looked back at Matt. "I don't think there's much. Hails is going to need to head over to the clinic to make sure the animals there are fed, and Dumbass is good to go. Would ask you to help there, but both Chris and Sam reminded me how temperamental DA can be. Could you maybe give her a ride? She came with me and Brooke."

Matt stepped up to her side and nodded. "Sure."

"I got Hailey," came Luke's deep voice behind Dwayne.

Dwayne's back went straight, and he turned to face their newcomer. An interesting reaction. Juliette tilted her head at the sudden undercurrent that entered the room. She glanced at Matt to gauge his reaction but only found his eyes serious and on his two brothers.

"I don't know if that's a good idea," Dwayne said, his mouth tight.

"I don't care," Luke responded. "I'm heading back that way anyhow. Makes more sense for me to take her since I need to go that way. Why drag these two out when they don't need to do the twenty-minute hike?"

"It's really no bother," Juliette inserted, wanting to de-escalate the rapidly rising situation. Luke's voice held a lethal edge that reflected off of Dwayne's body language.

"Guys," Matt said in a calming voice. "Let's just all take a breath."

"I think you know why," Dwayne said, his voice sharp as a butcher's knife.

"Stop it," came a fresh voice from the doorway. Hailey stood there looking at both men. "I'll go with Luke," she said, angry eyes on Dwayne.

Dwayne's chest visibly lifted and dropped, as if he'd taken a deep breath for patience. "Hails," he murmured, but the fight had gone out of him. The tension was still there, but she knew he wouldn't push against her. His back slumped against the wall, but his gaze softened as it landed on the stunning young woman.

More than ever, Juliette was curious about what was going on but figured she'd ask Matt later.

Hailey stepped inside and lifted a cautious gaze to Luke. "I'm ready now if you are."

Luke glanced in her direction but didn't meet her eyes. "Let's go." Then he walked to the front door without another word.

Hailey followed, stopping briefly at Dwayne before giving his hand a quick squeeze, then she, too, went out the front door.

Juliette turned to Matt, giving him wide eyes. His hand came to her nape and squeezed. He mouthed, *Later*.

She turned back to Dwayne, who stared at the front door as if he wanted to chase after Hailey. His troubled gaze seemed millions of miles away.

"D," Matt said.

Dwayne turned and blinked at him.

"You have to let her go. Trust them to do the right thing."

Dwayne just shook his head, frowned, and opened his mouth as if he wanted to say something, but instead lifted a hand and went out the back sliding door.

Juliette turned again toward Matt with wide eyes. He took one look at her and laughed, the sound deep and hearty. His expression, the laughter, all of it moved through her with an intensity unlike anything else.

His head dipped down, and he kissed her hard and quick, then leaned back and met her gaze. "You still want to keep us at a distance?"

She sighed softly, then smiled. "I'm thinking it's best if I'm on the inside, especially with all that's going on. Babies on the way, drama unfolding with young women and men. Looks to be a pretty intense period for you. You're going to need me."

He met her smile with one of his own and kissed her again. "I will always need you, no matter what."

****

Seven hours later, a healthy baby boy weighing in at eight pounds, three ounces, was delivered. Samantha Eagen and Chris Gonzalez named him Liam Christopher Gonzalez. The last name had been a surprise to many, seeing as Sam and Chris hadn't announced their engagement yet.

Back at Juliette and Matt's house, they cheered when receiving the news, clinking pints filled with beer, bellies full of food, with Mike and Don, who'd stayed behind to welcome Juliette into their fold.

The End

D.C. STONE

EVERNIGHT PUBLISHING ®

www.evernightpublishing.com